MIRROR, MIRROR

VALERIE STEPHENS

ZEBRA BOOKS
KENSINGTON PUBLISHING CORP.

ZEBRA BOOKS are published by

Kensington Publishing Corp.
850 Third Avenue
New York, NY 10022

Zebra and the Z logo Reg. U.S. Pat. & TM Off.

First Printing: December, 1994

Printed in the United States of America

One

When Amanda and James arrived at the party the house was already full, alive with voices and laughter and music. James left her standing alone by the stairs and went off to get them drinks. An hour later Amanda was still alone, still drinkless. She glimpsed him once through the melee in the living room, bent over a dark-haired woman, smiling, handing her a glass.

Was she the one? Amanda wondered.

Probably not. But somebody *like* that. Slim, beautiful, elegant, a glistening thoroughbred. Everything that Amanda was not.

Tonight was to have been a surprise, but Amanda had known about it for a week. Even James had known. The hours leading up to the party had been charged with anticipation as each of them pretended they were simply going for dinner at Patrick and Shelly's. Amanda wished it had been true.

Shelly, James's sister, emerged smiling from

the zoo in the living room and sauntered like a catwalk model toward Amanda.

"Having fun?"

"Have you seen James?"

"In there somewhere." She nodded to the wall of people. "Why so glum?"

"If I tell you something, will you promise not to think I'm crazy?"

"My goodness, I touched a nerve!"

"Is there somewhere we can talk?"

Shelly looked around, obviously dismayed at the idea of leaving her party even for a few moments, but finally nodded and put an arm around Amanda's shoulders.

"Upstairs."

They pushed their way through the group lounging on the landing, and made their way to the master bedroom. In the silence, Amanda leaned against the sink and took a deep breath. Shelly looked into the mirror and touched the corners of her lips with her finger.

"So, I promise I won't think you're crazy."

"I think James is having an affair."

Shelly's look of preoccupation evaporated. She stared at Amanda with wide eyes, looking more catlike than ever.

"Think it, or know it?"

"Know it."

"He told you?"

"It's just a lot of little changes."

"Like what?"

"I don't know, Shelly. Too many to count."

"Tell me one of them."

"We haven't made love in nearly three weeks, and it was nearly a month between that time and the time before."

"That's all? I haven't made love with Patrick in twice that long."

"I just know it, Shelly. He's seeing somebody. I don't know what to do. We've only been married for a year!"

Shelly put her hands on her hips. She looked at herself in the mirror, then back at Amanda.

"Are you looking for sympathy?"

"You're my friend! I just wanted to tell somebody!"

"Okay. I'm your friend. So I'll be honest with you. If I were James, I'd be seeing somebody else, too."

Flabbergasted, Amanda did not know what to say.

"Look at you," Shelly said. "Have you ever thought of going on a diet? Getting some exercise? Buying some nice clothes? Hasn't it ever occurred to you that you should take care of yourself a little?"

Amanda felt sick. She lifted a hand to her mouth.

"I'm sorry it hurts to hear this," Shelly said. "I'm saying it because I'm your friend. Maybe James *is* having an affair. I don't know. If you want to stop it, look to yourself first. That's all I've got to say, Amanda."

Amanda said nothing.

What she had needed from Shelly was commiseration, not a catalog of her deficiencies. The small enclosure of the bedroom suite seemed claustrophobic. Amanda felt as if she were trapped in an elevator with a stranger, a stranger to whom she had inadvertently blurted out her deepest, darkest secrets. At this moment, Shelly did not feel like her closest friend, not like a friend at all.

"I better rejoin the party," Shelly said quietly. Without meeting Amanda's eyes, she edged past her to the door. "Think about what I said."

Amanda stared into the mirror, trying not to see herself as Shelly had seen her. When she got downstairs, she resumed her guard duty in the living room doorway. Petra, James's mother, approached her with a holy smile. Her platinum blond hair hugged her skull like a helmet.

"You really should try to have fun," she said.

Amanda tried to smile. "I am."

"It's not fair to James for you to mope like this."

Petra walked away without waiting for a reply. Amanda fought back a surge of anger. After a few minutes, reeling from the constant chatter, she leaned against the doorframe and closed her eyes. She felt more alone than she had ever felt in her life. Outside, the September air would be cool, and she wished she could step into it—wished she could get away from the party, away from these people she did not know, away from their looks and their muttered comments. Did all of them see what Shelly saw? When she opened her eyes again, James was standing next to her.

He kissed her cheek. "Surprised?"

"Not really."

"Are you having fun?"

"I don't know anybody."

"To tell you the truth, I'm not sure that I do, either."

"Where were you?"

"Just mingling."

"With whom?"

"Everybody. Why?"

"Who was that woman you were talking to?"

"Oh, I don't know. One of Shelly's friends, I suppose."

They stood together a few minutes, saying nothing, as if they had just met and failed the first-impression test. Amanda felt conspicuous and ugly. Did James see her as Shelly saw her?

"Listen, why don't we go," he said. "You look tired."

"I'm not tired."

"You look uncomfortable. You're not having fun. I'll take you home, come on."

"I want to stay."

"Amanda, don't be silly. You hate parties. Let's go. I don't mind, really."

He went away to get their coats. When he came back the corner of his mouth was smeared with lipstick.

He grinned. "Ready?"

Amanda grabbed her coat and went outside. The sounds of the party reached out to surround her, then shut off as James closed the door. They walked down the drive, separated by a full yard, then along the street toward the car.

Amanda saw it first, and stopped in her tracks.

"What is it?"

"The car."

The bronze Mercedes was parked away from the streetlight, but even from here the damage was visible. The passenger-side window was smashed. Splinters of gleaming glass littered the street like stars. The door was a map of scratched lines.

"Oh, Christ," James muttered.

Amanda stood back as he inspected the damage. He circled the car and came back to her side shaking his head.

"Just your door. Thank God. In this neighborhood, can you believe it? Some night, huh?"

Amanda shivered, looking along the line of cars. None of the others had been touched.

"Some night," she said.

She turned away and walked back toward the house.

At Shelly's and Patrick's insistence they left the Mercedes on the street and borrowed

Shelly's Lincoln for the night. The drive home was silent and uncomfortable. Amanda's suspicions flirted with Shelly's hurtful comments until she was dizzy and could hardly think.

Their home on Park Avenue had once been a four-unit apartment building. She had sold it to James long before marrying him, and within a year the building was unrecognizable. He replaced the dilapidated red-brick exterior, brick by brick, and gutted the suffocating, dark interior.

Although she had lived in the building a year now, the scale of the place continued to impress her. After the clamor of the party, however, its quiet, open spaces welcomed her. She climbed the stairs to the bedrooms on the second floor, reluctant to use an elevator in her own home. James followed like a lazy shadow.

She undressed quickly and slipped into bed. James slowly stepped out of his clothes. At forty-two he was still slim, almost boyish. If she herself had ever looked girlish, those times were long gone.

Although she had earlier hoped they would make love tonight, she now dreaded the possibility. Shelly's comments had hurt her deeply, and had opened within her a chasm of self-consciousness. Still, it was their anniversary, and despite her doubts and suspicions, despite the vandalism to the car, she was not going to spoil it. Besides, wasn't it possible that she was wrong? How could she know for certain that James was being unfaithful? He deserved the benefit of the doubt.

She got out of bed and approached him from behind, winding her arms around him, pressing her breasts into his back.

"Happy anniversary," she said.

He turned to her, and she kissed his mouth. It took only a second or two to realize that he was not responding.

"Darling, I'm . . ." his words trailed off.

"What is it?"

"I'm sorry. I thought I told you. I'm going back to the party. I just wanted to change."

"Back?"

"It's hardly fair for both of us to leave. It took a lot of work to organize, and all those people . . . Besides, I thought I'd return Shelly's car and pick up ours."

"I thought you *wanted* to leave!"

"It's you who wanted to leave. I didn't think you'd mind."

"James, it's our anniversary! Shelly said we could keep the car until tomorrow."

"I'll make it up to you, I promise. I don't feel comfortable leaving the Mercedes out on the street like that. Not after tonight."

"I want to make love!"

"I think the mood has been broken," he said quietly.

Face burning, Amanda turned away from him and went back to the bed. She had not felt so embarrassed since Willy Oberman had scrambled from his car when she had tried to kiss him after their senior prom. She wanted to pull the sheets over her face.

James put on a crisp white shirt, a tie, and a dark jacket. Now, he would fit in at the party. He stopped at his dresser to splash cologne on his face, then came to the bed and kneeled by her.

"One of us should be there. They went to a lot of trouble."

"Just go, James."

"I'll make it up to you."

"Please, just go."

He kissed her forehead.

He was at the door when she called his name. He turned, half smiling.

"What?"

"Are you having an affair?"

"What made you say that?"

"Who is she, James? Just tell me who she is."

He laughed softly. "I am not having an affair. And even if I were, I wouldn't tell you. I doubt you'd really want me to. And even if I were to tell you, I wouldn't tell you with whom." He shook his head slowly. "But I'm not. I don't know who put the idea into your head."

She rolled over and stared at the window. James left without another word.

* * *

13

Amanda could not sleep. She could not stop thinking about what Shelly had said. The words lashed at her.

As rain began to patter against the window, she got out of bed.

Standing naked before the mirror, she regarded herself with unforgiving eyes. She had always considered herself an averagely attractive woman. Now, she wondered if she had been deluding herself. *Look at yourself!* Her hair was stringy, lifeless, dull. Her breasts were loose, shapeless gourds. Her belly swelled like a large purse into the formless tangle of her pubic hair. Her thighs rippled like jelly. She turned away from the mirror with a moan of despair.

She felt a stab of hatred for her body, then for herself, and then for James. She hated him for making her feel this way, hated him for seeing another woman, and hated that other woman with such intensity that even thinking about it for a few seconds brought her close to physical pain.

She forced herself to face the mirror again. With savage fingers she pinched her midriff, finding a handful of loose skin and flesh. She was a swollen, corpulent, disgusting creature!

She wondered now if James had *ever* really wanted to make love to her. It suddenly seemed more likely that he had simply been fulfilling what he perceived as a conjugal duty. Keep her happy, and he could get his real pleasure elsewhere.

Her heart galloped. Nausea filled her up. Dizzy, she sat heavily on the end of the bed. Bending close to the mirror, close enough to fog the glass, she opened her makeup drawer. She applied coral pink lipstick, her summer color, and blush. Without the benefit of complementary clothes, her makeup was so harsh she looked like a clown. As bad as Petra.

With a tissue and cold cream she cleaned her face. Nothing could improve her appearance. Nothing.

Despair brought weariness, but she could not sleep. As rain battered the window she got out of bed and opened the blinds. A dark September sky loomed overhead, rippling with lightning. As Amanda watched, a fork of brilliant light arced overhead, seemingly jumping from building to building. For barely a moment it illuminated a figure on the street below. Amanda pressed her face to the cold glass, shielding her eyes with her hands.

Somebody was standing by the corner of Peavey Park, shrouded in a dark raincoat. Was the pale smudge of face angled up at this window? Rain spattered the dark pavement around the figure. Amanda backed quickly away and sat down on the bed. The skin on her shoulders and neck crawled.

Why would somebody stand outside on a night like this? Why had she got the impression that whoever it was, was watching the window?

Steeling herself, she edged back to the window. The sky remained dark. The corner by the park was empty, the figure gone.

A feeling of unease settled upon her as she slipped back into bed. She hugged the blanket and quilt up to her neck, but even those coverings brought no warmth. She stared at the ceiling as light from the street, diffracted through glass and dripping rain, shimmered on the plaster.

At 12:30, when the front door opened, she was still awake. James had hardly been gone at all!

She turned off the light, and put her head back down.

James entered the room quietly. He did not turn on the light, and she sent out a silent prayer of thanks. She did not want to be seen. When he lifted the sheets and pressed close to her she stiffened. He kissed her cheek, then her neck. His skin was smooth. He smelled of cologne. He touched her.

"I'm sorry about earlier. You were right. I shouldn't have gone back. I promised you I would make it up to you. I meant it."

His erection pressed into her thigh. She wondered how he had managed to produce it. It certainly had not come from looking at her, or thinking of her. It couldn't have.

He kissed her breasts, moving his fingers between her thighs. He shifted his weight on top of her, touching her, kissing her. She put a hand behind his neck and held his face to her shoulder. The sounds she made, though they seemed to excite him, were mostly her muffled sobs of despair.

Afterward, they did not talk. Amanda was glad. She rolled away from him. The feel of his semen, sticky across her thigh, sickened her. Surely, surely he had been fantasizing about some other woman to bring himself to climax.

She watched the falling rain. Buildings across the street leaped in sporadic lightning.

Questions and suspicions filled her head. She wondered if he had seen anybody at the party. Had he even returned to the party? Who was the woman who had stolen him from her?

As sleep took her, a shadowy female figure slipped into her dreams, concealed in darkness, spattered by rain, illuminated only by lightning, watching, waiting.

"Who are you?" Amanda cried.

The answer was a soft, satisfied laugh.

Two

The woman at the Merit Health Center was tall, blond, and slim. Her white smock did little to disguise the perfect figure beneath it. Her name was Chrissy.

"Late night resolution?"

"Of a sort," Amanda said.

"First, let me ask you a couple of questions. Answer as honestly as you can."

"Okay."

"I assume you are here to lose weight and improve your appearance."

"Yes."

"Why?"

Amanda's mouth froze. Her mind went blank.

"Let me put it this way. For whom do you want to lose weight?"

"I want to do it for myself."

"Nobody else is in the picture?"

"I suppose there's my husband."

"Okay, that's very good. That means you're going to have support."

Amanda shook her head. "He doesn't know I'm here."

"Are you going to tell him?"

"I don't know."

"We like our clients to be honest about their goals. It's difficult to lose weight. It's ten times more difficult when you try to hide it. On the other hand, with support, anything is possible."

"I have a friend I can tell," Amanda said, thinking of Shelly.

"Well, that's a start."

Chrissy came to Amanda's side of the desk. "Let's put you on the scale. Then I'll run through our program with you and, if you like, give you a tour of our facilities. Do you know anything about us?"

"Just what I've seen in the ads."

"Well, we don't aim simply to take the weight off, Amanda. We like to keep it off. We do so through a strict regimen of diet control, behavior change, and a nationally renowned exercise program. Step over here."

Amanda followed Chrissy to a scale in the corner of the office.

"Should I take off my shoes?"

"If you like."

She did like. She took off her coat, kicked off her shoes, and stepped onto the scale. Chrissy stood close to her and adjusted the counterweights. Amanda's heart sank as the weight moved farther and farther along the bar.

19

Finally, the pointer wavered, rose, hovered a moment, then settled.

"One hundred and thirty-five and three-quarters pounds," Chrissy said. "Those quarter pounds are important when you're trying to lose them."

Amanda tried to smile back, but could not manage. One hundred and thirty-five pounds was worse than she had expected.

Chrissy measured her height, bust, waist, and thighs. Afterward, she checked a guidebook and wrote a number at the top of the page. She showed it to Amanda.

"Twenty pounds?"

"I know it sounds like a lot, but it isn't really. You may have considered yourself only marginally overweight. By insurance charts you're right. We prefer to be a bit more stringent in our guidelines, especially when appearance is a priority."

"I've never lost weight before."

"We guarantee results, Amanda, or we'll refund your money."

Amanda looked at the pink sheet in her hands, at the discouraging number. The resolve had gripped her in the middle of the night, and she had woken to stare at the ceiling, to listen to the still-falling rain. Now, in the face of the number she was looking at, she wondered if she could carry through. She remembered the woman James had been talking to at the party. Was she the one? Somebody like her, probably. Slim and perfect.

She nodded sharply. "Okay. I'll try it."

Chrissy smiled a deal-closing smile. "I know you think you're facing a very difficult situation. I want to show you something encouraging."

She opened her desk drawer, pulled out a photograph, and handed it to Amanda. The photo was of a very obese woman sitting on a sofa. Her thighs looked like tree trunks, her face a pumpkin. The eyes, so blue and clear, were unmistakable.

"That's you?"

"It's me, three years ago. I lost nearly two hundred pounds through the Merit program. I just wanted you to see that."

Amanda nodded, stunned. The change was profound. Chrissy now looked as insubstantial as a ghost. She wondered if the lines around her eyes and mouth, so deep they looked painful, had been visible three years ago.

It was nearly thirty minutes later that Amanda signed a check and handed it over at the front counter. Her program was to begin immediately. She would return tomorrow morning to have her progress measured and to begin her exercise program. She would return every day after that except Sundays, for two months, or until she hit her goal-weight.

When she left the building she felt dizzy, but relieved. She was doing something, at least.

In her mind she saw the other woman, mouth smiling. *Nothing you do will win him back. He's mine now.*

The shadowy face spoke with Shelly's voice. Amanda shuddered as she got into her car.

Traffic was surprisingly light as Amanda drove back toward the office. The clouds from last night had cleared for the most part, and blue sky opened overhead.

She had stopped at a light near the office when the red sports car pulled up beside her. Amanda glanced over at the other driver and found herself looking into a striking, feminine face. Dark eyes regarded her coldly. Amanda averted her gaze. Something about the face tugged at her memory.

When the light changed she pulled quickly away. The red car roared ahead and turned directly in front of her. Amanda slammed on her brakes to avoid rear-ending the smaller car. She leaned on her horn, but the red car was already receding in the distance. Amanda swore softly.

A horn blared behind her and she jumped. She applied gas, but the engine remained silent. The Buick had stalled.

"Damn it! Damn it!"

With other horns blaring now, Amanda twisted the ignition with trembling fingers. The engine roared to life and she put the car in gear immediately. It leapt forward with a squeal of rubber. In the rearview mirror she could see the other driver shaking his head.

She turned off quickly into a mall and brought the car to a halt. As she sat there, shaking, the face of the driver in the red car came to her, and connected with another memory. She saw it under falling rain, made harsh by lightning.

It was a full five minutes before her trembling had subsided enough to pull back into traffic.

James worked through the morning. He spent most of his time on the phone with worried, hesitant, or zealous clients, composing a symphony of equal parts reassurance, flattery, entreaty, caution, and speculation. The rest of his morning he spent writing the weekly *James Sanders Investment Newsletter.*

From the moment he entered his office his mind never strayed from his work. That was his chief talent. His ability to focus, to block out everything but the work at hand. It was a major factor in his success. As lunchtime approached, however, stray thoughts broke through the barrier of his concentration.

Amanda was one of them.

He remembered her face as she asked him if he were having an affair, the deep hurt in her eyes, the downturn of her mouth. It had torn him apart. Knowing he was responsible made it worse. She was not meant to suffer! He had never meant to hurt her!

Still, the fact was that she suspected something.

Feminine intuition, or feminine perceptions, or something, had caused her to look at him far too closely.

The more he thought of her, the less he could concentrate on his work. As noon approached he stopped working entirely. He leaned back in his chair with his hands behind his head. Through the blinds of his office, Park Avenue was brilliant in the autumn sunshine. Perhaps he would take a walk soon, or a drive; anything to pull his mind from the turmoil that was awakening in his life.

Last night, while making love, Amanda had been somewhere else. Her mind had been wandering. Perhaps she had been imagining him with another woman. Perhaps she had been blaming herself for the infidelity of which she suspected him.

Poor Amanda!

Outside, a car honked long and hard. A pedestrian shouted in anger, with a voice so loud it was clear even here in the office.

The phone rang.

He knew even before the caller spoke, simply by the moment of expectant silence, who it was.

"Hello, Lydia."

"Meet me this afternoon at two."

"I don't think that's a good idea."

"I need you."

The line went dead. James hung up and leaned back in his chair. The feeling of guilt gnawing relentlessly at him suddenly fell before the sweep of another, more compelling emotion.

Desire.

He felt it first in his stomach as a soft fluttering, then as a tension across his shoulders and chest.

There was no use fighting it. There never was.

By the time he arrived at the Sojourn Lodge in Edina it was closer to two than he had hoped.

He felt dizzy as he walked across the hotel's parking lot, but the crisp afternoon air invigorated him.

The clerk at the front desk, a young blond woman with very green eyes, cheeks pitted with old acne scars, recognized him and smiled.

"You'll be staying overnight again, Mr. Page?"

"I'll pay now, and I'll be out very early."

"Yes, sir."

She knew as well as he that he'd be gone in a few hours, but she said nothing.

He carried his only bag to the room and closed the door behind him. He did not lock the door.

He stood at the window and looked across the parking lot. His bronze Mercedes was conspicuous amongst the few domestic cars. Even from here he could see that the front passenger window was missing.

He checked his watch. It showed 2:00 P.M., on the nose. He had made an appointment for the window repair at 4:00. Surely, he would make it.

He lay on the bed with his hands behind his head and looked at the ceiling. He waited.

It was not long before Lydia arrived. James got off the bed. He studied her in the dresser mirror. Her black hair, impeccably styled, fell across her shoulders like a sable stole. He did not know how old she was, but she seemed not to have changed one bit over the past . . . my God, had it been 25 years? Even at the beginning she had been a good many years older than he. She looked ageless. Her reflection smiled at him.

"Have you been waiting for very long?

"I just got here a few minutes ago."

"That's good."

She applied her makeup. First eyeliner, then eye shadow, then mascara. She did it slowly, smiling, because she knew he liked to watch. Her small, dark eyes, blossomed, transfixing him. Next, she brushed blush on her cheeks, shaping and sharpening her features. Finally lipstick, deep red and moist until, at last, her face was born anew.

James's erection was painfully hard.

26

Lydia studied him in the mirror without turning to him.

"What did you mean on the phone about meeting me being a bad idea?"

James tried to calm his breathing. He could hardly think clearly now.

"Amanda suspects."

"Does she?"

"I think so."

"Does she know about me?"

"Not about you specifically, but she suspects I'm seeing somebody."

"Are you seeing somebody other than me?"

"Of course not!"

James turned away from her and went to the bed. He lay down and closed his eyes. Lydia's perfume surrounded him, filled him, unmoored him.

"I don't care if she knows," she said.

"I don't, either."

"You're lying."

"I just don't want her hurt. She's so fragile."

"Don't hurt her, then."

He kept his eyes closed as she touched him. Her nails felt like daggers against his flesh.

As she moved her fingers over him, he forgot Amanda. Forgot everything.

Nothing mattered at all.

It was nearly 5:00 P.M. The street beyond the dirty window was growing dark. Lincoln

Fowler sipped his coffee and waited with apparently infinite patience for Amanda to continue.

"I want to find out if my husband is seeing another woman."

"That's straightforward enough."

"I don't know what else to tell you."

"I'd like to ask some questions, as long as it won't make you uncomfortable."

"No. I mean, go ahead."

"You suspect your husband is seeing somebody?"

"I think so."

"You're sure it's another woman?"

She frowned at him. "Well, yes. I mean, I presume so."

"Have you asked him?"

"He said he wasn't."

"Do you believe him?"

"I don't know."

Fowler regarded her with curious but patient eyes. He was not what she had expected. Not at all like those television detectives, or even the book detectives with whom she was familiar. He was, to be frank, simply nondescript. She was not sure, had he turned away from her, that she could have described him with any accuracy.

His clothes were neutral. His jacket, pants, and shirt, sat somewhere between gray and brown. His mottled tie might have gone with a hundred different combinations. His face was roundish, perhaps a bit long, with pale, emotionless eyes. His hair was sandy, combed neatly, thin. She could not tell his age, though she guessed he would fall in the immense ballpark of twenty to forty. Even his voice had a neutral quality to it, as if one had simply overheard a conversation in passing.

"Have you thought this through, Amanda?"

"What do you mean?"

"Have you really considered this step you're about to take? Thought about what it means? Up to now you may have had a happy marriage. That involves trust. Very deep trust. If you hire me, you're as good as throwing it all away."

"I just need to know, that's all."

"Many people come here, wives and husbands alike, and they haven't really thought about it clearly. When they do, the answer becomes clear. Most of them really do still trust their spouses. They come to realize that the pain they're considering is unnecessary."

Amanda looked down at her hands. She thought of James's denial. Yet, she could not so easily discount the changes she had noticed in their relationship these past months.

"I trust my own intuition."

"You don't have to sleep with your intuition, Amanda. If you hire me, it's not going to matter what I find out. Either way, your relationship with your husband will suffer."

"I don't know how else to put it, Mr.

Fowler. I want to know. I need to know who he's seeing. I need to know."

"I just wanted to be certain you understood what you were asking. If you still want to pursue this matter, then we have to get into details."

"What kind of details?"

"Where does your husband work, Amanda?"

"He works mostly at home. Sometimes he visits clients out of town, but mostly they come to him. I have a picture of him, if you want it."

She held out the wallet-size photograph, and he took it from her.

"He has opportunity to see other women?"

"I suppose so. He's out some nights. I don't see him at all during the day. For that matter, he spends nearly every day by himself. He doesn't have to keep set hours."

"I don't suppose you have any women in mind?"

Amanda thought of the figure standing in the rain, and the woman in the red car. "There's something else," she said. "Last night our car was vandalized. Only my side. My window, my door. And later, at home, I saw somebody standing outside, watching the building. This morning, on the way to work, a car cut me off. It was a woman driver. I mean, she *looked* at me before she did it."

Fowler put his pen down on the desk and looked at her carefully. He frowned slightly.

30

"You think the woman you suspect your husband of seeing, is also trying to hurt you?"

Hearing him say it, Amanda realized how ridiculous it sounded. She laughed uncertainly. Suddenly the car's broken window was just one of those things, the figure in the rain was simply waiting for a bus, and the woman in the red car was just another rude rush-hour driver.

"I suppose not. It sounds silly."

"Oh, it happens sometimes," Fowler said. "Usually the other way around. Wives attacking mistresses."

"I guess my nerves are jangled, that's all."

Fowler picked up his pen again, apparently satisfied. "Well, it wouldn't hurt to be sure. But first things first. Is the information I get for you meant to influence a divorce or separation settlement?"

Amanda stared at him, feeling a relief that he had listened to her without laughing, but getting angry now. "I haven't even thought that far ahead."

"So you won't require a notarized deposition?"

"I doubt it."

"What evidence will satisfy you?"

"Do you mean of his guilt, or of his innocence?"

"Guilt. If he's innocent, of course, you'll just have to take my word for it."

"Photographs."

Fowler scribbled everything in a notebook, then brought a pad of printed sheets out of his desk. He handed it to Amanda.

"This is a contract. Sign two, and we'll each keep one. It says you've hired me and give me permission, if needed, to tell anything I discover to any law enforcement agency that asks for it. At my discretion."

"You mean to the police? But why?"

"It's just a formality. You'd be surprised how tangled some of these cases can get."

Amanda read the contract, filled in her name on both copies, and signed them both. Fowler ripped them from the pad and handed her one. He put the other in a crisp new manila folder, and put it in the top drawer of his desk. Amanda wrote him a check. He took it from her and studied it.

"This check is from your private account?"

"Yes."

"Does your husband see the statements?"

"No. Why?"

"Do you want him to know you hired a private investigator?"

Amanda blanched. "No."

He handed her one of his cards. "Keep this out of sight. The easiest way to handle this is for you to phone me in the evenings before he goes out. I'll cover him during the days for a little while. That should be a wide enough window. We'll catch him if he's up to anything."

Amanda put the business card in her purse. "That's everything?"

"Have you reported the vandalism on your car to the police?"

She shook her head. "I don't know. I'll have to ask my husband."

"Find out. If he hasn't done it, do it yourself."

"Is it important?"

"It might be, later, if you have to prove anything."

Amanda did not like the sound of those words, but nodded anyway.

"I won't be phoning you again until it's over, Amanda, but if you need to talk to me for any reason, just call."

"Thank you."

He rose from his seat and opened the door for her. As she walked down the hall she could feel his eyes on her back, but when she reached the stairs and turned his office door had closed.

Three

Amanda returned home feeling on edge, hungry, and dizzy. Her head throbbed. The first day of her diet, ending in the interview with Lincoln Fowler, had exhausted her. Thankfully, she was not paged to show any of her listed properties. She could not have borne to drive anywhere, or to see anybody.

James got home after seven. He had been visiting clients. He hardly looked at her when he talked to her. Her accusation last night had raised a wall between them, it seemed.

At ten, Amanda looked into the library. James was seated by the window with a copy of *Field and Stream* in his lap. Behind him, the various guns of his collection looked like toys.

"I'm going to bed," she said.

"Are you feeling all right? You look pale."

"Just tired."

"I'll be in soon."

"James?"

He looked up again from his magazine. "Yes?"

"Did you call the police about the car?"

"This morning. They said there had been a number of reports of vandalism in that area last night. Some kids out joyriding, that's all, looking for trouble. Nothing we can do about it. The deductible on the insurance is more than the cost of the repair."

She left him and went to bed. Whatever time he came through, she did not know, for as soon as she lay down, despite hunger and headache and fatigue, she was asleep.

She returned to Merit the next morning at 8:30 and met Chrissy.

"How was the first day?"

"Hell."

Chrissy smiled. "Good. Stand on the scale, please."

Amanda slipped out of her shoes and stepped up onto the scale. Chrissy adjusted the counterweight. Amanda watched the pointer float and settle.

"Very good," Chrissy said. "One hundred thirty-three and a half. That's down . . . two and one quarter pounds."

Amanda was shocked.

"That much?"

"The first two or three days you'll notice a fairly dramatic loss. Primarily it's water. You did drink your eight cups, didn't you?"

"Every one."

"You'll likely lose another four pounds over the next two days, and after that the rate will drop to about a half pound a day."

"That's incredible."

"How do you feel?"

"Better, now."

"It's encouraging, isn't it?"

"Very."

She had hoped that the following days would prove to be easier, but they were not. Each day seemed like an eternity of temptation, of hunger, of pain. There were only two things that kept her going. One, her determination to win James's attention from whomever had stolen it from her. And two, her daily counseling sessions with Chrissy.

There were no other signs of the woman in the red sports car, no figures skulking in the night outside the building, and soon Amanda could not even bring the memory of the woman's face to her mind. It was lost. And lost, she did not think about it.

For the next week, the weight came off exactly as Chrissy had promised. By the following Tuesday she was down to 127 pounds. Her headaches soon disappeared, and the consumption of water became almost second nature. She found herself drinking water instead of coffee, and by the end of the week her hunger pangs had flattened out to a feeling of continual near hunger.

There was no point in hiding the diet from

36

James, and after a few days she admitted, when he asked, what she was doing. He protested, but not much.

"If it's what you want," he said.

Amanda was not sure whether to be pleased at his neutrality, or not. He certainly was not a source of support, but then, she did not want him to be. What she wanted was for him to look at her with new eyes, with appreciation. That, she promised herself, would come. Since the night of her accusation, she had not brought up the subject again. The next time she did so, she wanted to be armed with facts.

She waited for Lincoln Fowler to call her, but he did not. There was nothing to do but wait. Besides, she had other things to worry about. By midway through the second week of the diet, she had run into problems.

On Friday, September 24th, exactly a week and a half after starting her diet, she reported to Merit in her now typical high spirits. When she stepped on the scale however, her good mood vanished.

"Hmmm," Chrissy said. "Up nearly a pound today."

"What?"

She stared at the pointer, steady, unmoving, and then at the counterweight. It was balanced at 126, exactly a pound more than the 125 it had balanced at yesterday morning.

"It's nothing to be concerned about."

But Amanda could only stare, feeling sick and angry.

"I just . . . don't understand it."

"It's what we call a plateau," Chrissy said. "Sometime in the past, as you were slowly gaining the weight that brought you to where you were last week, you must have hovered at this point for a while. Your body thinks this is a reasonable weight. It's been here before. It's comfortable here. That's all."

Amanda could hardly speak. She was close to tears.

"How long will it last?" she asked finally, as Chrissy led her back to the chair.

"That's hard to say. A day or two. Maybe even a week."

That wasn't what she wanted to hear. Chrissy saw it in her face.

"Of course, we could help things along, if you really want to."

"How?"

"Well, you'd have been starting your exercise program in another week anyway. You could start early."

Amanda did not hesitate. "Okay."

Chrissy chewed her lower lip. "We don't usually recommend this, but in certain cases it's been known to work wonders."

"What is it?"

"We could take you completely off milk and bread, and put you on zero-calorie vitamin supplements. A calcium tablet and a B-complex vitamin. That, combined with the exercise, should push you past it."

Again, she did not hesitate.

"Okay."

She began the supplements that day. Up until now she had been consuming one slice of whole-wheat bread every day, as well as one eight-ounce glass of skimmed milk. Now she stopped both.

She began the exercise program the following day.

The routine was simple and effective. One half hour of step aerobics, and another half hour of supervised weight training. It exhausted her, pushed her to her limits both physically and mentally, and nearly broke her.

As September faded away she was down another three pounds. She ached in nearly every part of her body, from her groin to her toes, from her fingertips to her buttocks, and her headaches were back. But the weight was coming off.

On Saturday, October 2nd, her weight now 122½ pounds, Amanda got up and could hardly move. Her entire body felt like a huge bruise, and her head pounded. When she held her hands out in front of her they trembled. James was already up, and was spending his morning at the shooting range with whatever new gun he'd purchased recently. She was glad he was not here to see her.

She studied herself in the mirror, but despite

the narrowing of her waist, the slight thinning of her thighs, the shrinking of her buttocks, and the definite sharpening of her features, she did not feel good. She felt on the verge of collapse. She was due to be at Merit in an hour, but she knew that she would not make it.

Holding back tears of frustration and pain, she dressed and left the house without eating. When she arrived at Shelly's and Patrick's she was crying openly. She had nearly crashed the car twice on the way over, dizzy spells overtaking her, rising to fill her head with blackness.

It was Shelly who answered the door.

The look on her face turned from one of brusque annoyance at having a Saturday morning disturbed, to one of utter shock. This was the first time Shelly had seen her since she had started the diet.

"Amanda? My God!"

"I think I'm going to die."

With Shelly holding her arm, she allowed herself to be led into the house, nearly collapsing into the sofa in the living room.

"It's a diet. It's killing me. I feel empty. I feel like I'm being drained."

"But, my God! You look fantastic! I've never seen you look so young!"

The words, so welcome and flattering, had their effect. They seemed to cut through the malaise that was surrounding her, seemed to clear the cobwebs from her head. She brushed tears from her eyes and looked at her friend steadily.

"You really think so?"

Shelly kneeled by the sofa. Her dark red hair looked as if it naturally grew into a pageboy cut. She reached out and held Amanda's shaking hand.

"I mean it."

"But my face . . . I look sickly. I hardly recognized myself in the mirror this morning."

Now Shelly grinned. "You think I look like this when I wake up? This is an hour with makeup, kiddo. If I looked first thing in the morning like you do now I'd be happy as hell."

"Really?"

"Really."

Amanda shook her head, confused and now feeling pangs of hunger.

"I just don't know, Shelly. The diet is working. I'm losing weight. But I don't want to get sick, you know? I don't know, I'm losing my incentive, I think."

"How's James reacting?"

"He hasn't said a thing. I don't think he's even noticed."

"Give it time."

Amanda breathed deeply, took back her hand, and leaned back in the sofa.

"I don't know," she said.

Shelly went away, leaving Amanda alone in

the living room. Amanda focused on the signals her body was sending her. Through the aches and pains of the exercises, she could still feel the pangs of hunger. She needed to eat something. She watched leaves fall from the two oak trees in the front yard—red patches drifting down.

"Hello, gorgeous!"

Patrick came over to her and lifted her chin. He pushed her head from side to side, looking into her eyes.

"Am I going to die?"

"The truth or lies?"

"Truth."

"Shelly told me about the diet. These symptoms are normal. Nothing to worry about."

She did not know why, but she suddenly suspected that he was lying to her, trying to make her feel better for some reason.

"I told you," Shelly said.

"If you want, I can give you something to make you feel better. Pick you up a little."

"Like a diet pill?"

"If you want."

"Isn't that supposed to be dangerous?"

"Unsupervised, maybe. But I'm your doctor."

Amanda considered this, then shook her head.

"No. Thanks anyway, but no. This has just been a bad morning, that's all. Really, the diet is working fine. Today, I just felt lost. I couldn't see the worth of it."

"That happens sometimes," Patrick said.

His smile was genuine and warm and she wondered why she thought he had been lying to her. She was not in top form, she decided.

"Just think of it like this," Shelly said, kneeling again and squeezing her hand. "It's for James. It's to keep him out of the clutches of some tawny young bimbo. Just keep thinking that."

"I do," Amanda said thoughtfully, looking out the window again. "I just forgot, I guess."

A red sports car drove slowly past the house. A pale face turned toward Amanda, then away again. Amanda stiffened. The car picked up speed and disappeared around the corner.

"Pretty soon, he's not going to let you forget. I promise you that," Shelly said. "Am I right, Patrick, or what?"

"She's right," Patrick said.

But Amanda wasn't listening. Her hunger and pain were forgotten. The face she had managed to forget was back again. This time, it brought with it a stab of icy fear.

As October rolled around, Lincoln Fowler waited for word from Amanda Sanders, Amanda *Burns*-Sanders that was, about her husband. His own surveillance had netted nothing. Sanders seemed to be the perfect husband, and he spent his days mostly at home. On the few occasions he went out, Fowler followed him to other businesses, or periodically to the Eastman Gun

Club in St. Paul. James Sanders was an avid shooter, apparently. It reminded Fowler that he would have to report to the shooting range himself sometime soon.

The call came on the afternoon of Wednesday, October 6th. He returned to his office and got the message on his answering machine. On the tape, Amanda sounded angry, and relieved. Like him, she wanted to find out the truth.

Fowler canceled all his other appointments, packed up his surveillance case, and drove over to Park Avenue.

At five minutes to four the front door of the apartment building opened and James Sanders came out. He locked the door, then disappeared into the alley beside the building. Fowler started his car and waited. A minute later a bronze Mercedes entered the street then moved south on Park Avenue toward Lake Street. Fowler followed.

He had grown accustomed to Sanders's driving patterns this past week, and it was no different this time. Sanders hated the freeways and used them as little as possible, choosing instead to take circuitous, minor routes, even should they add considerably to his driving time. He was a careful driver, and very easy to follow.

Fowler hung back and kept the Mercedes a few cars ahead. Sanders drove west on Lake, then turned south again on Excelsior Boulevard, heading into Edina. No shooting ranges out this

44

way. Either another client, or the payoff. Although he had liked Amanda, he hoped it was confirmation of his suspicions. That way, at least, he would feel as if he had earned his fee.

When Sanders turned off Excelsior into the parking lot of the Sojourn Lodge, a midsize, inner-city, salesman's hotel, Fowler grinned.

"You sly dog," he muttered. He drove past, then looped back, and parked his car across the lot from Sanders's car. With the surveillance case slung across his shoulder, he walked briskly to the hotel.

If this was what it appeared to be, and if Sanders was true to type, then he'd been here before. He might even be a regular.

Fowler went to the front desk. The clerk was a young woman, thin but ugly, who knew right away that he wasn't going to be a paying guest. She glared at him and pursed her lips.

"A guy just came in here," Fowler said. "About forty-five, over six feet tall, graying hair, good-looking, one bag."

"So?"

Fowler put a twenty on the desk. "What room is he in?"

She was used to this. Most desk clerks were. She pulled the twenty from under his fingers and put it away somewhere.

"Room 216."

"He come here often?"

"Sometimes."

45

"Anybody meet him here?"

"You got twenty bucks' worth already."

Fowler leaned closer. "I want more, or I'm going to tell the manager what you told me, and the guy in 216 as well."

She didn't look scared, but she knew she'd shortchanged him.

"Somebody meets him. A woman. I don't know her name. He comes here once in a while. Maybe once a month. He broke off for a while, but he started again a few months ago."

"Happy trails," Fowler said.

He took the stairs up to the second floor, and walked the halls until he found 216. He kneeled by the door and pressed his ear to the wood. The voices from beyond were clear.

". . . hasn't said anything else," a man said.

"James . . ." A woman's voice. Bingo.

Fowler opened the case and brought out the conductive microphone. He pressed it to the wood until it stuck, then activated the recorder. He plugged the earphone into his ear.

". . . you're so beautiful."

"I make myself that way for you."

"I love to watch you put on that stuff."

"I love you to watch."

Sanders moaned. The woman was silent. A minute later, Sanders spoke again.

"That's a new lipstick."

"Do you like it?"

"I love it."

Footsteps, whispering fabric. Then Sanders again, groaning. A woman's moan. Bed springs creaking. Fabric rustling.

"Oh, God, Lydia . . ."

"James, be quiet."

Then only silence, the rustling of sheets, moaning, both male and female. Fowler disconnected the microphone, put it back in the case, and backed away from the door. He walked to the end of the hall and took a position near a window with a distant view of Methodist Hospital. From his case he took the camera, and prefocused it on the doorway of 216. Then he sat back to wait.

Time passed slowly. A teenaged maid came by, looked at him without interest, and disappeared down the adjoining corridor. An older couple, deeply tanned, supporting one another by the arms, waddled by. He smiled at them. They smiled back.

It was an hour before the door to 216 opened.

Fowler crouched, camera ready. In the frame, he watched the door open. Saw light from within the room. Then a leg appeared, clad in black silk. Low, sensible heels. A black coat. Tall, slender. Black hair. Raven. She said something to Sanders, then closed the door. He took a picture. Another.

"Hello, Lydia," he whispered. "Look this way, baby. Look this way."

And for a moment, just before she turned

for the stairwell, she was looking right at him. Huge eyes, lips so red they looked bloody against her pale skin.

"Jesus Christ," Fowler muttered.

She was striking, but not beautiful. She was older than he had expected. Older than Amanda, certainly. She had the look of a woman trying hard to look attractive and younger. The kind of look that a lot of men found hard to resist. He was so startled that he nearly forgot to take the picture. His finger, fortunately, acted without him.

Holding his breath, he watched her walk for the stairs. After she had disappeared he stood, shaking his head.

Was she a hooker? He considered the possibility and dismissed it in the same breath. Way, way too much class there. That was money he had looked upon. Was that what attracted Sanders? Somehow, he doubted it. Sanders had enough money of his own.

He put the camera away. He walked back to 216 and listened at the door. No sound from within. She had worn Sanders out.

The smell of her perfume was heavy in the air, and it nearly made him dizzy.

He walked quickly for the stairs, then down. He entered the parking lot in time to see a red Mazda turn onto the street. He raised the camera for a shot, but by the time he was ready the car was gone. He swore under his breath.

Jesus Christ.

Poor James Sanders.

Poor Amanda.

Amanda was pleasant-looking, the way a wife should look. But this creature. Lydia. My God. She had something that Amanda did not have. A kind of sexual aura that even from fifty feet away Fowler had felt. A man would do a lot for that.

He knew one thing for certain.

Amanda Burns-Sanders didn't stand a chance against her.

On Thursday, Fred Cooper treated Amanda to lunch. They went to a new restaurant in a mall north of the office, a bright, metallic, modern-looking place called Chills. Amanda had heard that the salad bar was unbelievably good.

Amanda and Fred had been friends a long time, both having joined Midwest as rookies eight years ago. They often went to lunch together, and even saw each other socially on occasion. Fred was not married, and Amanda was well aware that he looked upon her with great fondness. He was the only agent from the office whom she had invited to her wedding. Although he had come, accompanied by a date, and had seemed to have a good time, she knew that he had been hurt.

"So, where's my compliment?" she prodded,

as they relaxed with coffee afterward. "Don't I look good?"

Fred looked at her seriously.

"What do you want me to say?"

"Don't you think I'm slimmer?"

He grinned coldly. "Hey, Amanda, you're looking thinner."

"That's not very nice, Fred."

"But it's true. You *are* thinner."

Exasperated, she said, "Well, don't you think I look good?"

"You don't look better, Amanda, just thinner. I'm sorry, I'm not trying to offend you."

"You don't."

"It's just . . . you really don't look well."

She could not argue with him. Although she was slimmer, and felt far greater self-confidence than she had ever felt in her life, she woke every morning feeling nauseated, aching terribly in her limbs and lower back, and with a splitting headache. Dark lines had appeared under her eyes, and her face was very pale.

"Dieting is stressful. I can't deny that. But in the end, it's worth it."

"But you look positively sick. I mean really, Amanda. Your face is gaunt. Your skin looks rubbery."

"This is the most convoluted compliment I've ever heard. Does it get to a point soon?"

"Your skin looks like it's lost all its resilience. You've got sacks under your eyes. And I've seen you grimacing when you move. You look and walk like an old woman now. A thin old woman, but still an old woman."

"Thanks a lot. Just what I need to hear right now."

"I'm just trying to be honest."

"I don't need that kind of honesty. I need support. This is not easy."

He sipped his coffee and regarded her concernedly. He really was an oafish looking man, and for the first time Amanda wondered what she saw in him. The doubt, however, was short-lived. Fred Cooper was one of the nicest men she knew, unconcerned with superficial things, honest and kind.

"Do you mind if I ask you something?" he said.

"Like what?"

"How much weight have you lost?"

"Since I started, just over sixteen pounds. I want to lose roughly five more."

"In slightly over three weeks."

"That's right."

"That works out to more than five pounds a week."

"It's a very good program."

"I did some reading on weight loss and dieting the other day. Almost everybody recommends two pounds a week as the limit."

"Those are insurance companies."

"Doctors. People concerned with health, not just appearance."

Amanda sipped her coffee, angry rather than

disturbed at this revelation. On the one hand she was touched that Fred was concerned enough to check into what she was doing, but on the other, she was furious that he assumed she needed looking after.

"At two pounds a week I doubt I could have kept going. It's just not enough."

"I think you're hurting yourself."

"I think you're wrong."

"You looked just fine before you went on your diet. How much did you weigh then? One-thirty-five?"

She was shocked at how accurate his guess was.

"Around there."

"And you're not a short woman, Amanda. You're what, five foot six?"

"Yes."

"According to insurance charts, at one-thirty-five you were nearly perfect."

"I don't care about insurance charts. I care about what I look like. And if you don't understand that, I'm sorry. I'm not going to have you undermining my self-confidence when I need it most!"

She came close to tears as she spoke, and the look of hurt and astonishment on Fred's face only made it worse.

"Listen, I'm sorry," he said. "I just think you should slow down. For your own good. I know you're doing this for James. It can't be for yourself. You're not the type. But no man is worth it. No person is worth torturing yourself for. If he doesn't love you for what you are, then he's a fool."

"This has nothing to do with James."

He knew she was lying, but he only nodded and looked down. Amanda could not bring herself to speak, afraid her voice would tremble. They finished their coffee in silence.

Four

Drizzle came down like mist on Friday morning. Amanda watched the gray sky and falling rain from inside Lincoln Fowler's office. On the desk between them sat a tape recorder.

Fowler had poured cups of coffee for them both, and now Amanda sipped hers. After three weeks, she did not mind her coffee black.

"You've lost a bit of weight," Fowler said, offering a good-morning smile that looked artificial and out of place.

"A little bit."

"Worry will do that."

"I suppose." She did not tell him about her diet.

"It suits you."

"Thank you."

The small talk seemed to make him uncomfortable, and finally he got down to business.

"I followed your husband yesterday afternoon, after your phone call. He drove to a hotel in Edina and checked in under a false name.

Page. I went to his room and discovered that a woman was already there."

Amanda swallowed hard, trying to keep the strong black coffee from coming back up.

"If you don't want to hear more, just tell me. I can give you a written report, if you prefer."

"Go on, please."

"I managed to tape some of the conversation through the door."

He turned on the tape-recorder and adjusted the volume. The voices that came into the room were muffled, but there was no doubt that one of them was James's. The other was a woman that sounded at once familiar, and totally strange. Lydia, James called her.

It's somebody I know, Amanda thought.

Fowler let the tape play long enough so that Amanda got a good idea of what was going on in the room. She could not look at the detective. She stared down at her hands, wringing them, twisting her fingers.

"I got a photograph of her as she came out of the room. I'm sorry, but I didn't manage to get one of them together."

He pushed a file folder across the desk.

Amanda picked it up with trembling fingers and opened it. The photographs were the kind you often saw in books about the Mafia, or true crime. Gritty, high contrast, the subjects caught in moments when they were least prepared.

The first photograph showed a woman leaving a hotel room, turned slightly away from the camera. Her coat was long and black. Her hair, too, was dark. What Amanda could see of the face was shadowy. She noticed the low heels, the black stockings. Elegant and wealthy, she thought.

The next photograph was a blowup of the woman's face as she had turned, momentarily, toward the camera. Amanda felt her blood turn to ice as she studied the photograph. She had seen this face before. It was the face beyond the glass of the red sports car, and it was the face that had looked up from the rain-soaked street at her bedroom window. So poised, so perfect, so unreal. Beauty manufactured by makeup, but still, beauty that was undeniable.

The woman was not looking directly at the camera, just slightly away, unaware of being photographed.

Amanda's stomach did a flip-flop. "The slut," she said softly. "This is the bitch who nearly ran me off the road."

"Are you sure?" Fowler said.

"Positive. I've seen her since then. She's followed me."

"This is not good, Amanda."

"He lied to me," Amanda said, hardly aware that Fowler had been speaking to her.

Fowler leaned toward her across the desk. "Now, I want you to listen to me, Amanda."

Amanda stared at the pictures, and kept staring until Fowler gently took them out of her fingers and closed the folder.

"Listen to me."

"I'm listening."

"You're hurt right now, and you're angry, and maybe you're thinking of hitting back."

She said nothing, but realized that he was right. If James were here right now she would pound him and kick him and scream at him until she killed him. She hated him.

"You've got to keep those feelings in check. They'll die down soon, I guarantee it."

"I don't want them to die down."

"That doesn't matter. They will, anyway. And if you run out of here right now and do something silly, you're going to regret it very, very quickly."

Amanda looked at him.

"What am I supposed to do?"

"Stay calm. Take the day off work. Go to a movie. Spend some money. Don't even go home tonight if you feel you're going to blow up at him."

"I have to go home. It's his birthday. The bastard."

"I know he seems like a real creep right now. He probably is. But soon enough you're going to realize that he's just human, just a stupid man, and that this means relatively little in the big picture of your marriage. It's just one of those things."

"Just one of those things."

"Give it a few days before confronting him. Think things through. Be logical."

"What about her?"

"If she approaches you again, call the police. Simple as that."

Amanda took a deep breath. "Are the pictures mine?"

"Yes. The negatives are in there, too."

She took them and put them into her bag. Then she stood and looked at Fowler disdainfully.

"I know it's just your job, and I know I asked you to do it, but I'm sorry I ever met you."

"I'm sorry, too, Amanda."

She left his office and went down to her car. In the car she sat silently for a few minutes, watching the rain, and then she started to cry. She was not even sure why she cried. It wasn't for James, really, or for his infidelity. That seemed distant, somehow. Unreal. This was for something else. Something closer to herself.

It was for all the pain she had suffered these past weeks, all the hope, all the effort. All for nothing!

He was seeing another woman!

She did not take Fowler's advice, but went directly from his office to work. She spent a desultory morning at the office, unable to concentrate on anything long enough to do effective work. All she could think about was James. About the picture of Lydia. About James naked with Lydia. About that dark, painted mouth whispering in James's ear.

How could he have betrayed their marriage like that? And after only a year!

And that started another train of thought she found equally as upsetting. How long, exactly, had this been going on?

She had become aware of James's withdrawal in July, after the trip to British Columbia. He had seemed like a different man after they returned. Quieter, shyer almost. He began to spend more time alone than he had ever done, sitting in the library with his gun collection, or off visiting clients. She had attributed the change to trouble in the markets. James's whole life, after all, was at the mercy of forces over which he had no control, his survival dependent on his ability to read and predict those forces. Was it any wonder that he was prone to mood swings?

Up until then he had been the perfect husband. Attentive, passionate, supportive. Even after that, she really had nothing to put her finger on except a vague unease, a sense of furtiveness in their relationship.

They had only been married a year!

That's what hurt most of all. She had always thought, hoped, expected, that her marriage would somehow, miraculously, through effort and love, escape the pressure of statistics. Not every marriage need fail. Hers, she had thought, would be one of the exceptions. How wrong she had been!

Her bitter reverie was interrupted by Tanya, who knocked on her door and stuck her head in.

"Delivery for you," Tanya said, and held out a small envelope.

Amanda composed herself. "Thanks."

She took the envelope and closed the door, then sat at her desk. It was a plain brown envelope, letter-sized. On it was her maiden name, without the hyphenated Sanders attachment. Amanda Burns.

She slit it with her letter opener and pulled out the single sheet within. She realized immediately what it was. It was a single page, torn from a junior high-school yearbook.

Her own yearbook. Joseph Walker Junior High, 1976. A picture of herself she had somehow managed to forget was circled in red ink. She looked at the round, spotted, shiny face in the picture and her stomach flip-flopped as spiteful memories rushed upon her.

The caption read: *Amanda Burns. Still waters run deep . . . and wide! Just kidding, Amanda! Voted most likely to succeed in a BIG way. Har Har.*

At the top of the page, in the same red ink as the circle around her photograph, were the words: "UGLY BITCH!"

Who could have found this yearbook? Who would have known where to look?

James, she realized, had been talking. Talking to Lydia.

Who else could it have been?

Anger so powerful that it made her hands shake, swept through her. She slowly crumpled the torn yearbook page and tossed it into the wastepaper basket by the desk.

Lincoln Fowler's entreatment for rationality and calm seemed nothing more than an annoying twitter at the back of her head. She pushed it aside.

Tonight was James's birthday.

She would give him a present he would never forget.

Amanda wandered the downtown skyway system in a daze, hardly realizing where she was going. She had the vague idea that she needed to get James a gift, something to maintain, for just a little while longer, the normalcy of their relationship. At a gun shop across from the Plymouth Building, a small outlet that James frequented, she bought a leather gun case James had looked at during a recent visit. A part of her was sure he would like it, and was concerned that he would. He often carried his guns to the shooting range in a plastic grocery bag, or wrapped up in a T-shirt. Yes, he could use this. It gave her a feeling of satisfaction to be taking such care in buying his gift.

She bought a coffee in a coffee shop in the

skyway overlooking South Fifth Street. She drank it slowly, watching cars move on the street below. Rain was falling.

She took the photographs from her purse. There were two or three that showed Lydia's face clearly, and she chose the one in which the woman seemed to be looking directly at the camera. Hate flowed out of her as she looked at the picture. She wanted to kill the woman. With her hands. While James watched.

Instead, she put the photograph in the gun case and closed it again. Perfect fit.

In the Crystal Court she paid to have the case wrapped at a customer service desk.

She spent the remainder of the afternoon wandering aimlessly, sometimes even leaving the skyway system to walk on the streets. She felt not at all a part of her surroundings, not even a part of the world.

By the time she arrived at Rand's her legs ached painfully, her feet throbbed, and she was damp from sweat and rain. James was already at the restaurant. The maitre d' led her to the table. James, dressed casually in slacks, an open-necked shirt, and a jacket, stood as she was seated.

"You look beautiful."

He was lying. She looked awful. She had seen herself in a mirror in the lobby, and she looked as if she'd been walking in the wind all day.

She handed him the present.

"Happy Birthday."

"I'll open it later."

"If you like."

Although his manner was bright, and though he appeared for all the world like a dutiful husband, and though she wanted to maintain the image of a happy marriage until the last moment when he opened the gift, she could not rise to the occasion. She was exhausted from her day of revelation and despair. She could hardly even look at James.

Their meal was quiet. James tried often to initiate lingering eye contact, but she refused the bait. She feared he would see her knowledge in her eyes. And besides, in his eyes she was forced to look upon the lies she had lived with for so long. Instead, she studied her plate as she ate.

They were waiting for dessert when he reached across the table, touched her chin, and moved her head so that she could not look away from him.

"Amanda, I love you."

She could not respond.

"I'm sorry for the way I've been acting. There's been a lot on my mind. Sometimes, I don't even feel like myself."

She tried to turn away, but he held her fast.

"All I know is that I love you. You're the best thing that ever happened to me. I'll make it all up to you. I promise."

Now, she did look into his eyes, and could

not look away. What she saw there could only be confirmation of his words. No man could look upon a woman the way he was looking at her, and not love her. Confused, she lifted her chin and looked away.

She ordered an unsweetened fruit salad for dessert, while James ordered a slice of torte. The sugar from the fruit rejuvenated her, and by the time she was finished she knew what she had to do.

James was her husband.

Lydia was the interloper here.

Confronting James would only end their marriage. There would be no chance of repairing the damage then, no chance of reconciliation. Confrontation would be the final slamming of the door. Lincoln Fowler knew what he was talking about.

If she wanted to fix things, then she had to proceed more cautiously. She would have to fight for James, as she was already doing, but she would have to do it surreptitiously. What better way to hit back at Lydia than to steal her husband back?

Confrontation could come later. Much later, when it would act as purifier rather than destroyer.

She realized she was smiling, and James smiled, too.

"I'll open my gift now."

"Not yet. I forgot to put something in there.

Something important. Please, just give me a moment."

She took the gift to the ladies' washroom. There, facing the mirror, she carefully unwrapped it. She removed the photograph of Lydia and put it in her purse. At the gun shop she had picked up a pamphlet for a new gun. She replaced the photograph with the pamphlet, then rewrapped the case as best she could. Before heading back to the dining room she brushed her hair and touched up her makeup. Her face was drawn and tired, but she smiled anyway.

At the table, James took the gift from her and opened it. His eyes brightened at the sight of the case, and he grinned when he saw the pamphlet.

"I love it. I love them both. I love you. Thank you."

He leaned across the table and kissed her on the lips.

"Happy birthday, darling," she said.

After being blocked at another plateau at one hundred eighteen pounds, Amanda finally reached her goal weight of 115 pounds on Thursday, October 14th. When she stepped on the scale at Merit, Chrissy grinned.

"Well done, Amanda!"

Amanda stared at the pointer, balanced perfectly at 115 pounds. She stared at the numbers a long time, unwilling to step down from the scale.

"You've completed the first phase of bringing your weight down," Chrissy said. "The most difficult part, yes, but there's still a lot of work to do."

Brought back to earth by these words, Amanda sat down by the desk and listened while Chrissy laid out the stabilization program she would have to follow, and the behavior modification classes that she would now attend once a week. Her exercise program would continue as it was for a while longer, and slowly be modified to suit her needs. For now, Amanda was to remain on the vitamin supplements and stay away from milk and bread. Slowly, Chrissy assured her, she would begin trying normal foods again.

When she told James she had reached her goal he smiled.

"That's great."

It just didn't mean that much to him, apparently. Which meant that he was either satisfied with the way she had looked before, which couldn't be true, since he was sleeping with another woman, or he didn't care.

He didn't care. That had to be it. He just didn't care.

Two days later, on Saturday morning while James was out shooting, she felt depressed. She moped around the house, looking in the fridge every ten minutes, tempted nearly to the point of breaking by what she found in there. If it had not been for the surprise arrival of Shelly and Patrick before lunch, she knew she would have fallen off the diet wagon with a loud, unmistakable thump.

Patrick appraised her as he came through the door.

"You're looking considerably better," he said.

Shelly held Amanda at arm's length and studied her. "Pretty soon you'll be able to fit into some decent clothes!"

"I guess so," Amanda said without enthusiasm. "I sense a note of unrest," Patrick said.

Amanda did not answer. She led them into the kitchen and poured three cups of coffee. While Shelly and Patrick sat at the table, she leaned against the counter. The temptation to eat was gone, but the feeling of futility remained strong.

"What's wrong, Amanda?" Shelly said.

"I don't want to bother you with it. It's my problem."

"All right," Shelly said firmly. "Spill it."

Amanda sipped her coffee. Without looking at either of them, she said, "James doesn't care that I've lost weight. He just doesn't notice."

"I'm sure you're wrong," Patrick said. "I can't see how he'd fail to notice."

"Well, he has."

"Give him time," Shelly said.

Amanda now looked at them squarely. "He's seeing somebody else."

"I think you're wrong," Shelly said. "I know my brother. I think you're wrong."

"I hired a detective."

If she had dropped a bomb in the kitchen, she could not have hoped for a more profound effect. Shelly and Patrick went white, and stared at her with open mouths and wide eyes.

"You what?"

"I had to know, Shelly. I had to know for certain."

Shelly stared at her. "I can't believe you'd betray James's trust by . . ."

"I'm not the one who's having an affair!"

Patrick regained his composure quickly. He looked at Shelly, and some sort of message seemed to pass between them that Amanda did not catch.

"Did you find anything definite?" he asked.

"He met a woman at a hotel. I have pictures. I think she's been following me."

Shelly and Patrick looked at each other again, pale as ghosts.

"I'll show you if you want."

They both nodded.

Amanda went upstairs and got the pictures. When she returned, Shelly and Patrick were leaning across the table, whispering. They sat up and became quiet. People just didn't know how to react when faced with this kind of thing.

"Her name is Lydia."

Strangely, she found herself in complete control of her emotions. Patrick and Shelly studied the pictures and looked at each other and finally looked at Amanda. She was struck by the impression that they were not as surprised as they appeared, that somehow they already knew about Lydia.

"I haven't confronted James yet," she said. "I just couldn't. I thought it might ruin everything."

"I think that was wise," Patrick said.

"But I don't know what to do. Look at her. She's older than I am. What happened to men going after younger women? I could understand that. What is she giving him that I'm not?"

"Don't give up, Amanda," Shelly said.

"I don't know what to do. She tried to run me off the road a couple of weeks ago. She even followed me here once. I think she sent me a note at work, a nasty note. And I'm not sure, but I'd be willing to bet she's the one who broke our car window on the night of your party."

Again, Patrick and Shelly looked at each other, and again Amanda had the feeling they knew something that she did not.

"I think she's trying to scare me away from James. As if I'd just pack up and leave my husband. She can't really believe I'd do that, that I wouldn't fight back."

Shelly and Patrick said nothing.

"Is there something I should know?" she said, unable to hold it back any longer.

Patrick rubbed his chin.

"To tell you the truth, we've been thinking about you for weeks now."

"If you've got something to say, please just say it."

"What are you doing this afternoon?" Shelly asked.

"Nothing. Why?"

"Feel like coming for a drive?"

She looked at them, saw the concern in their eyes, realized they were trying, in some way yet unspoken, to offer support.

"I guess so. If I have to."

Patrick smiled. "Good. I think we've got a way to help you."

Five

"What is this place?"

Patrick had driven them to Hopkins, and now they were parked beside a low metal and glass building nestled in a parklike setting with a small, man-made lake behind it.

"The Annandale Cosmetic Clinic," Patrick said, turning to look at her.

Shelly, too, turned. Neither of them was smiling.

"I don't think I want to be here."

"Amanda," Patrick said, "we knew this would be the only way to get you out here. Please. Just humor us for another hour. That's all. If you don't like what you see, we won't ever bring up the subject again."

"But I've heard so much about this, Patrick. So much bad stuff."

"You said you wanted to fight for James. Okay. So, prove it. Give us one hour."

Amanda sighed, realizing that she had no choice. She'd allowed them to bring her this far. To back out now would be to slap their faces. They thought that they were helping her, and in their own way she supposed they were. One hour. That much, at least, she could afford.

"One hour."

Patrick grinned. "You won't regret it."

The inside of the clinic seemed as sterile as the outside. Metal and glass everywhere, low ceilings, green plants in every corner looking lost and frightened. Apparently she was expected. A man in a white smock met them in the lobby. He was in his late thirties, Amanda guessed, tall and thin with blond, styled hair that hung over his forehead in a swoop. He smiled and shook Patrick's hand.

"Dr. Whitman, this is Amanda, the woman I was telling you about."

Amanda glared at Patrick. "Was all of this planned?"

"Don't blame him," Dr. Whitman said. "Sometimes people can be very devious when they're trying to help people they love."

Amanda smiled nervously.

"This won't take long," Dr. Whitman said. "We'll do a full assessment, then we'll have a little talk, and that will be it."

"Assessment?"

"I think you'll find this exciting."

Fifteen minutes later, after much cajoling from Shelly and Patrick, Amanda found herself standing alone in a small, white room. The walls appeared to be made out of translucent plastic, and light came from everywhere evenly. She was naked. On one wall was a mirror.

As she stood there, hugging herself, a voice came from a speaker above the mirror.

"Don't worry, Amanda, I'm alone behind the glass. Your friends are waiting in another room."

"I'm not worried."

"Good. Then I'll ask you to stand on the black footprints near the wall opposite the mirror."

Amanda found the footprints. She stood on them, facing the mirror.

"That's good, Amanda," came Whitman's soothing, melodious voice. "Now, relax, please. Let your hands hang at your sides. Feet slightly more apart. That's good. Look at the mirror, at about eye level. That's good. Don't move."

The lights behind her brightened, then faded.

"Now, face the wall to your right, same stance, focusing on the target at eye level. Good. Good. Now, face the wall to the left of the mirror, same stance. That's very good, Amanda. Excellent. And finally, face away from the mirror. Good. That's perfect, Amanda. You can get dressed now. We'll meet you in the display room."

The brightening and dimming of the lights had made her dizzy, and she was relieved when it was over. She shuffled into the dressing room and put on her clothes as quickly as she could. Although Whitman was a doctor, she felt as if she had just performed an exhibition. It made her feel sleazy.

Whitman led her down a brightly lit corridor to another room where Patrick and Shelly waited. The room was like a small theater. On one wall was a large CRT screen, and facing it three rows of chairs. At the back of the room was a sophisticated control desk, part computer terminal, part video-editing deck.

"Amanda," Dr. Whitman said. "We're going to look at your assessment now. If you'd prefer, we can do this alone, or Shelly and Patrick can stay. It's up to you. Some of this you might find a bit personal. Whatever you prefer is fine."

Amanda only knew one thing. She did not want to be alone. She looked from Shelly to Patrick. Patrick smiled warmly.

"I'll wait outside."

Amanda smiled her thanks at him. Then, holding Shelly's hand, she sat down in the front row.

"I don't even know why I'm doing this," she whispered to Shelly.

"You'll see why. Just wait."

The lights dimmed. The screen brightened. Amanda held her breath as an image formed.

"What you're looking at now, Amanda, are

the unedited, but computer-enhanced images of you in the assessment room."

The woman on the screen looked like a mannequin. Definitely human, or human-shaped, but made of plastic. Amanda recognized herself, recognized the sagging breasts, the flabby thighs, the protruding belly that even a twenty-pound weight loss could not fully eradicate. She blushed.

"It's obvious that you're a very attractive woman to begin with, Amanda," Dr. Whitman said.

That only caused Amanda to blush even more deeply. Was he looking at the same image as she was?

"However, there are some minor changes we could make that would subtly alter your appearance."

On the screen, the slowly spinning image of her body began to shift. At first, Amanda was not sure she was seeing any change at all, but soon there was no doubt. Her thighs, after two revolutions of the image, seemed to contract on themselves, until on the front-facing shot there was an actual triangular space beneath her pubis through which she could see white light.

"A bit of lyposuction on the thighs and buttocks," came Dr. Whitman's voice over.

The revolving computer enhancement began to shift again. Her belly seemed to rise and pull into itself, until only a slight swelling remained, voluptuous and nothing more.

"My God," Amanda whispered.

"A very minor tummy tuck," came Whitman's voice.

And then, on the screen, her breasts began to transform. They lifted up, became malleable, and seemed to withdraw into her ribs, until all that remained were two high, firm peaks.

"And to finalize the torso a modest mastopexy, or breast-lift."

Amanda stared, eyes wide and unbelieving, at the transformation on the screen. All thoughts of the horror stories she had heard, of possible complications, were eradicated in the face of new possibilities.

"Finally," Whitman said, "some minor adjustments to the facial features."

On the screen her face, still rotating, suddenly filled the screen. The computer-enhanced image made her skin look rough and textured. Her eyes looked almost somnambulant. On the profile of her nose she had to look down. My God, was she really that ugly?

"Again," Whitman said, "you can see that we have fine features to work with, and not much needs to be done."

Amanda's blush deepened.

"A slight shaving of the dorsum, perhaps a slight reshaping of the nostrils and tip cartilage."

On the screen her nose reshaped itself, the

hump in the middle shrinking, the tip rising slightly.

"Perhaps a face-lift would soften the naso-labial cleft, but this is only a possibility. In any event, it will help to reduce the excess flesh below the chin. Blepharoplasty, a very minor eyelid-lift to enhance the eyes and to bring balance. Finally, perhaps, dermabrasion to smooth minor defects."

On the screen, the computer-enhanced face seemed to sharpen up. The cheeks rose, the chin and flesh beneath tightened, and her eyes, so sleepy before, were suddenly striking.

"Of course, the image presented here is without enhancement. No makeup. When that is added, the changes will appear much more pro-found."

The changes, Amanda thought, were already profound.

When the lights went back up she was trembling. Shelly squeezed her hand.

Whitman helped her from the chair and led her into the hall.

"I'm sure you've got a lot to think about now," he said. "I'm also sure that Patrick will be able to counsel you if you choose."

Patrick came up beside Amanda and held her arm. "Of course I will."

Amanda was speechless. She followed Patrick and Shelly out to the car like a puppy. Only when she was in the back seat, and Patrick was leaving the clinic grounds, did she find her voice.

"Could I really look like that?"

"You could, Amanda," Shelly said, turning to look at her. "You really could. You've got the money. And think of the cause. Not only for yourself, but for your marriage."

"Let her think about it," Patrick said softly. "No need to push."

Shelly turned around.

Amanda, left alone in the back seat, watched traffic pass on the freeway. She thought of the photograph in the yearbook. Sometimes, at the worst moments, she thought of herself as still looking like that. Recently, she had thought that a lot. The images she had seen at the Annandale Clinic were something out of a fantasy. She tried to imagine Lydia's reaction to a change like that.

You want me to run, but I'm not going to. If you want a fight, you bitch, I'll give you a fight.

They were nearly downtown before she spoke again. "What, exactly, is the next step?" she asked.

Both Patrick and Shelly turned to her, but said nothing. The feeling came to Amanda that she had arrived right where they wanted her to arrive, right where they had been leading her from the very start.

* * *

Things moved quickly after her initial "assessment"; so quickly that Amanda felt everything was progressing without her direct involvement. A behemoth in motion, unstoppable. Perhaps that was for the better. The more she contemplated what was happening, the more she worried.

Patrick was wonderful. He visited her at work, taking time from his own pediatric practice to counsel her, and to encourage her. She met with Dr. Whitman twice after her assessment, each time to discuss thoroughly the procedures she was planning, to consider possible complications carefully. Though he expressed surprise at her apparent haste to undergo surgery, he was reassured and placated by Patrick, who talked to him quietly while Amanda was out of earshot. Once, she heard Whitman sound reluctant, even angry, something to do with the planned breast-lift, but saw him acquiesce in the face of Patrick's reassurance. Patrick was well respected in Twin City medical circles.

She could not escape the feeling, however, that she was on a roller coaster, that somewhere along the line it had gone out of control and that now she was on board until the end of the line, wherever that might be. In her worst moments, she could not help feeling that it was not she who had made these decisions, but Patrick and Shelly, and that she was simply a pawn in some sort of game.

What vanquished her doubts and reinforced her determination, was James's continued distance from her. He seemed, at times, almost frightened to touch her, and treated her, in bed, with a reverence that frustrated her beyond belief. He was saving his passion, apparently, for Lydia.

As if Lydia knew this and were satisfied with her work, there were no more letters to Amanda, no more near misses on the freeway. Amanda waited patiently, hopeful that her own counterstrike would be a knockout punch. She was doing the right thing. She was doing the only thing she could do.

She grew concerned only when Patrick asked her to lie to Whitman about her diet. Some people lost strength during dieting and weight loss, he said, but Amanda was not one of those. Better not to throw a wrench in the works for no good reason. Although she felt uneasy about it, she agreed.

The hardest part was keeping it all from James, something that both Patrick and Shelly agreed was probably a good idea.

"He'll fight it if he learns about it beforehand," Shelly said. "But if you present him the result—ipso facto, he'll realize he loves it."

James was planning a weeklong business trip, beginning on the 25th, taking him to Winnipeg, Toronto, Montreal, and then New York, returning to Minneapolis on the 31st. Patrick agreed this would be the best window of opportunity. The first surgery would be performed on the 25th, giving Amanda a week of recovery time before James returned. If all went well, he might never suspect what had happened until Amanda was prepared to tell him.

On the morning of the 25th, Patrick and Shelly came to pick her up. Patrick took one look at her then gripped her arm and steadied her.

"Amanda, calm down. Breathe deeply. Relax. Everything is going to be fine. Everything is going to be just perfect."

"Honey," Shelly said, squeezing her hand, "when this is all over, you're going to feel like a new person."

The morning was sunny and warm. When they arrived at the Annandale Clinic she was reluctant to enter the building. Once through that door, she knew, everything was irrevocable. But Patrick's hold on her arm was strong, and he led her up the path and into the reception area.

Whitman was waiting for them. His manner this morning was brusque, almost rude. He disengaged Patrick and Shelly. Shelly managed a kiss on Amanda's cheek. "We'll be here when it's finished," she said.

The next half hour was so rushed, so full of activity, that it seemed very much like a dream to Amanda. At the end of it she found herself lying in a small white room, naked beneath a thin sheet. Whitman was standing over her, looking concerned.

"We'll perform the abdominal surgery as planned, but I'm still concerned about your breasts," he said. "There's no indication of hypertrophy, and thus no justification for the removal of tissue."

"But Patrick said . . ."

"I know what Dr. Farren said. He's a pediatrician, not a cosmetic surgeon. That may qualify him to counsel you, but it does not give him the right to make a final decision. No breast reduction. I have, however, decided to go ahead with minor mastopexy. A little bit of a lift. It's far less traumatizing surgery, and it won't require you to be inactive for weeks on end. I think it will be satisfactory."

Earlier in the week he'd shown both her and Patrick the computer simulations of both the reduction and the mastopexy on her breasts, and Patrick had been adamant about the reduction. Now, however, she found herself feeling relieved. She'd agreed with Whitman all along.

She nodded to him with a nervous smile.

"Whatever you think, Doctor."

He still looked concerned. "What I think, Mrs. Sanders, is that you're rushing into this. I realize the whole concept may be appealing, but there are ramifications that are impossible to consider seriously in only a week."

"I've made my decision."

"Was it your decision, or was it Dr. Farren's? Patrick can be persuasive, I know that."

She looked at him, shocked that he had vocalized her own doubts. But she shook her head.

"Mine."

He smiled wryly. "Normally, we have a monthlong waiting list for the procedures you're undergoing today. Dr. Farren got you to the top of the list. He's got friends in high places."

"I know," she said.

His look softened, and he smiled. "Well, I had to speak my mind. I hope I didn't offend you. I do respect your decisions."

"I'm glad you're so honest."

"You can trust me when I tell you that it's all going to be fine. Just relax. A nurse will be in momentarily to administer mild sedation, and then we'll wheel you into the operating room. I'll see you again in about four hours."

"Thank you, Dr. Whitman."

He smiled, a thin smile covering deeper concern, and left the room. Amanda waited for the nurse to arrive. She thought of James. She thought of Lydia. She smiled grimly.

Amanda sat on the edge of the bed and lifted her arms. Beyond the window, the leaves on the trees were morning fire.

"Now, remember what I told you," Dr. Whitman said, bending close to her to study the dressings around her breasts. "It's not going to look very nice right now."

Dr. Whitman on one side of her, a nurse on the other, Amanda watched as they cut the dressings. Dr. Whitman began to unwind the long strips of white cloth. As Amanda's breasts appeared, she breathed deeply and looked away.

All she had glimpsed was white skin, marred by long red lines, swollen and ugly.

"Beautiful," Dr. Whitman said.

She felt the touch of his fingers on her flesh, so gentle and caring, yet so unlike a lover's.

"Much better than I expected," Dr. Whitman said, stepping back. "Don't you think?"

Looking down at herself, Amanda had to admit that they were not nearly as bad as she had originally thought. Despite being swollen, they were higher, it seemed, than they had been before. Her nipples, dark buds, were hard. The scars were across the top of each breast and down the sides, where he had removed wedges of skin. A plastic tube protruded from the side of each breast to drain what Dr. Whitman had called "residual fluid."

"They look kind of perky," Amanda said.

"They'll look even better in a few days. The scars will diminish over a period of a couple of months, but they should be noticeably less fiery even a week from now. We'll remove the drains tomorrow morning."

There was a mirror on the door leading into the room, and Amanda pushed herself off the bed. The nurse moved to stop her, but Dr. Whitman held up a hand to ward her off.

"Have a look," he said to Amanda.

Amanda stood before the mirror and studied herself. The breasts were definitely hers, but they were a younger woman's breasts. A girl's breasts.

When the swelling went down, and when the scars diminished, they would look beautiful. She realized she was smiling, and turned to Dr. Whitman with a small laugh.

"There's still a long way to go," he said. "You'll have to wear a bra day and night for at least three weeks, except when you take a shower. And as for sexual intercourse, well, you'll have to tell your husband to steer clear of your breasts for at least a few weeks."

No problem there, Amanda thought.

She sat on the bed again, and Dr. Whitman removed the dressing from her midriff. Again, Amanda stood to study herself in the mirror. Her belly was flatter, curvaceous but not bulging. Was her navel slightly higher than it had been before? She was not sure. A bright red line ran across the top of her abdomen, and down the sides of her belly. She stepped closer, noticing with surprise that the flesh around her mons pubis seemed firmer. The entire dark triangle seemed more pronounced somehow, and she felt a pang of envy, as if she were studying the photograph of a model.

"Very nice," Whitman said.

Amanda sat down on the bed, shaking her head. "I didn't realize it would look so good."

"We know what we're doing," he said.

The incisions were cleaned, new dressings were applied, and afterward Amanda lay down on the bed. Her doubts were gone, and along with them the post-op blues. Dr. Whitman had warned her that she might feel down about herself, about her body, for a few days. Staring now at the ceiling she felt only excited, and eager to leave the clinic.

Her whole life, she decided, was going to change.

"Do you feel like seeing visitors?" Whitman asked.

"Patrick and Shelly?"

"They've been waiting for about an hour. I had a hard time getting rid of them yesterday, and I doubt they'll take no for an answer today."

Amanda smiled. "Okay. Show them in."

She straightened the bed a bit and sat herself up. When Patrick and Shelly came into the room she greeted them with a smile. Shelly came right to the bedside and squeezed her hand.

"I know you probably feel terrible right now, Amanda, but it will get better. Operations can take a lot out of you."

"I feel fantastic."

"You do?"

Patrick came to the other side of the bed. "You look well."

"I just saw what was beneath the bandages."

"And?" Shelly prodded.

"It's fantastic. I can't believe it. I look like a girl of twenty. It's incredible."

Patrick grinned. "I'm glad, Amanda. I talked to Whitman about the breast reduction, and he's agreed to go ahead with it later. I know he was doubtful at first, but he's seen it my way."

"I don't want to, Patrick."

"Listen, I know he talked you out of it, but it's okay now."

"That's not it. I like them the way they are now. I don't want the reduction."

He stood up straight, looked at Shelly, then back at her.

"Well, we can talk about it later," he said.

Amanda did not want to argue, and she refused to be brought down. She grabbed both their hands and squeezed tightly.

"Shelly, when you first told me, at the anniversary party, to look at myself, I can't tell you how angry and hurt I was. But now, I see you were right. You were a true friend. I don't know how to thank you."

"You don't have to thank me."

"I just wish Lydia could see this. I can't wait."

When they left her, half an hour later, she

was tired. She lay gratefully back on the bed, and closed her eyes. Even the coming of sleep could not wipe the smile from her face.

Six

Amanda was discharged at 10:00 A.M. on Thursday morning. Patrick and Shelly were there to pick her up. Dr. Whitman gave her a small plastic bag. The bag contained extra dressings, which she would have to change herself, and two bras, rather heavy-duty things, she would have to wear constantly, and a bottle of analgesic tablets.

"I'll see you on Monday or Tuesday to remove the sutures," he said.

In the car, Amanda was silent. Her breasts ached, and her stomach felt unnaturally tight. Dr. Whitman had told her to expect it as muscle and flesh reshaped themselves, but still the discomfort bothered her.

Patrick and Shelly offered to come in with her, to stay overnight if necessary, but she refused. She wanted to be alone. She promised to call them every day.

Studying her body in the bedroom mirror, she was exhilarated. The scars were already turning paler, shrinking, and, if not for the sutures, would need a close look to see properly. The swelling in her breasts had gone down substantially, and for the first time she got a good idea of what they would look like weeks from now. Absolutely incredible. The clothes she could now wear!

Sleeping that night was tough. She ached considerably, and ended up having to take the tablets Dr. Whitman had provided. On Friday morning she was exhausted, and spent most of the day in bed. When she showered, later in the day, even the water spraying her breasts and belly seemed to burn. She debated calling Dr. Whitman to ask if these symptoms were normal, but did not want to seem childish.

Saturday was better. Though tender, her breasts had stopped aching, and her stomach felt quite comfortable. She was eating normal foods again, or as normal as her Merit diet allowed, and went back onto the supplements she had been using. No point in getting all this surgery and then putting weight back on.

By Sunday, she was feeling almost normal. The aches had diminished to dull background static, and she was even able to walk downtown and back again. Although James had asked her not to, she decided to pick him up at the airport when his plane arrived.

Excited by the prospect of his reaction to her new appearance, she wore a dress she had not worn in many years. Even with the operations and weight loss, it was a tight fit, and she knew that Dr. Whitman would not be pleased. But this was for James. It was all for James.

By the time his plane arrived from New York it was nearly 10:00 P.M. She had not eaten anything since lunch; and she was feeling light-headed. She watched the stream of passengers emerge from the arrival gate, praying that he would hurry up.

When he finally appeared, she waved at him. For a few seconds he did not recognize her, then his mouth opened in surprise. He waved, and worked his way toward her.

Amanda loosened her coat and opened it so that her dress and new body were visible. James, looking tired and nervous, pecked her cheek.

"Amanda, what are you doing here?"

"I thought I'd surprise you."

"You did."

He was not looking at her, but over her shoulder, to his left and right, furtive and worried. He was looking for somebody.

"This is really nice of you, Amanda," he said, still avoiding her eyes.

Amanda surveyed the milling crowd, looking for Lydia's familiar face. Nothing. If she was here, she knew well enough to remain concealed. Amanda's mouth was suddenly dry and bitter.

"How have you been?" James asked.

"Fine." He had not noticed the change in her appearance.

"You look a bit pale. Lot of colds going around."

"I'm fine."

On the drive back to Park Avenue he talked continuously about his trip, about the clients, about the weather. Rain pattered against the windshield, falling from a bleak sky, mirroring perfectly Amanda's mood. When they got home he went immediately to the library, promising to come through soon.

Amanda undressed, positively nauseated now. She had not eaten in nearly ten hours. The thought of eating made her feel worse. She could not stop thinking about Lydia. She knew who James had expected to see at the airport. He had worked hard to hide his disappointment, but not hard enough.

She put on one of Dr. Whitman's bras, and over top of it a flannel nightdress. In bed she lay on her back. The fatigue and hunger and anger brought out the aches and pains again. Sleep, she hoped, would bring oblivion.

Some time later she opened her eyes. She had slept, apparently. Her breasts ached terribly, and her stomach growled. She knew she would have to eat something. She could not wait until morning.

The clock radio showed 12:47. James was not in bed.

Still depressed, still angry, she got up. She

went to the library. James was sitting in his favorite chair, glasses resting on the tip of his nose, flipping through some papers. Amanda stood in the doorway and stared at him.

After a few seconds he seemed to realize she was there and looked up at her.

"You weren't in bed. I thought I'd get something to eat."

He stood up and, with a look of horror, came toward her.

"My, God, Amanda, what have you done to yourself?"

He finally noticed, she thought.

She smiled and looked down at herself. She saw the dark spots on the hardwood floor at her feet. She saw the glistening red swath below her right breast, reaching to her hips. It took only a second to realize the mess on the floor was blood, dripping from the hem of the nightgown. Then she collapsed.

Amanda felt warm all over. Comfortable, dozy, but not yet ready to slip into sleep. Voices, bells, clattering steel . . . all these sounds seemed distant, muted. She knew she was in a room, somewhere in the Hennepin County General Hospital, but it didn't seem very important that she was here. In a way she felt absolutely helpless, and the feeling provided some comfort. If there was nothing she could do, then there was nothing she *had* to do.

Whatever had happened had happened, and whatever was going to happen was going to happen.

"How are you feeling?"

Amanda opened her eyes. Dr. Whitman, wearing civilian clothes, was standing by the bed.

"Cozy."

"They've sedated you. You'll sleep well."

"Mmm." Smiling, she closed her eyes. "I should be angry with you, Mrs. Sanders."

"Why?" She opened her eyes again.

"For a number of reasons. Mainly because you lied to me."

"Lied?"

"You've been on a low-calorie, low-fat diet for a month now. You've lost over twenty pounds."

"I'm sorry. I didn't think you'd go ahead if you knew."

"You're right about that. And there are reasons why I wouldn't have. Mostly they have to do with the strength required to recover from surgery. Your resources are substantially depleted, Mrs. Sanders. You're very lucky not to have suffered more severe complications. Not to mention that if you regain any of that weight in the near future, you're going to lose any benefits of the surgery."

For the first time, she felt a spark of interest at her condition.

"What happened?"

"Nothing overly serious. One of the incisions

on your right breasts opened and the wound bled."

"Oh."

"It wouldn't have happened if you'd followed my instructions and taken it easy. "

"I had to pick up my husband."

"You didn't have to wear that form-fitting dress. It put far too much stress on your breasts."

"I'm sorry."

"Well, no real harm done, this time. Dr. Chapman resutured the incision. I've inspected the work, and I don't think you'll suffer any extra scarring."

"I'm sorry I lied to you. I'm sorry I wore that dress."

"You don't have to apologize, Mrs. Sanders. But I should tell you that I'll be withdrawing as your cosmetic surgeon. I just wouldn't feel comfortable about it. I already don't feel comfortable, partly because I have a feeling that Dr. Farren instructed you to withhold information from me, and partly because I feel he may be giving you advice not in your best interest. I don't like to work this way. I will, however, perform all the necessary steps to help you recover from the surgery you've already undergone. Don't have any fears about that."

Funnily enough, Amanda wasn't worried at all. Even Dr. Whitman's withdrawal meant little to her. She was inside a soft, warm cocoon, through which the worries of the world could not pass. She smiled up at him, then closed her eyes. At last, the darkness of sleep closed around her.

Voices woke her.

The room was dark. Parking-lot lights made the lateral window blinds green in places, and cast shadow bars on the wall behind her head. She was still within the cocoon, still sedated. Her eyes followed the clear plastic tube running from a bandage on her right hand to a half-full intravenous bag hanging overhead.

Other shadows crowded into the room from the area by the door, which she could not see because of the bathroom wall. Somebody, she thought, must be standing in the doorway. The shadows were cast by lights in the hall.

Then the voices again. She recognized them.

James. Patrick. Shelly.

James was angry. He said something to Patrick, voice hushed but very harsh.

". . . had a right to know! I'm her husband!"

"James, please . . ." that was Shelly, attempting to placate him.

"She decided herself," Patrick said.

And then they were all talking at once and Amanda picked up little. After a few seconds their voices turned into the crashing of surf. Amanda drifted away again.

And then, from the surf, a single, sharp, distinguishable word.

". . . Lydia . . ."

96

Amanda opened her eyes. She was not sure who had spoken, but the word seemed to hang in the air, stopping all conversation.

"I don't know," James said.

Shelly whispered something. Then James.

"Have to do something," said Patrick.

And then another voice, a new voice, a female voice, hushed but commanding. A nurse, ushering them along, clearing the hall.

Moments later the light from the doorway snuffed out. Amanda fought to remain conscious, but the bars above her head began to ripple and sway. A warm, dry sensation spread across her skin, from fingertip to fingertip, from head to toe, soothing her.

She closed her eyes and slept.

"Good morning!"

James came through the doorway grinning, a small vase of flowers in one hand. Amanda put down her magazine and smiled at him. He bent over and kissed her. His lips lingered for a moment, then he parted from her.

"Something to brighten up the room."

"You didn't have to do that. I'll be out tomorrow."

"That soon?"

"Dr. Chapman said I could go home today, but Dr. Whitman wanted me to stay an extra day."

"Can't say that I blame him."

He sat down in the chair next to the bed. For a few seconds, as they looked at each other, an uncomfortable, unnatural silence enveloped them. It was James who broke it.

"I wish you had told me what you were doing."

"I wanted it to be a surprise."

"I wouldn't have allowed it."

"As if it was your choice to make."

"I didn't mean it like that. I meant, I would have tried to argue you out of it."

"Would you?"

"Of course I would! I love you as you are! As you were. You don't have to do this sort of thing."

"What if I did it for myself?"

"Did you?"

"In a way, yes.

"I still wish you had told me."

He seemed honestly hurt, and she knew it was not an act. He did love her, despite his affair. She wondered what he would say if she brought up Lydia again, showed him the photographs that Fowler had taken. Would he still deny it? Would he still feign ignorance? What if she told him about Lydia's attacks? And they *were* attacks, however you wanted to look at them. The whole affair was an attack, when you got right down to it, a frontal assault on her self-esteem, on her very life.

Then, for the first time, she remembered the

conversation she had overheard in the hall last night.

"You were here last night."

"I stayed for a few hours after you were admitted, but you were sedated."

"You were standing in the doorway with Patrick and Shelly."

"It could be. They were here, too."

"You were arguing about something."

"Were we? I don't remember."

Something in his voice made her end her line of questioning. She did not want to confront him yet, and the vague suspicion that had flowered in her mind was too hideous to speak of openly. Not yet, anyway.

Their conversation turned to other things. He assured her that he had straightened things out with her office. She was not expected back until the following week, and he relayed her co-workers' concerns and best wishes. He had told them, despite protests from some quarters, not to visit her, to allow her to rest, and for that she was grateful. She did not know if she could stand to see anybody from the office right now. Not in the state she was in.

After an hour, James became fidgety. She knew that he hated hospitals, and his presence was beginning to make her nervous and tense. She suggested he leave, and he agreed without argument.

After he was gone, she lowered her bed and lay back. Her mind returned, unbidden, to the conversation she had overheard last night. The horrible suspicion she had so far managed to squash, slid like a snake back into her mind.

"Lydia," one of them had said.

As if the name were of long-standing familiarity to all of them. As if Patrick and Shelly had known of her existence all along. As if, in fact, Amanda had been the very last to know.

Seven

On Friday, November 5th, Amanda returned to the Annandale Clinic to have her sutures removed. Dr. Whitman studied the scars on her breasts and belly closely.

"Much better than I had hoped," he said.

And much better than anybody had led Amanda to expect. Already the scars were losing some of their fiery redness, fading to pale pink lines that looked nothing worse than the indentations from bra straps or from the tops of pantyhose.

"No indication of infection, or swelling. This is really good."

Studying herself in the mirror, Amanda was amazed at what she saw. Between neck and hips she was a brand-new person. She had the breasts and belly of a twenty year old, but not the twenty year old she had been herself. These were the high breasts and flat belly she had envied in other girls. Now they were hers.

"I'd like to ask you to consider not going

101

ahead with any additional surgery," he said to her as she was dressing.

"Why?"

Dr. Whitman touched his chin and frowned, looking almost fatherly.

"Amanda, I'm the first to admit that cosmetic surgery is exactly what some people need. They may have lived all their lives with flaws that made them ashamed, or made them feel ostracized. Or they may have suffered disfigurement in accidents, or in fires. I can even defend surgery that will make a definite improvement in appearance. In your case, I was doubtful even of the mastopexy and abdominal surgery, since the results, while not insignificant, were also not radical. You were very attractive before the procedures."

Amanda did not smile. She did not say anything.

"I just don't feel that further surgery will do anything to improve your appearance. It will simply change it. And change, of itself, is not worth surgery."

"What about how I feel inside?"

"There are doctors who deal with that."

"I don't need a psychiatrist, Dr. Whitman. I mean I feel better inside, looking this way on the outside."

"I'd like to know what made you feel bad about yourself to begin with."

"Nothing made me feel bad," she lied. "I just saw the way I looked."

"Well, I just had to speak my mind. Your body is your own."

"Thank you."

"As I've already said, however, I will not participate in further surgery."

"I understand that. Patrick—Dr. Farren—has already picked another surgeon. He'll see me when I'm ready to proceed."

"May I ask his name?"

"Raymond Lowell, at the Matrix Clinic."

For a moment she thought that Dr. Whitman was going to turn away. His face went white.

"Mrs. Sanders . . ."

"Burns-Sanders, please."

"I don't usually criticize fellow surgeons, but I feel it is my duty to tell you that Raymond Lowell is considered . . . reckless, by some of his peers."

"He came highly recommended."

"He's recommended by those who seek surgery outside the medical mainstream. I ask you to reconsider."

"Will you do the work?"

"No, I won't."

"Then there's nothing more to discuss."

But in the following days, Amanda did reconsider. She was not eager to go under the knife again, and looking at her face in the mirror she realized that she would not know what to feel if she saw another face reflected there. A face-lift was much more personal than the changes she had undergone so far. Her breasts and belly with their pale, fading scars, were hidden behind clothes, the overall effect being that she was slimmer, more shapely. But work on the face . . . that would be visible for all to see.

Returning to work took her mind off all that. Although Fred Cooper had covered her listings there was still a lot of catching up to do. She arranged for four open houses within two weeks of returning.

In addition, she returned to Merit to continue with the stabilization and behavior modification phases of her program. Chrissy saw the difference in her immediately, guessed she had undergone surgery, and told Amanda that she would need written permission from a physician before reentering the program.

"But, God, you look fantastic!"

Patrick provided the written permission that night, and a day later Amanda was back in the full swing of her stabilization and exercise program.

By mid-November there was snow on the ground, and the National Weather Service was warning of a major blizzard by the end of the week. The bleak weather became a perfect match for Amanda's mood.

Patrick kept asking her when she would be ready for the lyposuction and the face-lift, and she kept putting him off, not even sure why. Dr. Whitman's words had sunk in, apparently.

But in the end, as with her earlier decision,

it was Lydia who finally pushed her into making up her mind.

The November blizzard started on the afternoon of the 17th. Amanda left work early, not wanting to be trapped at the office for any length of time. Instead, she found herself trapped at home. Alone, with James.

As snow filled the streets, blocking freeways, Amanda and James reached a crisis. They had not made love since well before Amanda had undergone surgery, and now that she was fully recovered, he was still reluctant to touch her. While an eerie, winter silence descended upon Minneapolis, Amanda resolved to break their sexual fast.

During the first night of the blizzard, while James read in the library, Amanda sequestered herself in the bedroom and began to transform herself. Sitting before her dresser mirror she applied makeup. Not much, but more than she usually wore to bed. From her lingerie drawer she chose a bra and high-cut panties she had purchased recently.

When James finally came to bed, she was ready. She left the light on. When he looked at her, his eyes widened, and she could see, immediately, that he was affected.

"I want you to make love to me," she said.

He sat down on the bed and stared at her. But he did not touch her.

"James, please."

"Darling, you haven't completely recovered yet."

"I have."

"I don't want to damage you."

"Damage me? James! I'm not a fragile piece of equipment that gets broken when you touch it! I'm your wife. It's your duty to make love to me when I want you to!"

But he only shook his head. "Soon. I promise."

When he undressed, she saw that he was erect. But in bed he turned away from her.

Something was holding him back, and it was not simply his fear of hurting her. His mind was elsewhere. And she knew where. With Lydia. Despite the diet, despite the surgery, Lydia was winning. Lydia had him, controlled him.

"I'm just tired," he said, as she turned off the light.

Amanda rolled away from him. Through the half-closed blinds she watched snow falling.

She thought of Lydia.

If I ever meet you alone, I'll kill you.

They were stuck together in the house for three days while the blizzard raged and the city shut itself down. They hardly talked at all, and made no further attempts to make love.

On Saturday, November 20th, after the snowplows had cleared the streets and traffic was once again moving, Amanda left James alone at home and drove to Patrick and Shelly's house.

Patrick answered the door, eyebrows rising when he saw her.

"I'm ready to go ahead," she said. "Any time."

The Matrix Clinic differed notably from the Annandale Clinic. Here, she found no comforting decoration, no atmosphere of easy relaxation. Matrix was all business. Institutional green walls, parking lots on one side, an incinerator/laundry plant on the other. This was an industrial complex. Doctors, nurses, even orderlies, bustled along corridors with severe expressions, as abrupt with patients as they were among themselves. The clients here were of a younger variety than at Annandale, men and women alike, in for nose-jobs and eyelid-lifts.

Dr. Lowell, too, was a change from Dr. Whitman. At least twenty years Dr. Whitman's senior, his experience showed in nearly everything about him. His voice, his facial expressions, his touch, all revealed his self-assurance. He expressed no doubts, suffered no qualms.

On the one hand, Amanda's confidence that she had made the right decision strengthened. On the other hand, the moment she set foot in the clinic she felt that all choice had been taken from her. The train had left the station, and there were no stops until the last.

Dr. Lowell visited her only briefly in pre-op. He studied her breasts and abdomen.

107

"Dr. Whitman is a fine surgeon. I wish we could convince him to come over."

She smiled at that. Dr. Whitman would never work here.

"The operation today will last about four hours. I'll be performing the face-lift, the rhinoplasty and the blepharoplasty. My assistant, Dr. Thomas, will tackle the lyposuction on your thighs. You'll be under general anesthesia."

After that, he left her alone. She spent the next half hour smiling nervously at a nurse who uttered only two or three words while they were together. Minutes before the operation, the nurse injected a sedative into Amanda's arm. When they rolled her gurney into the operation room, her head was swimming and nausea tightened her stomach.

Lights circled above her, brightening and dimming, while the corners of the ceiling faded into darkness. Two faces bent over her. Dr. Lowell moved her chin from side to side, his touch rougher now than she had ever felt it. The other face drifted in and out of focus, and when it bent close to her she stopped breathing. Patrick.

"Hi, Amanda. Dr. Lowell has agreed to let me observe. How are you feeling?"

She said something, but her mouth groaned. Patrick being here with her was strange, and she felt uneasy about it.

"Just relax. The anesthetist will be in shortly."

108

Then Dr. Lowell was bending over her, blue eyes studying her face intently. Dr. Lowell and Patrick started talking. Arguing. She heard her name a few times. A nurse appeared from nowhere and hovered over her, then another man, fatter and younger than Dr. Lowell. He must be Dr. Thomas. When the anesthetist arrived, tall, rail thin, black, and the youngest person in the room, he smiled at her. His hands were gentle when he touched her. He droned on about the weather and had her count backwards, the sound of his voice filling her as she plunged through a long, winding tunnel, and into darkness.

Wednesday was the worst day of Amanda's life.

Dr. Lowell and a nurse came to her room early in the morning. Lowell was cheerful, but businesslike.

"The nausea has passed?"

"Yes?"

"How do you feel?"

"Excited."

"Don't expect much. The first days after removal of the dressings can be disappointing."

For two days, head swathed in bandages, she had felt like a Minnesota Vikings nose-tackle. Now, as the dressings fell to the side of the bed, she felt light-headed.

"Excellent healing," Dr. Lowell said.

He touched her chin and moved her head from side to side. "Excellent."

"How do I look?"

"Let me show you."

He helped her from the bed and walked her to the bathroom area. Amanda stared at her reflection in the mirror and started to cry. Her face was purple and yellow. Her eyes were mere slits, recessed in swollen flesh.

"Oh, God."

"The swelling will go down in a day or two. The bruises will fade to an acceptable level in a week, possibly two. The sutures will fall out by themselves over a period of ten to twenty days."

"Oh, God."

He led her back to the bed.

"Get as much rest as you can. You're going home today."

When Dr. Lowell and the nurse left her, Amanda continued to cry. The tears trickled down her swollen, misshapen face, soaking the pillow. When Patrick and Shelly stuck their heads into the room she was still crying.

"Go away."

"Amanda, what's wrong?" Patrick asked.

"Look at me!"

"You look fine. Bruising and swelling are normal. It's nothing out of the ordinary."

"James is waiting outside," Shelly said. "He'd like to see you."

Amanda sat up straight. The tears stopped instantly.

"No."

"He's sick with worry. He wants to see how you're doing."

"I said no, Shelly. No. I don't want him to see me like this."

"What are you going to do when you get out of here this afternoon?" Patrick asked. "You have to go home."

"No. I can't. I won't."

"Where will you go?"

"I'll go to my parents."

"Amanda, you're being silly," Patrick said.

"I don't care. I'll phone them. They'll come to get me."

Shelly sat on the edge of the bed and held her hand. "Don't phone them. We'll take you up there, won't we, Patrick?"

"If that's what you want, yes."

"That's what I want."

"Then I suppose I had better go and tell something to James."

"Please, Patrick, tell him I'm sorry. It won't be for long."

He nodded and left the room. Shelly continued to squeeze her hand.

"Don't you worry, sweetie. When this is all over you're going to feel like a million bucks."

Amanda said nothing. She turned away from Shelly and started to cry again. She had hoped the change in her appearance would be a knockout punch to Lydia, a winning stroke to reclaim her husband. Instead it had turned back on her. Her face was a mangled pulp, she was down for the count, and somewhere, laughing delightedly, Lydia was moving in for the kill.

Eight

Amanda spent a week and a half at her parents' home in St. Cloud. Her parents' reaction to her new surgery was worse than she had expected. Her father hardly talked to her at all. The time there, however, allowed the swelling and bruising to fade.

On Saturday, December 11th, she stood before her dresser mirror and studied herself. Even with the scars on her thighs, face, and torso still visible, thin red lines curving here and there, she was stunning. She stared for minutes on end, eyes wide. She dared not believe what she saw. Her soft curves had become hard edges. Her face was angular now, cheeks high, with a narrow upturned nose. Her breasts and belly were firm. Her once-thunderous thighs were thin and shapely.

She applied some makeup. A touch of lipstick, eyeshadow, and blush, brought her face into sharp definition. She used no more than usual. Even that was enough to transform her completely.

The effect was compelling.

For most of her time here she had doubted she would ever look or feel beautiful. Now, those doubts were banished.

It had been ten days since her surgery, ten days for Lydia to have her way with James. Long enough. Too long.

An hour later, she carried her single bag downstairs. Her parents, sitting in the living room, stared at her silently.

"I'm going back now," she said.

Amanda opened her arms and hugged her still-silent mother. She moved toward her father, but he stepped away from her.

"Dad, please."

He shook his head. "Who are you? You're not my daughter. I don't know you."

"I'm sorry you don't approve, Dad. But it's my life."

"God gave you beauty enough," he said, and turned away from her.

Her mother helped her on with her coat. "He doesn't mean it, dear. It's just the shock."

"It's a shock to me, too," Amanda said.

In the car, driving back to the Twin Cities, she could not stop smiling.

Amanda opened and closed the front door as quietly as she could. She took off her coat and hung it up. She stood in the foyer and listened. From James's office came the sound of his voice.

She walked toward the office door, and poked her head around the corner. He was talking on the phone. When he saw her his eyes widened and his mouth opened.

Into the phone, he said, "I'll call you back tomorrow. I've got an emergency here."

"Hello, James."

"Amanda?"

She lifted her arms and turned for him. He could not close his mouth.

"You're beautiful."

"Thank you."

"You were always beautiful, but now . . ."

"I know, James."

"I can't believe it."

His eyes roamed her body, top to bottom, lingering on thighs, breasts, and finally face. The desire in his expression was so obvious that she began to feel it herself. She could not remember the last time he had looked at her like that.

"Make love to me, James."

"Now?"

"Now."

She held out her hand to him. He came toward her like a teenager being seduced by an older woman. He still had not closed his mouth.

She led him upstairs. In the bedroom, she

slipped out of her dress. If he had looked shocked before, he now looked astounded.

"Amanda . . ."

Amanda started to take off her bra.

"No, please. Leave it on. Leave it all on."

"Okay."

He came to her then, and extended a hand toward her. Gently, as if touching her for the first time, he slid his hands beneath her bra. His thumbs pressed against her nipples, moved slowly in circles. His touch was cool, electric, and it sent shivers through her entire body.

"I can't believe this," he said hoarsely.

Their lovemaking was the most animalistic of their entire relationship. Amanda felt he was using her, and she used him back. When it was over, she stared at the ceiling. Her legs shook. Her heart pounded. Every inch of her felt used and battered, yet she had never felt so fulfilled in her life.

When her breathing had slowed to normal, she slid off the bed and went to the dresser. From her purse she got the picture of Lydia and went back to the bed.

James looked at it and turned pale. He put it facedown on his chest. He closed his eyes. His upper lip trembled. His breathing had returned to normal, but now his breath came from his mouth in a rush.

"Will you end it with her?" Amanda asked.

He opened his eyes and looked at her. His

face showed no guile. He did not try to deny it.

"I'll end it."

Despite protests from James, Amanda returned to work on Monday morning. After avoiding it as long as possible, afraid of his reaction, she looked in on Fred Cooper.

He appeared neither surprised, nor shocked, nor appreciative. He had known she was here. He had been waiting.

"Hello," she said.

"Hello."

"Can I come in?"

"Have a seat."

She went in, closed the door, and sat down. He closed the magazine he'd been reading and put it down on the desk. He looked at her, still smiling.

"You're back much sooner than I expected," he said.

"I feel pretty good. I wanted to get back into the swing of business."

"That's probably a good idea."

The strained formality between them was almost physically painful for Amanda. Other than Shelly, he was the only person she felt she could treat as a confidant. They lapsed into silence, and she could not look at him.

"Fred, why are we acting this way?"

"How are we acting?"

"Like we hardly know each other. Like we're just co-workers, or maybe even less."

He stared at her. All pretense of civility had gone. He nodded slowly.

"I don't know who you are any more, Amanda."

This echo of her dad's sentiments cut her, but it also made her angry.

"You're talking nonsense. I'm me. I haven't changed."

"How do you know?"

"I know what's inside."

"Do you?"

"Yes, I do. I want you to stop acting like this. You're my friend, so be my friend. I don't need a judge!"

He took a deep breath. "I *am* your friend. You're right. I worry about you, as a friend. I tried to give you advice, but you didn't want it."

"Give it to me now."

"It's too late, now."

"I know you don't approve of what I've done."

"It's not simply a matter of not approving. What you've done is . . . dangerous."

"Don't be silly."

"I'm not being silly, Amanda. I checked out the kind of surgery you've had."

"Somehow, I knew that you would."

"Did you know that the normal wait between

surgeries of that type is about six months, sometimes a year?"

"They said I was in good health."

"Who said that?"

"My doctor told me."

"What doctor?"

"Fred, what's your point?"

"My point is that you moved far more quickly than is good for you. You decided one week to have surgery, and you had it done the next. Major breast and abdomen surgery, Amanda. You decided in the blink of an eye."

"I knew what I wanted to do."

"Then why had you never talked about it before? Why was it all so sudden?"

"It wasn't sudden. I don't always tell you what I'm planning."

"I know you don't. I just thought we were honest with each other."

"We are, Fred."

"We *were,* you mean."

Amanda took a deep breath. "I'm sorry if you don't approve, Fred, but it's *my* life. These are *my* decisions to make."

"I know that. In a way, I admire what you've done. I mean, taking charge of your life so completely that you'd alter your appearance. That takes guts, I guess. I just get the feeling that somebody pushed you into it. Somebody didn't give you the complete picture. I've never heard of surgery like this going ahead so quickly. Never."

"Don't you like what you see?"

"What am I supposed to see?"

"Come on, Fred. Objectively, don't I look better?"

"Objectively, you look like this year's cover model. I suppose next year you can have more surgery to put back everything they took out. Cover girls always change."

"You don't think I look better," she said flatly.

"I liked you the way you were."

"I didn't."

"Then I feel sorry for you."

Amanda stood up, angry. "I don't need you to talk to me like that!"

"I'm sorry, Amanda. Friends speak their minds."

"Maybe I should speak mine."

"Please, do."

"Okay, I will. You're a slob, Fred. You dress like a twelve year old. Nothing ever matches. Look at that shirt and tie. Jesus. You embarrass me! Look at you! Look at your hair. Don't you own a comb? Don't you care about yourself? About what you look like? Do you really not know why Tracy left you? Look at you!"

His expression did not change. "I like myself," he said quietly. "I always have."

Amanda sat down again, trembling. She had done a number on Fred twice as bad as Shelly had done on her!

"Oh, God, Fred, I'm sorry. I didn't mean to say any of it. You know I didn't!"

"You were just speaking your mind."

"I don't know what I was speaking."

She had hurt him. She knew that. He had always trusted her opinion, and they had always been honest with each each other. She had stuck in the knife, especially about Tracy, and twisted sharply.

"Let's go for lunch," she said. "Let's go and talk, like we used to. I'll buy."

He smiled, but there was no humor in it. It was simply a mask put on to hide something more painful.

"I can't today. I have to complete this deal." He waved at the desk.

Amanda stood, nodding slowly. "Maybe later," she said.

She returned to her office. There, door closed, she stared out the window for a long time.

Nine

Sparky's was a singles bar that Fred and Amanda never patronized. Many secretaries and low-level executives from the local businesses spent their lunch hours there. On impulse Amanda turned into the parking lot.

Loud music assailed her as she entered the lounge, heavy bass that drummed against her rib cage. She felt underdressed in her jeans and sweater, but not enough to bother her. She bypassed the tables and took a stool at the bar.

Immediately, the bartender delivered a strawberry margarita. She looked down at the drink, then up at the bartender.

"I didn't order this."

The bartender, a fat woman in a white blouse, smiled. "It's from the gentleman in the corner."

Amanda did not turn around. She blushed and looked down at her hands.

"You look like this has never happened to you before."

"Never."

"You're joking. The way you look?"

Amanda looked up. The fat bartender, whose name tag said Viola, was still smiling.

"I haven't always looked like this."

"Well, you'd better get used to it."

Amanda stared at the drink. She did not know what to do. If she accepted it, was she also tacitly accepting some sort of proposition? Would the man who bought the drink then approach her? She did not know if she could deal with that.

"Listen, honey, it's just a drink. It's free. That's all it is. He's not going to bother you any more, whether you drink it or not. Not unless you send him signals."

"Signals?"

"You could try turning around, smiling, and waving him over. If that doesn't work, try sticking out your tongue and licking your lips."

"I'm not going to do that!"

"So drink your drink and enjoy it."

Amanda smiled nervously. She picked up the glass and sipped from it. It was good.

"Now, that wasn't so hard, was it?" Viola asked.

Amanda shook her head, smiling now.

She ordered a basket of breaded shrimp, but only nibbled on one or two, remembering too late about her diet, and made the drink last through her lunch. Even so, she felt it. She

123

had not tasted alcohol in a long time. When she was ready to leave, she waved to Viola.

"Is he still there?"

"Sure is, and looking this way."

Amanda put on her coat. She turned around and looked toward the corner. In a booth, by himself, sat a man she guessed to be about thirty. He looked much younger than her. His face was striking, almost chiseled. Even from here she could see that his large eyes were blue.

Something flip-flopped in her stomach.

Thanks, she mouthed silently, and smiled.

He lifted a hand and nodded, smiling back.

As she left the lounge, Amanda could hardly breathe. She could not believe what had just happened had actually happened.

She sat in the car a few minutes, gathering her thoughts, then drove back to the office.

She came through the front door smiling.

"Must have been a good lunch," Tanya said.

"It was."

Amanda plucked the single message from her message box. She opened it and read the perfect handwriting. *We must talk.* There was no name at the bottom, no return number.

"Who called?"

"Nobody. They dropped by. Left something for you."

Tanya picked a large envelope off the desk and handed it to Amanda. Amanda took it, frowning.

"Who was it?"

"A woman. Good looking. Not an agent, I don't think."

"Did she give her name?"

"Lydia," Tanya said. "Yeah, Lydia."

Amanda bit back the gasp that wanted to come out. She smiled stiffly at Tanya and went back to her office. Sitting at her desk she slit the envelope open and pulled out the contents.

In her hands she held one of her own wedding photographs. Her face had been slashed with red ink, and deep red furrows ran the length of the white wedding dress. She flipped the photograph over. On the back, in the same red ink, was a message.

He's mine.
You can't have him.
Cunt!
I'll kill you!
I'll kill you both!

Amanda slipped the photograph back into the envelope, out of sight, then, trembling, closed her eyes.

As the glowing digits of his desk clock changed to 2:33, James let out his breath. The time had advanced beyond the usual window of Lydia's calls.

He had started to rise from his desk when the phone rang.

When the voice on the other end said his name, he knew who it was.

"Hello, Lydia."

"Meet me tonight."

"I can't. I'll be busy."

After a long pause, she said, "You're lying."

"I just can't."

"I could come there."

"I don't want to see you."

"You're lying to yourself if you think that."

"It's over between us. I don't want to see you any more."

On the other end of the line, the silence waited. He heard her draw on a cigarette.

"Is she making you do this?"

"No, she's not. But if she were, she'd have the right to, wouldn't she?"

"I meant to ask her this afternoon, but she was out."

For a moment, the words did not register with James. When they did, he stopped breathing.

"What are you talking about?"

"I went to see her at her office."

There was no malice in the words. No hint of anything untoward. Yet James felt himself slipping towards a chasm of fear and anger.

"Stay away from Amanda!"

"Nothing to be jealous about. Just girl talk. If we ever get together, that is."

"Lydia, I'm warning you, stay away from Amanda. You know I can make your life miserable if I want to. You know that."

"And I yours."

"Stay away from Amanda."

His tone left no room for argument. When she spoke again she sounded almost petulant. "You'll come back to me, you know. You always do."

"Not this time."

"You will. I *know* you will."

The line went dead.

With a trembling hand, James hung up the receiver. He stared at the phone, lost in thought.

She wouldn't dare disobey him in this. She knew very well he had muscles he could flex if he had to. It wasn't the threat of her seeing Amanda that bothered him so much. If it came down to it, Amanda could deal with Lydia quite handily, he expected. It was her certainty that he'd be back that troubled him. Even now, only seconds after breaking off with her, he felt flares of desire. He did not know how to contact her, but if he did, he might have phoned her right then to apologize.

He covered his eyes, breathing deeply. He was still sitting that way when the front door opened. He sat up straight as Amanda looked into his office. Her face was pale.

"She came to see me! Right to the office!"

"I know. She called me."

She stared at him, shaking her head. Even now, shocked and angered, she was beautiful. He followed the line of her thigh up inside her coat. The jeans were snug, but not tight. They accentuated her sculpted hips.

"She left a message," she said quietly.

She handed him an envelope. He took it and opened it. When the photograph slid out he gritted his teeth.

"Oh, Jesus Christ."

"Look on the other side."

He flipped it over.

"Amanda, I'm sorry. I don't know what to say."

"It's not the first time, James. She tried to run me off the road once. She sent me other messages."

"No, that's not like her."

"I'm telling you, it was her! I saw her! I think she's the one who broke the car window."

"But why would she do that?"

"Because she hates me. She wants to scare me away from you. But I'm not leaving, James."

Seeing Amanda so angry was almost as much of a shock as the photograph.

"I don't want you to."

"The bitch!"

"I'll talk to her."

"No. Let's call the police."

"No."

"But . . ."

128

"Amanda, I know her. If we call the police, it will only make things worse. We don't want that. Besides, I already talked to her. I ended it with her. We just want this to end. Right?"

Amanda stared at him, obviously uncertain. "How did she react?"

"She was unhappy, of course."

A tiny smile broke on Amanda's lips.

"How unhappy?"

He did not answer that.

"Let's go away," he said.

"Away?"

"Nobody buys a house over Christmas anyway. Let's go south for a week."

The frown on her face evaporated. "How far south?"

"Mexico. Cancún."

"Are you serious?"

"Very. We need to be alone together. A second honeymoon."

"What about your mother? We should visit over Christmas, shouldn't we?"

"To hell with my mother!"

"She'll blame me, you know."

"I promise I'll shoulder all the blame myself. I'll tell her you fought against it tooth and nail, and that I literally had to threaten you with divorce."

"I suppose I could get more time away. Another week isn't going to hurt."

"I'll arrange it, then."

She came toward him and slid into his lap.

With her arms around his neck she kissed his mouth. Her tongue touched his lips, then she pulled back.

"You really ended it with her?"

"Really."

"I hope she kills herself. I hope it's ruined her life."

He said nothing.

"It could be romantic, couldn't it?" she said after awhile.

"We'll redefine the whole concept."

"She'll hate it when she finds out, won't she? She'll just die." She grinned in an entirely unpleasant way.

He did not respond. She kissed him then, moving her mouth over his. Her body trembled through her sweater. She kept kissing him. Her hands moved down his stomach, between his legs.

Like Lydia, he realized, she had him where she wanted him.

On the morning of Thursday, December 23rd, Amanda and James boarded their flight at Minneapolis International. After an interminable delay due to sleet that had fallen steadily nearly all through the night, the plane took off and rose through the low clouds over Minneapolis. Initial turbulence made for some ohs and ahs from worried passengers, but when they finally broke through the cloudcover, and brilliant sunlight pressed down on the white fluff below them, Amanda turned to James and kissed his cheek.

"God, it's beautiful."

"You are easily pleased, Amanda. Five hours of this and you'll be begging for some rough weather."

"No, I won't. It's just so peaceful. Can't you almost imagine that there's no world down there at all? That it's just us up here?"

"If not for the two hundred others sitting beside us, I suppose."

"You know what I mean."

He only nodded.

He didn't share her exultation in being away from the Twin Cities. It seemed to her, as they entered the brilliant sky above the clouds, that as well as leaving behind snow, sleet, gray skies, and grimy streets, they were also parting, for good, with their old life. Amanda had left her old body behind her, had nearly forgotten it now, and James had left behind . . . Lydia. Willingly. She believed that now.

In the week since he had broken off with Lydia, Amanda had been the focus of all his desire. She could not doubt that for an instant. She had never known such attention before, and in a way it frightened her.

Occasionally she found time to contemplate their new relationship, and even to worry about it. She wondered if James were making love to her, or to some fantasy in his head. She had *become* that fantasy. That was foolish, of course, and when she caught herself thinking that way she stopped immediately. She had James. She had him completely. He said he had ended it with Lydia, and she did not doubt it for an instant. With what eros he spent on her, there could be little of that coin left for any other woman.

She thought often of Lydia. She wished pain and hurt on the other woman as she had wished misfortune on no other person in her life. It made her feel childish to do so, but she could not help herself. There were no more messages. Lydia, apparently, had admitted defeat.

For most of the flight they sat in comfortable silence, talking only when the clouds parted below and glimpses of green earth showed through.

That evening, both of them bone-tired from the flight, they entered their private villa on the Caribbean coast, halfway between Cancún and the ruins at Tulum. As the sun disappeared into the ocean, flattening into a rainbow of colors that filled the bowl of the sky from rim to rim, they made love. Afterward, invigorated rather than exhausted, they took chairs down to the beach. They listened to waves lapping at the shore, while above them, stars Amanda had never before seen, filled the night with soft light.

The following days were a dream. On their honeymoon they had gone to Brazil, and though she had enjoyed herself, she had found the hectic pace far too draining. For the first week in Mexico they did not leave the villa except to pick up groceries, and spent their days and nights in pleasant languor, content to be with each other, under the sky, by the sea. If she had imagined a fairy tale for herself, it could not have been as perfect as this.

Though James had originally talked of a week, he had arranged for what amounted to nearly two weeks for them. They spent eight days and nights at the villa, rented from a Mexico City businessman whom James knew, and on New Year's day they packed and drove their rented car up to Cancún, where he had reserved for them a suite at the Hyacinth Hotel.

"I want to celebrate the New Year," he told her.

After a week alone, Amanda did not argue.

The Hyacinth was luxury beyond all expectation. Amanda had never experienced anything like it. Every need was met with immediate gratification, every wish granted with a smile, every luxury provided as if expected.

Many Americans and Canadians were booked at the Hyacinth, as well as a few Europeans. On most occasions Amanda would have felt uncomfortable, but with James, this new, attentive, loving James, she felt protected, and part of the crowd.

As midnight of the 31st approached, the

guests of the hotel gathered around the complex pool area, a multilevel panoply of peanut-, almond-, and star-shaped waterways stretching from the rear of the hotel nearly down to the beach. There must have been nearly a thousand people milling around the water. Above, visible even amidst the bright pool lights, stars twinkled.

Amanda and James sat at a table close to the beach, facing away from the crowd. It was pleasant to hear the laughter and chatter behind them. Even Amanda, unaccustomed to crowds, enjoyed herself.

As midnight approached, James rose to get them drinks. Amanda reached out and grabbed his hand.

"I love you."

He reached down to kiss her. "I love you, too."

He smiled as he walked away. Everything was perfect.

Too perfect.

Ten

James wound his way through the crowd, toward the bar closest to them. His mood was warm. The week and a half they had spent together so far had been as close to perfect as he could have hoped. For the first time in his year of marriage to Amanda, he felt as if he knew her. And yet, this was a *new* Amanda. This was not the woman he had married.

Her appearance had changed. Yes, there was that. But the change was more profound than that. It went deep.

Sex between them had always been acceptably good. It was something they did regularly, and until he had started seeing Lydia again, there had been no complaints from either of them. Now, however, it was a brand new ball game.

He had never dreamed that Amanda could show such interest in sex, such imagination, such desire.

Faces in the crowd grinned at him as he

passed. A woman he had seen only once or twice gave him a come-hither look that only a month ago might have brought him to his knees before her, literally. Now he smiled back and walked on. He had Amanda. He did not need anyone else.

At the bar he ordered a double Glenlivet for himself, and a sling for Amanda. As the bartender mixed the sling, James watched the crowd in the mirror between the bottles and glasses.

Over by the main pool somebody yelled out, "Two minutes!"

"Hurry up with that, will you," James said good naturedly. "Or it'll be next year."

The bartender, a young Mexican who spoke with a flawless, American mid-West accent, grinned and pushed the drinks toward him. James smiled back and pushed him the credit card.

"Having a good time, sir?"

"Fantastic."

"New Year down here, it is different."

"Yes, it is."

In the mirror, the crowd swayed. Music, coming from a matrix of strategically placed speakers, flowed around the revelers as if it were a liquid, buoying them, moving them.

He accepted his credit card from the bartender, and moved to pick up his drinks. In the mirror, a face solidified in the crowd, and stared at him. James, still smiling, stared back at the reflection.

Only when the face smiled, red lips turning up to reveal perfect teeth, did he realize who it was. He spun around.

But she was gone.

His skin crawled, and goose bumps rose on his shoulders and neck.

"Everything all right, sir?"

In the mirror, he saw that he was white, his lips almost blue.

"Fine."

With trembling hands he picked up the drinks and walked back toward the table, eyes scanning the crowd, looking for any sign of her.

Amanda looked up as he returned, and took her drink. She was smiling, looking relaxed. James sat down. His hands were still trembling. He lifted the glass to his mouth and drank half the scotch in one swallow, cringing as the single malt slid down his throat.

"James, what is it?"

He looked at her and shook his head. But there was no use denying it. He wouldn't be able to, even if he tried.

"I saw Lydia."

"Here? Where?"

"By the bar."

She looked over her shoulder. Then she looked out over the ocean.

She reached for her drink, but her fingers

tipped the edge of the glass and it fell to its side, spilling across the table.

She looked at him, and her mouth was trembling.

As the ten-second countdown toward the New Year began, James lifted the glass to his mouth and drained the remainder of the scotch. Even the warmth of the alcohol in his stomach could not cut through the chill that had gripped him.

The flight back was tense and uncomfortable. The silence between them became palpable. James took the window seat and stared out over the wing, brooding, irritated, almost wrathful. Once or twice Amanda questioned him about Lydia.

"Who *is* she, James?"

"Just a woman."

"She must be well-off to come down here on the spur of the moment, to follow you like that."

He turned away, shutting her out, shoulders rigid against further inquiry.

Later, angry herself, she said, "I thought you had ended it with her."

"I did end it with her, God damn it!"

His vehemence shocked her. Across the aisle, a darkly tanned young man in jeans and T-shirt looked over with raised eyebrows. Blushing, Amanda turned away.

"What was she doing down here?"

"She's trying to make things difficult, that's all."

"She's succeeding."

He gripped her hand, his expression earnest. "We can't let her get to us. That's what she wants."

"You didn't tell her where we were going?"

"No."

"Then how did she know?"

He sighed, shrugged, and turned away.

The incident at the hotel had cast a pall over the entire trip. Even Amanda's memory of their days together, the secluded week at the villa, became infected with the presence of Lydia. At the time she had felt alone with James, but now she saw that shadowed, alluring face everywhere. They had never been alone. Lydia had been with them every moment. The other woman had not admitted defeat at all. She had simply regrouped to mount another attack.

It was close to midnight on Sunday, January 3rd, when they disembarked. They cleared customs quickly, having forgone the purchase of any souvenirs, and hailed a taxi home. The bitter cold—wet, dreary, and somehow closer than even the humid Yucatan heat—did nothing to cheer them. That night they slept with their backs to each other.

In the morning, James was determinedly cheery. He came into the bedroom with a tray on which rested a cup of coffee, a glass of juice, and two slices of toast with strawberry jam. He sat down beside Amanda and stretched the tray across her lap, then leaned over and kissed her mouth.

"I'll be damned if I'll let that bitch ruin everything."

"You sound as if you hate her," Amanda said, sitting up.

"I do hate her."

"Then why were you seeing her?"

"I don't know."

She believed him. He seemed almost childish sitting next to her, confused. Amanda felt a stab of hatred for Lydia.

"Are you going to talk to her again?"

"Do you think I should?"

Amanda sipped her juice and thought about it. The idea of James initiating contact with Lydia, whatever the reason, frightened her. Yet the thought of Lydia continuing to harass them frightened her even more.

"I think you should warn her off, yes."

"I will, then."

"Why don't you let me do it?"

He seemed to consider the notion, then shook his head.

"I don't want you to have anything to do with her."

She nearly argued with him, but instead bit into her toast. It was difficult to explain to him that Lydia, as a mystery, a virtual ghost, held more power over her than any normal person. She needed to bring Lydia down to the level of the real. She could not explain it. Sometimes she even found it difficult to super-impose the surveillance-photo face upon the dream image. The imagined Lydia coveted her very insubstantiality.

James kissed her again. "I'll talk to her. She won't bother us again."

Amanda smiled, again believing him. "Okay."

"Are you totally exhausted?"

"No. Why?"

"My mother called."

Amanda sighed, but nodded. "I suppose we should visit."

"We could do it this afternoon. Shelly and Patrick will be there."

"Okay."

"We could visit your parents, too, if you wanted."

"I think I may have outstayed my welcome there."

She had no desire to face her father again. James kissed her.

"It really was a great trip though, despite everything, wasn't it?"

"I suppose it was."

Eleven

Petra Sanders lived on an estate on the shore of Cedar Island Lake in Maple Grove, Minneapolis's most north-westerly suburb. Every time Amanda came up here she couldn't help writing the listing in her head. *Colonial classic on 7 acres in fantasy-park-like setting overlooking lake.* Something like that. Seven bedrooms, a fully finished basement with a separate entrance to the outside, indoor pool, solid oak island kitchen to die for. The whole works. The listing of a lifetime. But Petra Sanders would never sell. And even if she did, Amanda would not be the agent to list it. In a family like the Sanderses there were obligations that superseded the loyalties of family.

As they drove up the winding drive, Amanda grew tense. She hated coming here. From the start, she had been on shaky ground with James's mother.

If it had not been for Shelly, she doubted the marriage would ever have gone ahead.

In the dead of winter the surrounding land was pristine, breathtaking. The gnarled and leafless trunks of ash, elm, and cedar, reached like skeletons from the covering of snow.

"Don't leave me alone with her," she said.

"I won't, I promise."

Since this morning, James had been terribly solicitous, but she did not mind. As they rounded the last curve and the house appeared ahead, Amanda felt relieved. Patrick's Jaguar was parked at an angle by the front steps. She would not be alone in the enemy camp. She had not seen either Shelly or Patrick since the day they had driven her to her parents home in St. Cloud. She wondered how they would react to her new appearance, which had changed considerably since then. She dreaded Petra's reaction.

Amanda got out of the car, but waited for James to hold her arm before climbing the steps to the front door. It opened before they reached it and Shelly stuck her head out.

"My, my, don't we look brown!"

Amanda grinned. "Happy New Year!"

They hugged. In the vestibule, Shelly waved away the servant who came to the door, then helped Amanda out of her coat.

"You look stunning!"

"What about me?" James came in behind her and shut the door.

"You look fine."

Shelly took Amanda by the arm and led her

into the drawing room. Thin traceries of cigarette smoke hung in the air. The room was
sparsely decorated, only an antique settee, three
arm chairs, two long but low tables. The walls
were bare but for two brooding, abstract oil
paintings, and a brass rubbing of a medieval
knight that hung over the mantel. Patrick and
Petra were sitting at opposite ends of the settee. Patrick's eyes widened as he saw Amanda.
He rose and kissed her cheek.

"Happy New Year, beautiful."

Petra did not rise. She looked up at Amanda
from her seated position, legs crossed, hands
folded in her lap, and smiled. Amanda reached
down and kissed the cheek that was turned for
her, skin smooth and cool beneath her lips. She
knew that Petra was in her late sixties, but the
woman's skin, the application of her makeup,
the style of her platinum hair, all spoke of a
younger woman.

"Amanda," she said.

"Happy New Year," Amanda said.

"Well, we were discussing that," Petra said.

When James came into the room Petra stood.
She went to her son and held him at arm's
length, studied his face a moment, then kissed
him. Amanda watched their embrace, and felt a
moment's deep discomfort. The kiss, she
thought, lasted heartbeats longer than was appropriate. When they parted, James had a lipstick smear on his upper lip. He smiled,
embarrassed, and wiped his mouth with a hand-

kerchief. As Petra turned away, James looked at Amanda and shrugged.

Petra took her seat in the settee again. James put his arm around Amanda's shoulder.

"What do you think, Mother?"

"About what?"

"About Amanda!"

Petra turned to Amanda with cool eyes. Amanda blushed, at once furious with James for making her the center of attention, and yet pleased that he was showing her off.

"It's amazing what surgery will do," Petra said.

"Only when you've got very good basics to start with," Patrick put in.

"That's right," James said.

"I suppose," Petra said, and put a cigarette in her mouth. She lit it with a small silver lighter and exhaled smoke into the air. "Of course, having your appearance altered is getting common these days. I suppose there's nothing really wrong with it."

"Nothing at all," Patrick said.

Shelly, who had taken a seat by the window, said, "I think it was very brave of Amanda to do what she did, don't you? It takes courage to take your life in hand and to try to change the cards you've been dealt."

"Hmmm," Petra said, breathing smoke. "I understand you're on a diet, too. Is it going well?"

Blushing so deeply now that her face burned, Amanda said, "Fine, thanks."

She turned away and sat down, hoping they would talk about something else, but her appearance seemed the topic of the hour.

"I've been thinking about it myself," James said, taking the final seat. "Have this little ridge shaved off. What do you think?"

He fingered his nose, wrinkling his forehead.

"I forbid you to tamper with the looks you have been given!" Petra declared.

"I was only joking, Mother," James said.

Amanda cringed for him. With his mother, he became the little boy.

"Simply because it is acceptable for some people to change their looks, does not give such license to the rest of us."

Amanda could not speak. She tried not to look anyone in the face. It was only Shelly's timely interruption that saved her.

"Mother, stop spouting nonsense, will you?"

Petra glared at Shelly, drew on her cigarette, and looked away. The conversation, it appeared, was over. A heavy silence settled in the room, but in it Amanda began to relax. When, minutes later, James and Patrick started talking about guns, she heaved a sigh of relief. From across the room Shelly raised her eyebrows and winked at her. Amanda smiled back.

The afternoon passed as many others had passed before it, with Petra trying to control everything, but opposed at every turn by Shelly.

James was quite ready to submit to her, and Patrick cared neither way. Amanda was uncomfortably in the middle, well aware of Petra's dislike for her, and found herself repeatedly approached for support in ways meant to hurt her, but to which she could not react.

"Am I right, Amanda?" Petra would say. Or, "Amanda's an everyday girl, she know's what I'm talking about, don't you dear?" Or, worst by far, "Why don't we just ask Amanda?"

She put up with it, as she always did, with sparse help from James, and only occasional defensive aid from Shelly.

In the midst of a bitter discussion about religion, a topic on which Amanda had only the vaguest opinions, she left the room unnoticed, to use the toilet. The door next to the kitchen was locked, however, and the manservant, Gordon, whose name she knew but which she had never said aloud, touched her arm and quietly told her that the facility was under repair and would she please use the upstairs.

Amanda went upstairs, uncomfortable in doing so. She had roomed upstairs once, when James and she had stayed the night in their early courtship, but since then had not seen it. She felt like an intruder, waiting at any moment to be seen and accosted by the lady of the house. Nothing like that happened, however, and the moments went by without incident. She was tempted, in fact, to stay up here. She could hear voices from downstairs, sometimes raised to almost a shouting pitch. The Sanderses' family discussions were usually of this sort. What else could you expect with Petra the head of the household?

Finally, knowing she could delay no longer, she left the bathroom. Passing the master bedroom, she paused, her attention drawn to a number of framed photographs on an ornamental dresser.

Amanda froze, staring at the photographs, and almost against her will entered the room. Most of the photos were of James or Shelly as youngsters, teenagers, graduating from college. There were none, she noticed, of the children's marriages, or of their spouses, and this did not surprise her. One photograph was of Herbert Sanders, James's father, who had died when James was fourteen. But one picture, nestled in with the others, shocked her, and then horrified her.

It was of a woman. The photograph looked relatively recent, at least within the past ten years. It was a portrait, actually, and the woman in it was staring at the camera with an almost smug expression. Her hair was dark, winding around her shoulders in long coils. Her face, angular from makeup, verged on being severe. What horrified Amanda, what took her breath away, was the resemblance of the woman in the photograph to the woman she knew only as Lydia. They were not the same, this woman's features were finer, the nose a bit higher, the eyes wider, but the similarities . . . the curve of the lips, the shape of eyes . . . it was astonishing.

"Pictures speak a thousand words, don't they?"

Amanda started, heart tripping, and spun around. Petra was looking over her shoulder.

"I'm sorry," stammered Amanda. "I saw the pictures, and I . . ."

"Don't be sorry. You're not a stranger here, Amanda."

Petra stepped past her, closer to the pictures.

"You were looking at this one."

"Yes," Amanda said, still fighting shock.

"She's my sister. Paula."

"Oh."

Now she saw the resemblance, but it did nothing to diminish the horror she had felt.

"My younger sister," Petra said. "James's favorite aunt."

"He's never mentioned her," Amanda said.

"I don't suppose he has. They haven't seen each other in years. Paula moved to England just before James went to college."

"Oh, I see."

Petra turned away from the pictures, smiling at Amanda. "Seen enough?"

Amanda blushed. "Yes. Thank you."

She let Petra usher her out of the room. Petra moved toward the washroom, and Amanda stepped down the stairs. She was halfway down when she heard her name mentioned in the living room. The voices were hushed now. She heard James say something, and Shelly bark a reply.

When she came into the room a pall of silence settled.

"I was just upstairs," she said.

Shelly smiled nervously. "You could get lost in this house," she said.

"Yes," Amanda said.

She sat down. The others looked at each other. Patrick whistled softly.

"I suppose we should be going soon," James said.

"Us, too," Patrick said.

But it was a long time before anybody moved.

Neither of them spoke much in the car, each lost in thoughts not meant to be shared. When they got home, however, James took her in his arms and kissed her mouth.

"I'm sorry about this afternoon. Mother can be inhuman."

Amanda did not laugh at his little joke.

"When I was upstairs, I looked at some photographs in your mother's bedroom."

He took off his coat and helped her out of hers, not overly interested.

"Oh?"

"One of them was of your Aunt Paula."

"Oh, yes?" He turned to her again. "Did mother give you family histories?"

"She said Paula was your favorite aunt."

"Did she?"

"Yes."

"I suppose she was, when I was younger. Paula was the only one of my relatives who wasn't completely . . . square. She used to take me and Shelly to movies, sometimes."

Amanda frowned, hardly knowing where her thoughts were leading, but aware that she was approaching an area of shadow and darkness she might not want to enter.

"Do you know who she reminded me of?"

"Mother?"

"Her, yes. But also Lydia."

"Lydia?"

"There's a real resemblance."

"I never really thought about it."

"There is, though, isn't there?"

"I don't know."

"There *is.*"

He was frowning now. "Do we have to talk about Lydia?"

"We're talking about Paula."

"Let's not talk about either one of them. That's all over. Can't we just forget about it?"

"Is it over? Judging by Cancún, it's not."

"Amanda, why are you doing this?" He spoke softly, and looked directly into her eyes.

Amanda sighed, nebulous suspicion slipping away. "I guess I'm being silly."

151

"Let's put it behind us." He kissed her. "I'm going to work for an hour or so, then I'll be upstairs."

She went upstairs and undressed. In the shower she let the hot water soothe her, let it work on her muscles and seep into her bones. When she came out of the shower she felt languid, but totally clearheaded. She put on a robe, and went into the library to look for a book. The phone rang just as she settled herself. She knew that James would not answer the house phone in his office, so she rose and answered it herself.

"Hello?"

The silence on the other end lasted much longer than it should have, and when the voice finally spoke, goose bumps rose on Amanda's neck.

"Is James there?"

Smooth, mellifluous, precise. The voice from the tape-recording Fowler had let her hear.

"I'm sorry, he's busy right now," she said, mouth working before she had time to react.

"It's important," the voice said.

Amanda's skin crawled. The receiver was pressed so tightly to her ear that it hurt.

"Lydia?"

No answer. Amanda felt cold, detached, almost dreamy.

"Leave my husband alone," she said quietly. "I know all about you. If I see you again I'm going to call the police."

She hung up the receiver. She stood there silently, heart pounding, until she could breathe normally.

She went downstairs. In his office, James was flipping through a sheaf of papers.

He looked up, saw her, smiled.

"Who called?"

"Just somebody from work," Amanda said. "Coming up soon?"

He nodded, then picked up the phone.

"Soon."

Amanda went back upstairs.

Twelve

On Tuesday, Amanda met Shelly for lunch at Solaria. The restaurant, though considered trendy to the nth degree, seemed more like a cattle car to Amanda. There hardly seemed room enough to maneuver between stalls.

They took their seats in a booth looking east toward the Metrodome. Beyond the window, snow spiraled from a dark sky, falling the twenty-five stories to the street below. The sun's light remained trapped far above Solaria, far above the city.

When their martinis arrived, Amanda took a long swallow.

"Did James tell you about Cancún?"

"Yes, and I'm jealous as hell. I tried to convince Patrick to take me somewhere, but after Barbados last year he was determined to have a white Christmas."

"I mean, did he tell you about Lydia?"

Shelly's glass froze halfway between the table and her mouth. "Lydia?"

"We saw her down there."

Shelly took a sip of her drink.

"You did?"

"Well, James did. After we moved from the villa to the hotel. She followed us down there. She ruined everything!"

"I can't believe it."

"That's not all. Before we left to go there, she came to my office. She left a clipping from one of my old yearbooks, with my picture circled, and something offensive scrawled at the top. Before that, she tried to run me off the road in her car. And last night, after we got home from your mother's, she phoned the house."

"Mom?"

"Lydia!" She did not bite back on her anger soon enough.

"How do you know it was her?" Shelly said contritely.

"I recognized her voice. From the tapes. Remember? That detective I hired made tapes of James and Lydia."

Now, Shelly's face went white. "You never told me that. You showed me the picture, that's all."

"Didn't I? Well, there was a tape. And I recognized the voice. It was her."

Shelly finished her martini and waved to the waiter for another. Amanda finished hers and pointed to her own glass.

"Did you tell James?"

"Not about last night's phone call."

"Are you going to?"

"I don't know."

"Maybe it would be better to forget about it."

"Forget about it? Shelly, this woman is invading our life! She's trying to scare me. What if she decides to do more than that? What if she's a crackpot? I mean, a violent one?"

Shelly fidgeted. When their drinks came she took a swallow.

"At your mother's yesterday I saw a picture of one of your aunts. Paula."

Amanda opened her purse and put a photograph of Lydia down on the table. Shelly looked at it briefly.

"That's Lydia," Amanda said.

"You've shown me before. What are you getting at?"

"Don't you see a resemblance?"

"With what?"

"Between Lydia and your aunt!"

Shelly looked shocked. She picked up the photograph and looked at it closely.

"Not really."

"I see it, Shelly. I don't think you can miss it."

"I suppose, vaguely then, yes. Maybe in the hair."

"And the eyes and the mouth."

Shelly put the photograph back down. "What

exactly are you saying? That James is having an affair with our aunt?"

"You tell me. Is it possible?"

"That's really sick!"

"How old is Paula?"

"I don't know. Midfifties. Ten years younger than Mom, anyway."

"It's possible, then."

"Okay, so maybe the numbers are possible, but Paula lives in England. She hasn't been over here in years."

"Maybe she's here now."

Shelly's face hardened. "Amanda, I don't like this conversation. I'm sorry James was having an affair. But you're twisting it into something really perverse."

Amanda felt the air drop from her sails. She sighed and gathered up the photograph, then stuffed it back into her purse. The things she had just said turned starkly ludicrous as she thought about them.

"I'm sorry, Shelly. I don't know what's wrong with me. I'm jumping at shadows."

Shelly swallowed her anger and tried a marginal smile.

"You don't have to worry, you know. If James says he's finished with this Lydia, then he's finished with her. And if she won't leave of her own accord, he'll push her out."

"I hope you're right. The whole thing has put me on edge. I feel so strange, sometimes. I guess it's partly the surgery, partly Lydia."

"Strange, how?"

"It's so hard to explain. Since the operations, I've felt . . . different. I mean, it's still me here on the inside, but on the outside it feels like somebody else."

"I suppose that's natural."

"It doesn't feel natural. It's almost like my body and my soul aren't comfortable together anymore. It's like, Lydia has been trying to scare me away, and in one sense I *have* left. I mean, the old me has gone, hasn't she? So in a way, Lydia won."

"You're right, that sounds strange."

"I guess I just need to relax."

Looking at Shelly, she felt suddenly envious. Shelly was naturally beautiful, naturally slim. She used makeup and clothes to startling effect, raising herself to the level of being actually striking. Yet she was *real*.

Amanda felt distinctly *unreal*, a phantasm.

"You know, Amanda, you should be proud of what you've accomplished, and you should be thankful for what you've got. Things could be a lot worse."

Amanda sipped her drink but said nothing.

The girl at the desk of the Sojourn Lodge gave James a smile reserved for regulars.

"Nice to see you again, Mr. Page. You'll be staying overnight?"

"Yes, and checking out very early. I'll pay now."

As usual, he paid cash.

He took the stairs up to the second floor, and walked slowly down the too-bright, carpeted corridor to 216. He entered the room, closed the door, but did not lock it. He stood at the window and watched the parking lot, watched eddies of snow swirl along the asphalt. Sandlike particles of ice bombarded the window with the sound of tiny claws.

He checked his watch. It was almost 3:00.

"Come on, Lydia," he said to himself.

He paced the room, wringing his hands, looking at the floor. At 4:00 he phoned down to the front desk and asked for a pot of coffee to be sent up. When it arrived, ten minutes later, he poured himself a cup and drank it quickly. The hot liquid fortified him, but not to any great extent.

He drank another two cups, then lay back on the bed.

He looked at the door.

He waited.

He must have dozed off at one point, because he woke with a start.

Lydia was watching him in the mirror. He glanced at his watch. It was just past 5:00. Outside, streetlights glowed inside halos of swirling snow.

"I'm sorry I took so long," she said.

James fought the sleep from his brain. He

felt foggy, numb, as if he'd been sleeping for hours instead of only twenty minutes.

"I haven't been here that long," he said. "I just dozed off."

She smiled and opened her makeup case. She took out her eyeliner and applied it in smooth, deft strokes.

"Don't bother, Lydia."

Her eyes found his, questioning.

"I came because I wanted to talk to you in person."

She pursed her lips. From the makeup case she removed the tube of lipstick. She uncapped it, screwed up the vermilion finger, and touched it to her lips. The color spread smoothly.

"I said don't bother."

"What do you want to talk about?"

"Obviously you're not listening to me on the phone. I told you, it's over between us."

"It doesn't feel like it's over."

"It *is* over, Lydia."

She moved her lips together, smoothing the lipstick. Looking directly into the reflection of James's face, she said, "You were surprised to see me in Mexico."

"Yes, I was."

"You weren't very nice to me. You ran off."

"Are you doing this intentionally?"

"Doing what?"

"Not understanding. I told you, we're finished!"

160

"I tried to phone you the other night. Amanda wouldn't let me talk to you."

"You phoned?"

"I'd talk to her, if I were you. She's keeping you in the dark."

James took a deep, calming breath.

"Listen to me, Lydia. We're through. Stay away from Amanda. Stay away from me. Don't phone, don't write, don't do anything. Go to hell, for all I care. I'm free, now."

"It's only an illusion. Now *she* controls you, instead of me."

"Shut up."

"You can never be free, James. You don't have it in you. You're an obsessive-compulsive, pussy-whipped weakling, and you like being that way."

"I said, shut up!"

"Make me."

He forced her hand down to the dresser. She strained against him, but not hard. She continued to smile. And then her perfume seemed to fill him, and a rush of images crossed his mind, tangled limbs and open mouths. With a groan, James fell back on the bed.

"It's not so easy to fight, is it?"

He closed his eyes, shuddering. His body was something apart from him, acting alone. It sent him signals of desire. His mind was a slave to that desire.

Suddenly, the taste of her lipstick filled his

161

mouth. He felt her fingers run up between his thighs.

"It's not so bad, is it? Being controlled?"

He thought of Amanda. He thought of what she had demanded of him, of what she had done to win him away from Lydia. He groaned softly.

"I won't be angry about the things you've said," Lydia whispered. "There's no need to be, is there?"

James sat up straight and swung his legs off the bed.

"Leave me alone!"

He stood before she could reach for him again. He would not look at her, but looked only at her reflection in the mirror.

"You're disgusting," he said hoarsely. "And I am, too."

He grabbed a tissue from the box on the dresser and wiped his mouth clean of her lipstick. Her face, in the mirror, was shocked. Before she could move toward him, he opened the door and stepped out into the hall. He slammed the door hard behind him, and walked quickly for the stairs.

The desk clerk said something to him as he passed, but he did not understand her, and did not turn to find out what it was. In the parking lot he let the cold snow and wind swirl around him, bracing him, waking him.

He shuddered in the cold, knowing he had escaped only barely. Another second, another

162

touch, and he would have succumbed. He was *that* weak.

He sobbed as he got into the car. As he turned out of the parking lot, into traffic on Normandale, he glanced up at the hotel. His room light was on. For a moment he thought he saw her standing in the window, arms stretched to either side, and he almost turned back. But a car blared its horn at him, and he slammed on his brakes with a curse.

When he looked back up, the window was empty. Swearing softly, he accelerated into traffic.

Amanda went onto the upstairs landing when she heard James get in. He stared up at her as he was stamping his feet, face red, hair matted with snow. He looked as if he'd been walking. Even his pants were thick with snow.

"Did you get my note?"

"Yes."

"I had to see her again, to tell her it was over, to leave us alone."

As he climbed the stairs his movements were stiff, almost faltering, as if his age had suddenly caught up with him. His smile was weary, perhaps even a bit sad.

"Have you eaten, yet?" she asked.

"No."

"Come back down and I'll make you something."

He followed her wearily back downstairs, and into the kitchen. While she brought eggs, onion, cheese, and tomato from the fridge, he leaned on the counter and watched her. Something about his expression bothered her, but she could not quite determine what it was. He seemed almost smug.

Amanda cracked four eggs into the frying pan.

"How did it go?" She stirred them vigorously with a fork.

"I told her to stop bothering us."

"And?"

"She argued a bit. She came on to me."

"She won't bother us again?"

"I don't think so."

"I think she loves you." The words came out of the blue, and Amanda was shocked to hear herself say them.

James looked even more shocked. He stood up straight and blinked hard.

"What?"

"That's why she was making things difficult. She loves you."

"That's ridiculous."

"It's probably true. How long have you known her?"

"I don't want to talk about her."

If he had seemed open to discussion only moments ago, he was open no longer.

"It's not fair that I know nothing about her. I bet she knows a lot about me."

"Can't we just forget about her?"

The eggs in the frying pan were hardening, and she tossed in the onions and tomatoes, then flipped the whole mass with the spatula.

He came up behind her and put his arms around her. His face nuzzled her neck, and she tried to twist away from him. He held her fast and whispered into her ear.

"It's over. It was a mistake, and it's over. If you can forgive me, then we can both put it behind us."

The feel of his warm breath on her neck, his arms holding her, brought new thoughts. Maybe Lydia *did* love James. Would that be so unusual? Weren't most of these *other women* simply looking for love?

The idea now gave her a thrill. If Lydia *did* love James, then his breaking it off with her would have been a savage blow. Painful, humiliating.

Good.

"I bought you a present," James said.

His hold on her loosened and she managed to twist around to face him. From his jacket pocket he pulled out a small, black, Saks bag. He held it out for her, but snatched it away as she reached for it.

"James!"

"First, say that you forgive me."

"Give me that bag."

"Say it!"

"All right, damn it, I forgive you!"

165

"Say that you love me."

His tone was only half playful.

"You say that *you* love me."

"I love you, Amanda."

"I love you, too."

He grinned and handed her the bag. She took it from his fingers and opened it up. Inside was a silver box, which she now plucked out and pried open. A small bottle of perfume slipped out into her hand.

"Calantha," she said. "My God, this is worth more than gold."

"Platinum," James said.

She uncapped it and touched the cool glass to her wrist. The fragrance rose to her face, delicate, subtle, reaching fingers into her subconscious to pluck strings of memory, or even of instinct.

It was hauntingly familiar.

"It's gorgeous."

She held out her wrist for him to smell. He did so, and for a moment his eyes clouded over. A small line appeared in his forehead.

"Why did you choose this?"

"The woman at the counter recommended it. She said it was expensive enough to make you forgive anything."

Amanda brought her wrist to her face again, and closed her eyes. She allowed the fragrance to fill her, to move her memories.

Her eyes snapped open.

"It's hers."

The familiarity of it had suddenly clicked. She nearly dropped the bottle to the floor. James looked horrified.

"What?"

"It's hers, isn't it? It's Lydia's!"

"It's not!"

"I knew I'd smelled it somewhere. I thought it must have been one of the women at the office, but now I remember. It was on you! On one of those nights when you came back from a client visit. This is what I smelled!"

His face was white. He took the bottle from her fingers and opened it. He raised it to his nose and sniffed, his eyes closed.

"Oh, Jesus." He shook his head, mortified. "I didn't know, Amanda. Honest, to God. When the woman recommended it, I just said sure. I didn't recognize it when she let me smell it. I'm sorry."

"Lydia has very expensive tastes." Then, another horrible thought struck her. "Did you buy some for Lydia?"

"No! I've never bought her anything. I'll take it back. I'll get something else."

He started to put the bottle back into the box, but Amanda took it from him.

"No."

"You can't wear it."

"Why can't I?"

He looked at her, more shocked than horrified now.

"I thought . . ."

"If she can wear it, so can I. Aren't I good enough for Calantha?"

"Of course you are, it's just . . ."

Amanda opened the bottle again. She touched it to her wrists, rubbing some of the cool, almost oily liquid into her skin. She rubbed her wrists across her throat. The fragrance surrounded her like an aura.

"Do you like it?" she asked.

James had backed away, his expression unreadable. He appeared to be almost frightened of her.

"Do you like it?" she repeated.

He nodded. On the stove, the eggs sizzled. Amanda moved the pan off the burner and turned it off.

"I'm not hungry any more," she said.

James swallowed hard, still staring at her with disbelieving eyes.

"I'm going up to bed," she said. "You can come up soon, if you want."

His mouth made a dry sort of sound. Amanda walked past him, perfume in hand.

Thirteen

The following week-and-a-half burned into Amanda's memory. James had never shown such interest in her appearance. One day he was buying her makeup, the next clothes, the next shoes and lingerie, none of which she wanted to wear. If it had not been for the novelty of the attention, she would have exploded angrily after only a couple of days. As it was, half enchanted by his behavior, she allowed the gifts to keep coming without giving any indication that she would use any of it. James seemed happy just to keep buying.

On Thursday, January 13th, after her morning appointment at Merit, Amanda took the day off work and dropped in at Rhapsody, a hair salon.

After washing Amanda's hair, Simone, the stylist, ran her fingers through it.

"What did you have in mind?"

"Whatever you think fits."

"Ooh, I like that!"

Simone stepped back and studied Amanda carefully. She pursed her pink lips and pushed a hand under her chin.

"I say we thin it out, shape it a little. A bob, maybe?"

"If you like."

Simone frowned.

"Have you considered having your hair colored?"

Amanda shook her head.

"The brown and blond don't seem to go well with the face, but I suppose the face is easier to change, isn't it?"

"I like the face," Amanda said. "What would you recommend for the hair?"

"Darker. Even black."

Amanda stared at herself in the mirror. She felt as if she were looking at another person.

"Okay," she said.

Simone grinned, coming close with a pair of scissors and a comb. "Besides, mistakes don't last more than six weeks, do they?"

Amanda did not smile.

At home, she found James in his office. She waited in the doorway for him to look up at her. When he did so, his face turned pale. He blinked.

"Amanda?" His voice was hoarse.

"Does it suit me?"

"My God, yes."

He followed her around like a puppy for the rest of the day, and when they made love later that afternoon he seemed like a boy at her command.

Afterward, as James slept, Amanda lay wide awake in bed and stared at the window. She felt restless and troubled. Cars roared by outside as rush-hour traffic filled the streets. Already, the sky was growing dark.

Amanda swung her legs out of bed and got up. She sat at the dresser and studied herself in the mirror.

The sex had bruised her makeup. With tissue and cold cream she cleaned her face, wiping eyes and cheeks and lips until her face was bare.

She looked at herself with an empty feeling inside. Without makeup, she could glimpse the old Amanda. Just barely. Beneath the frame of hair so black it looked almost liquid, her face seemed pale. The scars from the face and eye-lifts were slightly fired from the rubbing with tissue.

"Hello, Frankenstein," she said softly.

She brushed her hair. Then, very carefully, she began to apply makeup again. Impulsively, she decided to take some of the advice James had been giving her over the past few days. She supposed she should be grateful he had shown so much interest in her appearance.

She wiped heavy, almost careless smudges above her eyes. With the red lipstick he had bought for her, which she had never worn, she touched her lips hard, almost with a slashing motion. With only eye shadow and lipstick she was again transformed. Her mouth looked cruel, her eyes cold. She smiled at herself, but even as she did so the smile froze.

"My God," she said.

With trembling hands she opened her purse and raked through it. She found what she was looking for and pulled it out.

In her fingers she held the surveillance photograph of Lydia. The mystery woman stared at the camera, stared at Amanda. Black hair, cold eyes, downturned mouth, sharp, almost angular features. Cruel. Judgemental.

The face in the photograph was the face in the mirror.

Identical.

James snored on, oblivious.

She wondered, hands shaking, if this were what he had wanted all along.

It was 8:30 when Amanda's pager notified her that a buyer wanted to see one of her listings. James, after sleeping for nearly an hour, was ensconced in the library with his gun collection. Amanda dressed and prepared herself. James kissed her chastely before she left, looking rather shocked. She had left her makeup exactly as she had applied it. The sudden change had affected him. She liked that.

The roads were quiet, the city somnambulant,

and she relaxed as she drove. Once, as she looked into the rearview mirror and caught sight of her own eyes, she gasped. For a moment she had thought somebody else was in the car with her. With her black hair, and new, darker makeup, she looked totally unfamiliar. She adjusted the mirror.

When she arrived at the house on Laxdale, the buyer was already there, waiting in a rented Cadillac in the driveway. He got out only when Amanda was standing next to his car.

His face was deeply tanned, his eyes pale blue. He reminded her of a young Paul Newman.

"Damn that's cold," he said. "You Amanda Sanders?"

"That's me. Mr. Tomkin?"

"Call me Tom." He grinned a Texas grin and put his arm around her shoulder as she led him up to the house.

Amanda gave him the grand tour. Afterward, she waited by the front door while he looked around by himself. When he came back down he was rubbing his chin, nodding.

"Looks damn good," he said.

"It's a wonderful house. A wonderful neighborhood."

"Well, I'll think about it."

"Do you have an agent?"

"Should I get one?"

"If you're serious."

"I'm serious. I'll be living up here . . . this

is the 13th, right? Say another month. I'm going to need a house. My wife has demanded a house."

Before he opened the front door, he said, "Upstairs, in the master bedroom, it looked to me like one of the windows was open. I couldn't close it."

"I'll do it. If you want to see the house again, or another property, please call me."

"I've got your card."

He left the house, closed the door behind him. Amanda went upstairs. In the master bedroom she found that he was right. Somebody, likely another agent showing the place, had opened the window and left it open.

In this weather, an open window would mean a high heating bill. She looked around and found a piece of foil with cigarette butts crushed out in it. Tomorrow, she would find out who had been here, and give them hell.

She checked the house one more time, turning off lights, then went out and locked up. The bitter cold stung her face, and she clenched her teeth against it.

If the house sold she would net $3,000. Twice that if she double-ended the deal and sold it to Mr. Tomkin before he found himself an agent. The thought of it made the cold seem less bitter.

Her thoughts were on Tomkin, the house, and the sale as she started to cross the street. She heard the roar of the engine before she saw the car, and when she looked up she found herself staring into a set of high beams only yards away.

Amanda cried out and jumped backward, tripping over her own feet. She fell hard to the street. The red sports car roared by only inches away from her. For an instant she was looking through the driver-side window, at the face illuminated by green dashboard lights.

The car squealed around the corner and disappeared behind a high fence. Amanda lay on the ground, shaking.

The face behind the glass had been female, stark, with dark lips, and eyes that glittered in shadowed hollows.

Lydia's face.

Amanda was still shaking by the time Shelly answered the door. Shelly stared at her for what seemed like a long time before recognizing her. Then her eyes moved to Amanda's scraped hands and torn stockings.

"Amanda? What happened?"

"I was attacked."

"My God! Patrick!"

Amanda allowed herself to be led into the house. Patrick appeared at the top of the stairs.

"Amanda was attacked," Shelly said.

He came down quickly. "Help me get her coat off."

Their hands seemed to be touching her everywhere, pulling, tugging. Then she was being led through to the living room, lowered onto the sofa. Shelly left the room, then returned a few seconds later with a bowl of warm water, a clean cloth, and an ointment of some kind. Patrick kneeled by her and inspected her hands and legs.

"Minor lacerations. I'll clean those up for you. Get her a drink, will you Shell? A large brandy. What happened?"

"I was showing a house over on Laxdale. A car tried to run me down."

"*Tried* to run you down?" Shelly said from the liquor table.

"The car didn't stop afterward?" Patrick asked. With very gentle fingers he dabbed at the palms of her hands. The soapy water stung, but once the ointment was applied the scrapes felt much better.

"It didn't stop."

"Are you sure it was intentional?" He tugged her stockings. "Maybe you better take these off."

"I saw the driver."

Shelly held out the glass of brandy for her. Amanda took it from her and took a large swallow. The alcohol slid down her throat like molten steel, and she shuddered.

They both looked at her earnestly, waiting.

"It was Lydia."

"Lydia?"

"Lydia?"

They looked at each other, then back at her.

"Take those off," Patrick said quietly.

Amanda nodded. She stood and went through to the kitchen alone. She unclasped the stockings from the garters and pulled them off. After this, she decided, she was going back to pantyhose. Her knees and shins stung. From the living room she heard Patrick and Shelly talking in hushed voices, almost arguing, but when she went back through they were silent.

As Patrick kneeled to clean her knees, Shelly paced back and forth in the doorway, hand pressed to her mouth.

"Have you told anybody yet?" Patrick dabbed at her knees.

"I sat in the car a while. I was too shaky to drive. Then I came right here. I thought I was going to crash the car."

Shelly said, "I doubt it was Lydia. It doesn't make sense, does it?"

"It was her. I recognized her from the picture. I've seen her enough times. It was her. It *does* make sense. You *know* what she's been doing, Shelly. *Shit!*"

After he'd applied ointment to her legs, Patrick stood up. Amanda took another large swallow of the brandy, and realized with a shock that the glass was empty.

"What are you going to do?"

"Call the police. Have the bitch arrested."

Again, Patrick and Shelly glanced at each

other, very quickly, but long enough to exchange a look of concern.

"What is it?"

Shelly sat down beside her on the sofa and took her hand. "Are you sure you should call the police?"

"She could have killed me!"

"What if it wasn't her?"

"Why do you keep saying that? It *was* her. I'd recognize her anywhere. She's angry because James has dumped her. She blames me."

"I just think you could exacerbate the problem if you were to bring in the police. If she's really that unstable, who knows what it might push her to."

Amanda took a deep breath. "Then what should I do?"

"Tell James," Patrick said. "Maybe he can talk to her."

"Fat lot of good that's done so far."

"Does he know, yet?"

"I came straight here."

"Let me phone him," Patrick said. "I don't want you driving home. Shell, get her another drink, will you?"

Shelly squeezed Amanda's hand and went to the liquor table. Patrick smiled reassuringly. "I expect we're blowing this all out of proportion."

He left the room and she heard him punching numbers on the phone. Amanda took the refilled glass from Shelly and sipped it. She was feeling the last glass as a pleasant tingling sensation at the back of her neck and through her limbs.

Patrick came back, frowning.

"He'll be here shortly."

"What did he say?" Amanda asked.

"He was shocked."

"Did he believe it?"

"Yes."

Amanda felt deep relief. She reclined her head on the back of the sofa and closed her eyes.

"I think Shelly's right, though," Patrick said. "From what you've told us about this Lydia, she's not the type of person you want to provoke."

"I'm not the one who's doing the provoking, am I?" She felt swathed in cotton now. The night's shock and the brandy were having a profound effect.

"By the way," Patrick said, "you're hair looks very nice that way. You look really good."

The quick change of subject startled Amanda. She opened her eyes and smiled. "Do you think so?"

"You look lovely, Amanda," Shelly said. "I didn't recognize you at the door. Everything is different."

"As in, I didn't look lovely before?"

"That's not what I meant."

Amanda smiled and closed her eyes again.

"You know who I look like, of course," she said dreamily.

"Who?" Patrick said.

"Lydia."

They did not answer her, and she did not open her eyes.

She must have drifted off then, for when she opened her eyes again she was alone in the living room and a fire was crackling in the hearth. Even from across the room she could feel the warmth on her face. The sweet smell of silver ash filled the room. She still felt thick-headed, but her body was suffused with a pleasant glow, almost a numbness. Her skin had the dry, warm feel of deep sleep.

Voices came from somewhere deeper in the house. She heard Shelly and Patrick, and then James. Their voices were low, hushed, but sounded argumentative. Amanda wanted to get up, but she seemed to have no energy. She could not even bring herself to speak.

Perhaps she was asleep. It certainly felt like it. Maybe all of this was a dream.

With that in mind she closed her eyes. The warmth and the sweet smell and the sound of the crackling fire sent her back down into darkness.

When she opened her eyes again the fog was gone. James was sitting in the easy chair across from her. He smiled at her.

"How are you feeling?"

"Better, now."

She could feel a slight stinging in her hands and knees, but that was preferable to the apparent drunkenness that had anesthetized her earlier.

"She's awake!" James called.

Patrick and Shelly came through. Patrick gave her a quick inspection.

"You look much better," he said.

"What time is it? "

"Almost midnight."

"Midnight!"

That meant she had been sleeping for nearly two hours! She sat up straight. Alcohol had never had that effect on her before.

"What did you put in my drink?" she asked, half jokingly.

"Nothing," Patrick said abruptly. "You had a bit of a shock, that's all."

James stood and came over to her. He held out his hand and helped her off the sofa.

"Come on, let's go home," he said.

With Shelly's help, Amanda got back into her coat. At the door, she kissed Patrick on the cheek and gave Shelly a hug.

"Thanks," she said.

"I'll bring your car tomorrow," Patrick said.

In James's car, heading back downtown, they did not talk. Amanda sat with her head pressed to the cool window. She could not stop thinking about Patrick and Shelly's advice not to call the police. It felt all wrong.

She watched every car they passed, or that passed them, looking for Lydia's face.

She saw it many times, reflected back at her in the night-darkened glass of her own window.

Fourteen

At home, James lost whatever composure had kept him so calm at Patrick and Shelly's. He poured himself a very stiff scotch and paced the upstairs landing, moving back and forth between the library and the living room.

"I don't understand it," he said. "It doesn't make sense."

Amanda, leaning in the library doorway, said, "Please stop moving about like that! You're giving me motion sickness."

He cast her an angry glance, then took a deep breath and nodded.

"I'm sorry. This whole thing has got me confused."

"She's angry about being replaced."

"Replaced?"

"Look at me, James. Don't I look a lot like her?"

He sipped his scotch. "I suppose you do, a little."

"I could be her twin!"

"The resemblance isn't that close."

"Maybe not, but we're definitely of a type."

"That still doesn't explain why she tried to run you down. How would she know? You only put on that damned makeup tonight."

"Maybe she saw the hair earlier. Maybe she's been watching me. I *know* she has. I could feel it. Oh, damn it, I *don't* know. I just know that it was her."

"But why?"

"Think about it. It's not simply that you told her it was over. It's not simply that you threw her over for me. What you did was throw her over for somebody who might as well *be* her."

He stared at her, face pale.

"My, God," he said softly.

Amanda laughed bitterly. "I didn't even realize what was happening," she said. "I didn't realize what you were doing, until it was too late."

"What *I* was doing?"

"You and your directions for my makeup."

"I wasn't the one who made you have those operations. I wasn't the one who dyed your hair."

"I had a part in it, too. I know that."

"It wasn't intentional," James said.

"Maybe not. That doesn't change the fact that it's happened."

"If you changed back, maybe she'd stop."

"Do you want me to?"

He sipped his drink, then shook his head, then shrugged. "I don't know. No."

"Then we have to call the police."

"No."

"Why not?"

"Because it will only make things worse."

"For who?"

"For her. And for us."

"You're worried about her," Amanda said.

"I'm worried about what she might do, that's all."

"She tried to run me down, James. She tried to kill me. That's not something you just *hope* will get better."

"I'll talk to her."

"Like you did before?"

He came at her then, furious. "Amanda, I want to keep the police out of it. We don't want to make our personal lives public."

She hadn't thought of that.

"It would ruin us. Me, anyway."

"I don't see how."

"Don't you? My clients trust me. If they find out I can't even handle my personal affairs, how can they expect me to handle theirs?"

He spun away from her and went into the living room. When he came back his glass was full. He seemed to be almost panicked.

"I just don't understand it," he said.

"James, that woman is in love with you."

"I don't believe that."

"It's obvious, isn't it? I don't know what you told her about your relationship, I don't know what you led her to believe, but somewhere along the line she fell in love with you."

"That's ridiculous."

"A woman doesn't follow a man down to the ends of Mexico simply to give him a hard time. She doesn't visit his wife at work, send her threatening letters, and then try to run her down, just to make him feel bad. She does that kind of thing because she believes the man she loves has been stolen from her, and she wants him back."

"Back?"

"It won't matter what you tell her. It won't make any difference how you explain it to her. She's not going to stop until she gets you back."

He stared at her, incredulous, and swallowed half his glass of scotch. He wiped his mouth. His eyes had the look of a trapped animal.

He turned away from her and leaned against the wall, head resting on his arm.

Amanda realized something then, and it shocked her. James was frightened. Lydia frightened him.

"We have to call the police," Amanda said. "She tried to kill me, James. You have to decide who you care about. Her, or me. Who are you going to protect?"

He stood there against the wall. His shoulders shook.

He said nothing.

Lieutenant Toni Kirk wore blue jeans and a leather bomber jacket. Silver highlights streaked her short blond hair. At first glance she looked about twenty years old, with an attractive, narrow face, and sharp gray eyes. Upon closer inspection her age increased to midthirties, but the attractiveness remained. Sitting beside her at the kitchen table was her partner, Jim Haley. He was a slim man, pale-faced, soft-looking, but with the same sharp eyes as his partner.

"From where do you know her?" Toni Kirk asked.

Amanda looked at the policewoman without speaking. Her hand trembled on top of the table. Toni Kirk looked poised, and comfortable. Amanda could see the butt of a handgun inside her open jacket. Toni Kirk's face was hard, implacable, self-assured. This woman would never have cosmetic surgery, Amanda thought.

"Maybe I should answer that," James said from behind her.

Toni continued to look at Amanda, but nodded. How long had James been standing there? Neither of the detectives had given any indication.

"Okay, Mr. Sanders."

"Amanda thinks the woman in the car was a woman with whom I had an affair."

"I don't think it, I know it."

"You've met her?"

"I've got photographs of her."

"There's no doubt in your mind about the identity of the woman in the car?"

"None."

"Who is she?"

"Her name is Lydia."

"Last name?"

Amanda shook her head, shocked to realize that she had never even thought to ask James the question. Now she turned to him. "James?"

"I'm afraid I don't know, either," he said.

Amanda stared at him, utterly flabbergasted.

"How long did you see this woman?" Toni Kirk asked him.

"I can't remember. A while."

"You never traded last names?"

"It wasn't like that," James said. He did not appear embarrassed, but he looked decidedly uncomfortable. "I wasn't the one to initiate . . . rather, it was she who called me when she wanted to . . ."

"What do you know about her?"

"Nothing."

"Nothing?" Amanda said.

"Nothing?" Toni Kirk said.

"I don't know her full name. I don't even know if Lydia is her real first name. I don't know where she lives. I don't know what kind of car she drives. I don't know her phone number."

Toni Kirk was quiet for a moment. Amanda continued to stare incredulously at James. He would not return her gaze.

"How did she contact you?"

"By phone. We would arrange to meet. Afterward, she would leave first, and then I wouldn't hear from her again until the next time."

"At what intervals did she call?"

Now, James blushed.

"It varied. Sometimes every other week. Sometimes every few days."

"When did you start seeing her?"

"I don't remember."

"When did you stop?"

James took a deep breath. "I stopped, the first time, when I met Amanda. I started seeing her again a short time ago, and now I've stopped again. For good, this time."

Toni Kirk looked neither skeptical nor credulous.

"Do you have those pictures handy?" she said to Amanda.

Amanda nodded and stood without looking at James. She went up to the living room, retrieved the picture from her purse, and brought it back down to the kitchen. Toni Kirk, Lieutenant Haley, and James were sitting quietly.

Kirk took the picture from Amanda. She

looked at it, frowned, looked at Amanda, then put it down.

"Why would she want to hurt you?"

"Because she's angry that James cut her off."

"Many other women are cut off by repentant husbands, Mrs. Burns-Sanders, but most of them do not embark upon campaigns of vengeance."

"I think she's more than angry about James cutting her off."

"What else might she be angry about?"

"Recently I had cosmetic surgery," Amanda said carefully. "If you'll look at the picture, you'll see there's now a resemblance between her and me. Sometimes it can be quite striking."

"This was intentional?"

Amanda shook her head. "No. It just . . . happened."

"You think she's angry that you've made yourself look like her?"

"Maybe."

"And so she tried to run you down."

"That wasn't the first time. Our car was vandalized, back in September, when I first suspected James was having an affair."

"That wasn't Lydia," James said abruptly.

"I bet it was," Amanda said without looking at him. "Then she tried to run me off the road once. It was the same red car."

"It could have been anybody," James said.

"She sent threatening letters to my office.

Pictures of me, defaced or mutilated. She even came to the office once, but I wasn't there. And when we went down to Mexico before Christmas, she followed us. She's harassing us. It's getting worse, that's all."

Toni Kirk looked at James.

"Mr. Sanders, while your wife has been talking you've looked skeptical."

James shrugged, and Amanda looked at him in horror. "I find it very difficult to imagine Lydia trying to hurt Amanda. She *did* follow us to Mexico, and she admitted visiting Amanda at work, she wanted to talk, but . . . the rest, I just can't see it."

Toni Kirk looked at Lieutenant Haley. He closed his notebook. Their coffee remained untouched in front of them.

"Well," Toni Kirk said.

"Can you do something about her?" Amanda asked.

"I'll be honest with you, Mrs. Burns-Sanders. No, we can't. You haven't been hurt. There's no indication that this Lydia has broken any laws."

"She tried to run me down!"

"But she didn't. And when there's no actual injury or property damage involved, it's very hard to prove intent."

"You mean there's nothing we can do?"

"What we *will* do is try to contact Lydia. Sometimes that's enough to end potential harassment."

"What about a court order restraining her from seeing either James or me?"

"That's possible, but we'd still have to find out who she is, and then you'd have to press charges in order for a justice to even consider a restraining order."

Amanda rubbed her eyes wearily.

"I will keep in touch, though," Toni Kirk said. "And if anything develops, you can call me."

After she had showed the two detectives out of the building, Amanda went back into the kitchen. James was still there. He smiled apologetically at her.

"How could you not know *anything* about her?"

"I just don't."

"How could you sleep with somebody you know nothing about?"

He took a deep breath and sipped his coffee.

"Did you at least use protection, for God's sake?"

"Amanda . . ."

"I suppose I should have an AIDS test. I suppose you should, too."

"I'm sorry."

"God damn it, James, I'm so angry!"

"I know," he said. "I'm sorry."

James lay facedown on the bed in room 216 at the Sojourn Lodge in Edina. It was nearly

3:00 P.M. Amanda had left the house just before 1:00 to show a property, and though he had tried to argue her out of it, she had remained determined. Lydia was not going to upset her whole life. The phone call from Lydia had come only minutes after Amanda had gone.

He had been waiting for an hour now. Much longer than usual. The thought kept coming to him that Lydia's call had been a ruse, something to take away his attention while she went after Amanda, but he managed to fight it off. Lydia would not play with him like that. She wouldn't dare.

At 3:30 she arrived.

"I'm sorry I took so long. I had trouble getting here."

He hadn't remembered the traffic being bad, but he did not question her about it.

"Don't bother getting ready," he said. "We're not going to do anything."

"Oh, but we are!"

"No, we're not."

"Why did you come?"

"Because obviously I didn't make it clear to you last time. It's over between us."

Her reflection smiled at him. It was a smug, almost condescending smile. She continued to smile as James wrapped his fingers around her throat. Her eyes widened and her mouth opened.

"James!"

"Now, listen to me," he said.

She struggled against him, twisting her head.

"Listen to me!"

She stopped moving and stared at him in the mirror. Her eyes were frightened.

"I know what you did the other night. You tried to hurt Amanda."

She said nothing.

"If you do that again, Lydia, I'm going to hurt you."

"You wouldn't dare."

"I *would* dare. I'll do it. I'll hurt you in ways you can't even imagine."

Her eyes misted.

"I love you."

James lessened the pressure on her throat. She continued to stare at him.

"I love Amanda."

"Why?"

"Because she's my wife."

"Look what she's become!"

"She did that because she loves me."

"I love you!"

"I'm sorry."

Now, her look softened, became wily.

"I want you."

"No."

He loosened his grip, and her mouth found his hand.

"Whatever she gives you, I gave you first," she said.

"Stop it."

"Whatever she can give you now, I can give you more."

"Lydia, don't."

She kissed his fingers, and now moved a hand between his legs.

"You *do* want me."

"No!"

He spun away and fell to the bed. He was a puppet, yanked this way and that.

"We were made for each other. We can't live without each other."

"No, Lydia, no."

"I can hurt her."

James stiffened. "I don't want her hurt!"

"Then come back to me. You can have us both. I don't mind. I'm not greedy. She's the greedy one."

"I can't."

"You can."

"If Amanda finds out . . ."

"We'll be more careful this time."

He groaned as she touched him.

"You won't hurt her? You won't bother her anymore?"

"Not if you come back to me. Any friend of yours is a friend of mine."

"You bitch," he said hoarsely.

"I'm *your* bitch," she said, and bit his lip.

195

Fifteen

Monday the 17th brought a low-pressure front, gray skies, and warmth enough to turn the streets into filthy quagmires. Late in the afternoon Amanda met Shelly downtown for a drink. They talked little, both uncomfortable. When Amanda left, she wondered what had happened to their friendship. There seemed to be secrets between them now, vast areas of unknown.

She walked slowly along the downtown streets, glad of the fresh air. As she was crossing Nicollet Mall, Amanda froze.

Lydia had entered the street ahead of her.

There could be no doubt about it.

The black hair and angular face, so much like her own, were unmistakable.

Lydia walked briskly, heading toward Hennepin. For a second, Amanda nearly turned around and walked the other way. A strange fear had flowered inside her, and her hands trembled. Curiosity decided the battle. Biting her lip, she forced herself to follow. She had not been seen.

Lydia was wearing a long, black coat. High boots. She walked stiffly erect.

"You bitch," Amanda muttered under her breath.

When Lydia crossed the street, Amanda followed. For a moment, as Lydia checked for traffic, her eyes passed across Amanda. Amanda held her breath and turned away. When she looked back, Lydia was still walking, oblivious.

Before they reached Hennepin, Lydia turned into a doorway and disappeared. The Radisson Hotel.

Amanda hurried along and entered the hotel. A doorman tried to open and hold the door for her, but she beat him to it. In the lobby, she found herself amidst a small crowd of men and women with paper badges taped to their chests. One chubby, red-faced man tried to get out of her way, but she ran into him. His badge said HELLO I'M BOB.

He grinned at her, blushing.

"Hello, I'm Bob," he said.

Amanda brushed him aside and forced her way through the milling crowd. She could not see Lydia.

She glanced toward the elevators, and saw doors closing. She glanced at the front desk. The three desk clerks, despite the noise and chaos, looked neither harried nor disturbed.

Amanda worked her way to the desk. A young man in a red jacket, with a very pale face and wire-rimmed glasses looked up at her and smiled.

"Can I help you?"

Amanda tried to smile, but nervousness turned it to a grimace.

"I'm looking for my sister," she said. "She looks a lot like me. She was checked in here and I was supposed to meet her in the lobby but she hasn't shown up yet."

"Her name?"

"Lydia," Amanda said.

"Last name?"

She blushed furiously. "Uhm, the thing is, she just got married, a secret ceremony, and nobody knows her name yet. I'm here to meet her husband. I'm sure you know who I'm talking about. She looks just like me."

He looked at her, frowning. Then his eyes widened.

"Yes. I've seen her. A bit taller than you."

"That's Lydia."

"She's not a guest, though. She must be visiting somebody."

Amanda's heart tripped in her chest. In a voice much calmer than she felt, she said, "Is a James Sanders registered?"

The young man typed something into his computer, then shook his head.

"I'm sorry, no."

"How about Page? Mr. Page?"

He typed something else. "Sorry again, no."

A wave of relief crashed over Amanda. She closed her eyes.

"Thank you."

She worked her way back through the crowd toward the entrance, then changed her mind. Damn it, no. She wasn't going to give up so easily. She veered off to her left, past a magazine and tobacco stand, toward the restaurant. She passed the cash register, and scanned the tables. The place was almost full at this hour, but she could not see Lydia.

The hostess approached her, smiling.

"Table for one?"

"I'll just sit at the counter."

Amanda walked in and took a stool. She ordered coffee and drank it slowly, eyes scanning the crowd in the lobby, watching the faces in the restaurant. When she had finished, the waitress came by and offered a refill.

"No, thank you, I was just waiting for somebody."

She paid for the coffee and left the restaurant. In the lobby she fortified herself with a deep breath, and fought her way through the crowd again. She was halfway across the floor when she ran into Bob.

"Hello, I'm Bob," he said, smiling. "Oh, we've met!"

She grinned stupidly at him and pushed past, toward the lounge. Faint pop music drifted through the open door. She stepped in and looked around. Mostly men here. Heads turned to her as she entered, eyes appraising. No sign of Lydia.

Beaten now, Amanda backed out. She wasn't going to find Lydia in here. Quite possibly the other woman had simply entered the front door and taken the stairs or the elevator to the skyway level. She could be anywhere.

Resigned now to failure, Amanda elbowed her way toward the front entrance. Across the lobby she glimpsed Bob, introducing himself to somebody else. To her left, one of the elevator doors opened. She turned toward it, quite by accident, and stopped dead in her tracks.

James came out of the elevator and walked quickly toward the entrance, looking straight ahead, face grim. Amanda stared at him, heart sinking.

"Oh, God," she said softly.

She watched him pass through the door and turn toward Marquette. She stared at the door a few seconds, unmoving.

It could have been a coincidence. He might simply have been down here meeting a client. That's all. She should not jump to conclusions.

But as she walked toward the entrance, elbowing her way through the crowd, she couldn't help herself. There was only one logical conclusion to jump to, and it wasn't a very big leap.

James greeted Amanda with an innocent

smile when she got home. After a quick look at her face, the smile faded.

"What's wrong?"

"I saw you!"

"What are you talking about?"

"At the Radisson! I was there!"

"I've been here all afternoon. All day."

Amanda stared at him in utter disbelief. How could he look her straight in the eyes and lie like this?

"I went downtown for a drink with Shelly," Amanda said quietly. "I tried to phone you, but there was no answer."

He frowned. "I didn't hear the phone, Amanda. Are you sure you had the right number?"

She pretended she had not heard him. "When I left the bar, I saw Lydia on the street. I followed her."

His face was pale now. He took a deep breath.

"She went into the Radisson. I followed her in there, too."

"Amanda . . ."

"I couldn't find her, but as I was leaving I saw you get out of the elevator. You didn't see me. You went right for the doors and walked away."

"If you'll . . ."

"Don't lie to me! I saw you!"

Her voice edged on hysteria, but she could not calm herself.

"Okay, I was there."

"Why did you lie?"

"The way you were acting, if I'd told you the truth you wouldn't have believed me."

"You saw Lydia."

"No."

"Don't lie!"

"I was there to meet a client. That's all. I promise you, Amanda, that's all it was."

"What client?"

"George Proctor, from Chicago. He was up here for a convention, and he phoned."

She stared at him, shaking, livid, thinking of the milling crowd in the lobby.

"I saw Lydia, James."

"I didn't see her, Amanda. I didn't."

His voice held no deception, and his face was solemn, yet she did not believe him. She stepped up to him and bent close. He smelled of fresh air and exhaust. Yet under the outdoor smell she caught a hint of Calantha.

"I smell her perfume!"

"It's *your* perfume, too, Amanda."

She reeled before his words as if she'd been struck. She had lost control, and she needed to attack him, needed to prove him false. She spun away from him and stalked into the lobby. At the front hall closet she pulled his coat from its hanger and pressed it to her face. Now, again, she caught a hint of Calantha. No doubt about it. And yet, it *could* be hers, she thought. It wasn't, but it could be.

She searched the pockets and found a wad of tissues. One of the tissues had a smear of red lipstick.

She spun, triumphant.

"You bastard!"

He was standing with his hands in his pockets, looking perplexed and concerned.

"That was from when we went for lunch. That was your kiss. Your lipstick."

"James, you're lying to me. I know it."

"I'm not."

"Look at me! Look at what I did to myself, for you!"

"I never asked you to, Amanda. You know I didn't."

"No, but you turned to another woman because I didn't please you!"

"That's not true!"

"It is true! Look at me! Look at what I've become! Just for you!"

"I loved you the way you were."

"But you like me better this way, don't you? Admit it!"

She dropped his coat to the floor. A calm anger descended upon her, and she returned his even stare.

"How would you feel if *I* had an affair? You wouldn't like it, would you? No, you wouldn't. You want to keep me as the pristine, untouchable wife, while you go off and screw whomever you please!"

"Amanda!"

"I could have an affair, you know. There were two men today at the bar, just ask Shelly. One word, and I could have had either one of them. Both of them!"

"You're being ridiculous."

"Or at work, there are men who find me attractive. How about Fred? You know Fred. If I wanted him, he would. You know that. He *would!*"

James looked stricken.

"Amanda, I'm sorry for all I've done. But I didn't see her today. I promise you that. That's all I can say. I didn't see her."

Amanda turned away. She ran for the stairs, and swept up them as James called to her. She ignored him and slammed the bedroom door behind her. She fell face first on the bed, buried her face in the pillow, and wept.

It was some time later, perhaps half an hour, when the door opened and James came in. He did not turn on a light. He sat on the edge of the bed and stroked her hair.

She turned over and looked up at him. In the light from the street his face looked gaunt, full of shadow.

"I'm sorry about everything, Amanda. It's my fault, I know that. If I'd never met Lydia, none of this would have happened."

Amanda sniffed and rubbed her eyes. "It doesn't matter anymore. We're falling apart."

"We're not."

"We are, James."

He leaned over her and kissed her face. His hand touched her breast.

"Let me prove to you that I love you!"

She pushed him away. "That's not love, James."

"Please, Amanda."

"No. Not now. Not tonight."

He stood, looking guilt-racked and concerned.

"I'm sorry, Amanda."

When he left the room, Amanda pressed her face back to the pillow. She hated herself. At his kiss, at his touch, she had felt herself responding. The only thing that had held her back was the knowledge that even if he had made love to her, even had his fervor and passion been honest, he would not have been with her. He would have been making love to her shell. The shell that looked so much like Lydia. Even when he made love, even as she held him tightly in her arms, possessing him, he was being unfaithful.

Toni Kirk was waiting for Amanda at MRS on Tuesday morning.

"Oh, hello," Amanda said.

"I wanted to talk to you, without your husband around," Toni Kirk said.

Amanda ushered her into the office. Toni slipped out of her coat, sat down, and looked at a picture of Amanda and James on the desk. It was an old picture, showing Amanda only months after their marriage.

"This is you?"

"Yes."

"How long ago?"

"Eight or nine months."

"My God."

Toni looked closely at Amanda's face, at her body. She looked back at the picture on the desk, and Amanda looked at it too. In the picture she was smiling and looked happy. She felt as if she were looking at a photograph of somebody else, a candid snap of a joyful moment. It seemed distant and unreal.

"Quite a difference."

"Yes."

It was obvious that Toni Kirk wanted to ask more questions. There is something intensely private about the body, about its appearance. A loss of weight due to diet you can praise, but the drastic changes brought on by surgery must be ignored. But Toni Kirk was a cop, and questions came naturally.

"You said the other day you had not intentionally made yourself look so much like this Lydia person."

"That's right. Well, it's mostly right. Lydia's more of a type than a person, wouldn't you say? I guess I was moving toward the type, and that's the similarity."

"You didn't like your old type?"

"Does it matter if I did or not?"

"I'm just curious."

"I liked my old type just fine. My husband, apparently, did not."

"So, all this was for him?"

"Partially," Amanda said quietly. "Do you object?"

"No."

"Yes, you do. You're thinking what a lot of people have been thinking but haven't said aloud to me. No man is worth it."

"You're right. That *is* what I was thinking."

"I put a lot of work into my marriage. I love my husband. I believe marriage involves compromise. If my looking like this makes my husband happy, if it keeps him away from other women, then I don't see what's wrong with it."

"I didn't mean to pry. I may not believe in changing myself to suit any man's preferences, but I *do* believe it's your choice and nobody else's."

"Thank you," Amanda said, and not for the first time wondered if *any* of it had been her own choice.

"I noticed the other day that you seemed reluctant to talk much. I thought if I talked to you alone, without your husband present, you might say more."

"About what?"

"About Lydia."

Amanda laughed softly. "I wish I could tell you more, Lieutenant Kirk."

"Just Toni, please."

"But I really don't know more, Toni. Lydia is the quintessential mystery woman."

"I got the impression you knew more about her than you were saying."

Amanda sighed. "I have suspicions, but they're totally unfounded, and if I told them to you and it ever got back to James, or any of my family, it would be disastrous."

"I can be very careful when I investigate. I'm good at that."

"I'm sure you are, but you wouldn't be *able* to investigate this without raising hell."

"You're not going to tell me?"

"For interest's sake and for no other reason?"

Toni Kirk rubbed her chin. "If that's the way it has to be."

"That's the way it has to be." Amanda took a deep breath. "I suspect . . . no, I don't suspect . . . it's just a feeling, and I'm sure it's off base . . . Lydia looks a lot like one of James's aunts."

Toni Kirk's eyebrows raised a notch. "I see what you mean. I wouldn't touch that with a ten-foot pole. Do you really believe that?"

"I don't know. I get angry, and I latch onto things. If I *did* really believe it, I don't know if I'd ever be able to . . . no, I don't believe it. It's just, I find it hard to believe that James knows so little about Lydia."

"I've seen cases like it before. Some women

play with men. Married men. You'd be surprised."

"Bet I wouldn't."

"Maybe not."

Toni took a deep breath and looked troubled.

"You haven't found her," Amanda said.

"I had hoped you'd be able to give me a bit more information. As it is, the license plate fragment didn't pan out, and we've got nothing. I really shouldn't have devoted as much time as I already have to this case, since really, there is no case. And now, well, I have to drop it."

"I understand."

Toni looked at her thoughtfully. "Nothing has happened since that night?"

Amanda pursed her lips, thinking about yesterday and seeing Lydia downtown. Overnight, she had decided to believe James's story. She *had* to believe it, or else she had to believe that he was still seeing Lydia, which meant believing that her marriage was over.

"Nothing," she said.

"Either she's given up, or you made a mistake when you identified her."

"I suppose so."

"Either way, we can't do much unless we know who she is."

"I *do* understand."

"If you really want to pursue this matter, you could hire a private investigator. If you can identify Lydia we can proceed. Do you love your husband?"

"Yes."

"Then the other option is to drop it right now and let it lie. Lydia, whoever she is, might have it out of her system. If you go further, you might stir the pot, raise some trouble."

"The private detective I originally hired said pretty much the same thing."

"It's part of the detective's creed."

Their quiet laughter was brittle and mirthless. When Amanda showed Toni to the door, Tanya watched her with questioning eyes. She returned to her office, closed the door, and stared at the picture on her desk. She did not know how much time passed but the knock on the door seemed to pull her from a dream that she could not remember.

"Yes?"

Fred Cooper stuck his head in. "Hi," he said.

"Hi."

He smiled nervously. A tension separated them that had never been there before.

"We haven't been for lunch in a while."

"No," Amanda agreed.

"Want to pick up where we left off?"

For the first time that morning Amanda smiled with pleasure.

"That sounds nice," she said.

Sixteen

"I've never been here before, but they tell me the salads are fantastic," Fred said.

They were at a window table in Olive's, halfway between the office and downtown. Olive's was popular with a younger crowd, and it was well known for its health-conscious menu. The outside of the building was brownstone, steel, and glass, but inside, a veneer of half logs and four happily roaring gas fireplaces produced the ambience of a near-rustic hideaway. Minnesota seasonal prints by an unknown artist decorated the wall. To their right a nameless northeastern lake glittered between green hills under a blue sky.

When the waitress came Fred ordered a beer. Amanda looked at the menu, then at Fred, then at the waitress. "Oh, hell, make it two."

They were silent until the beer arrived.

They sipped their beer. Fred seemed nervous. When they looked at each other for more than a few seconds he turned away, or looked down at his hands. He fidgeted continuously with his knife or fork.

"So, what do you call this new look?" he asked.

"I don't know," Amanda said.

"You know what it reminds me of?"

"No."

"Like, a 1950s housewife, or something. Like Mrs. Cleaver dressed to the nines. Oh, hell, I'm sorry."

"That's all right."

"I meant, it's attractive. Is it coming back in?"

"I don't know."

She hadn't really thought about it, hadn't really tried to pigeonhole her new appearance, but Fred was right. Hearing him say it, however, was disconcerting. It made her realize that the beauty she had attained, if you could call it beauty, was not the current ideal. She had become *one* man's ideal female. James's.

"One of the reasons I wanted to take you for lunch was to apologize for the way I acted."

"What way?"

"Like a disapproving parent. As if I had the right."

"You don't have to apologize."

"I think I do. The way I acted, it was as if I should have some say in the way you look, and I know that I shouldn't."

"It's okay, Fred."

"I mean, I don't *want* a say in it."

"Okay."

"I'm not making myself very clear, am I?"

"Not very."

He took a long pull on his beer and turned away from her. When he turned back he looked solemn and repentant.

"Whatever your reasons for changing your appearance, they were your own reasons. The way I acted, it was like saying that I approved of you only when you looked the way I wanted you to look."

"I didn't think that."

"Good. I'm glad."

When their food came they ate in silence, looking at each other across the table. It was good to be sitting with a friend again, somebody with whom she could be herself without putting on airs. As the lunch progressed and they started on their second beers, they loosened up considerably. Fred told jokes. Amanda followed suit. They laughed uproariously.

For the first time in a very long time Amanda felt like herself. When she smiled she did not feel the motion of her lips. When she lifted her arms she was not aware of her breasts brushing against the fabric of her bra. Her face stopped being a mask and became her own.

A change came over Fred, too. The more they talked, the closer they leaned toward each other over the table. The closer they leaned, the more intimate became the subject of conversation. They swapped gossip and secrets as they had done so often in the past. She thought of what she had said to James about having an affair with Fred. As he talked, his soft, insistent voice making her smile, she considered the possibility seriously for the first time. She had never looked at Fred that way before, and doing so was a shock.

He was young, roughly her own age, his face narrow and rugged. He had often told her how much he liked to walk in the country, and to cross-country ski. She saw, now, that he was very fit. Beneath his rumpled exterior was a very solid man.

Yet, he was her friend. Nothing more, nothing less. Just a guy. A buddy. A pal.

It was so good to be talking with him again.

For Amanda it was like having a hundred-pound weight lifted off her chest and being able to breathe deeply for the first time. It was exhilarating.

As they were served coffee, Amanda glimpsed the red car moving slowly in the parking lot. She stiffened, staring, breath caught in her throat. The face behind the driver's window was a pale smudge, but it was definitely looking this way. The car disappeared beyond the edge of the window.

"Is there something wrong?"

"Nothing. No." Just a red car, that's all.

She sipped her coffee. When she saw the

deep red smudge on the edge of the cup she started, thinking for a moment that the cup was dirty. Then she recognized the shade. It was her own. She could imagine how her lips must look.

Fred did not notice the small frown that marred her perfect forehead.

"It really is you in there, isn't it, Amanda?"

Amanda smiled stiffly.

"It's me," she said.

In here. Somewhere.

When Amanda got home that night the house was dark. James was sitting in his office, bent over the desk. He had not heard her come in.

Amanda stood in his office doorway and watched him. He had not yet seen her. He was sitting in darkness, still wearing his coat, scribbling something on a note pad. As she came between the lobby light and his desk, her shadow crossed his hand. He looked up.

For a moment she thought he had smiled at her. But he sat up straight, knocking papers from his desk. He took a sharp breath.

"Sorry I'm late," Amanda said. "How long have you been here?"

He stood now. His face was white, his eyes shocked. He stepped toward her, then stopped.

"God damn it," he said softly. "I told you. I told you never, ever to come here!"

Amanda stared at him, uncomprehending.

"I . . ."

He came at her. He smelled of outside, and a cold shell of air brushed across her. When he gripped her arm she winced.

"Damn it, Lydia! If Amanda . . ."

"It's me!"

He stared at her and his mouth fell open. He stepped back, face now full of horror.

"Oh, God!"

"It's me, James. It's Amanda!"

"Oh, God, I'm sorry. Amanda, I'm . . ."

With his face turned away from her he barged past. His coat rose around him like a cloak as he ran for the front door.

"James! Wait!"

But he was already out the door, and it closed behind him. Amanda stood by his office, staring after him.

She stared at the door a few seconds longer, as if waiting for him to return. Then, silently, she went upstairs.

Dr. Richard Whitman put down his book and looked at the springer spaniel by the door. Taffy wagged his tail at even this small movement from his master.

"Do you think I could get by for one night without taking him out?"

His wife Brenda, flat out on the sofa, her red hair splashed across one arm, looked at Taffy then back at the television. Her face was round and spattered with freckles, little islands in a creamy sea. Beneath the Vikings T-shirt her breasts were full, her tummy curved. He knew every slope, every crevice, every peak in her body. If she ever wanted to change anything, he had decided long ago, another doctor would have to do it. He would never touch her with anything harder than his hands. Well, that wasn't strictly true.

"How would you like it if we only allowed you to use the bathroom on alternate days?"

"I was going to put him in the yard, for goodness sake!"

"Well, I suppose we could let *you* use the basement on Mondays, Wednesdays, and Fridays, and you could use the bathroom on the other days."

"Okay, okay, I was just asking."

He stood and stretched, loosening a knot of muscle in his lower back. He groaned softly.

Brenda looked at him curiously.

"I had a damned complicated mammaplasty today," he explained. "I nearly froze up, bent over."

"Poor boy."

"If there were only a way to operate on patients *above* you."

"Then you'd get kinks in your neck."

"Well, I could alternate, then. Operate above one day, below the next."

Brenda shook her head. Her green eyes sparkled mischievously. "Take Taffy out, and I'll deal with your back when you return."

"Promise?"

"I promise, and more besides."

"Ooh. You shouldn't have said that. It's going to be a quick walk."

"The longer the walk, the more impressed I'll be."

"Blackmail! Didn't they ever tell you never to use sex as a weapon in marriage?"

"I'm not using it as a weapon. I'm using it as a reward. A carrot hanging in front of your face."

"Taffy! Get your leash!"

"Richard, go and tuck in Ann."

As Taffy pulled his red nylon leash from the shoe rack by the door, Richard bounded up the stairs. He stuck his head into Ann's room. She was sitting up in bed with a copy of Tolkein's *The Hobbit* open in her lap. At nine, she had her mother's red hair and freckles, but her father's pale, blue eyes.

"Dad, how big are eagles?"

"Oh, I don't know. Big enough, I suppose."

"Could they carry somebody? Like give them a ride?"

Richard sat on the edge of the bed. "I don't know. There are stories of eagles picking up babies and carrying them away."

"To give them rides?"

"Uh, no."

"You mean, to eat?"

"I suppose so."

She looked up at him with a disturbed expression. "That's gross."

"I guess it is. But no more tonight, okay? Time for lights out."

She slid down in bed, handing him the book. "Dad?"

"What?"

"Are you really going to take all that time off so we can go on holidays?"

"I am."

"Are you mad at Mom for making you?"

"Mom didn't make me. I wanted to."

She smiled knowingly up at him. He ruffled her hair. "Go to sleep. You hear too much."

He leaned down and kissed her, then stood and turned out the light.

"I love you, Dad."

"I love you, too, hobbit."

He closed her door and went back downstairs. Taffy's leash was attached and hanging from the dog's mouth. The dog's stubby tail lashed against the base of the door.

Brenda handed him his coat. He zipped it up and pulled on a hat.

"You look ten years old with that hat on," Brenda said.

"Don't treat me like a ten year old when I get back."

"Never."

She put her arms around him and kissed him. Taffy growled softly.

"Back soon," he said.

When he went out and closed the door, Brenda was already climbing the stairs. The cold air braced him and he took a deep breath. Taffy tugged him down to the bottom of the drive. As the dog lifted his leg against their own gate, Richard looked back at the house. Still lit with Christmas lights, snow on the roof, icicles hanging from the eaves, it looked like something out of a dream.

God, they had so much! Their lives were so damned good! He would change nothing, even if he had the chance. Nothing. Life was perfect. And how ironic, that he had what he had because of people who were not happy with what they had. People who wanted to change not only their lives, but their bodies, and their souls.

It made him sad, sometimes, to think about it. Sad, and a little guilty.

He let Taffy pull him along. Forest Lake Drive was deserted. Only the streetlights, few and far between, gave indications of life. How funny, that one of Minneapolis's most exclusive neighborhoods should seem so much like wilderness!

He pulled Taffy across the road, and for a while they walked along a thin trail by the edge of the lake. Across the frozen expanse of water the lights of the city glowed, a green haze rising into the night.

As Taffy stopped to do more business, Richard closed his eyes and listened. You could hear the world out here. Across the lake, ice cracked, a sharp sound that echoed for a moment, then diminished. The oak trees around him groaned with the weight of recent wet snow.

Taffy finished and lunged ahead. Richard followed.

They turned away from the lake, back toward Forest Lake Drive and lights. Taffy strained at the leash.

They were approaching the road when something slammed into Richard's back.

He stumbled forward, dropping Taffy's leash, gasping for breath. Across the lake, more ice cracked.

Jesus Christ!

He turned around, looking for what had hit him, but saw only darkness and snow.

Jesus!

The breath had been knocked out of him and his back felt as if somebody had punched him right between the shoulder blades.

He coughed, and thick fluid filled his mouth, splattering across his arm. Ten yards away, Taffy barked and wagged his tail.

"Taffy!" Richard called, but the sound came out as a gurgle.

He tripped on his feet and fell to the snow. His back was now numb, but his chest ached and throbbed. What had happened?

He lay on his back and stared up at the

low, gray clouds. They swirled above him. Darkness seeped in at the edge of his vision. When he breathed, something bubbled within him.

He heard footsteps in the snow, and suddenly a shape was standing over him. He blinked his eyes, trying to focus. He found the face and blinked hard, clearing his vision.

Something about those eyes, that mouth.

It took him a few seconds to place them.

"What are you doing here?"

Then he saw the gun, coming up to point at his eyes.

"Wait," he said, gurgling. "Wait. I've got a family. A daughter. Please . . ."

In his mind, Ann's face formed, shrouded in sleepy darkness, *I love you Dad.* But those lips, those red, waxy lips, only turned up at the corners.

Flame leaped from the barrel of the gun.

Ann's face disintegrated in a cloud of darkness, a roar of thunder, a blood red rushing tide.

Seventeen

The next morning, Amanda found James sleeping on the sofa. She did not disturb him. He snored softly as she left the house.

She spent the entire morning and most of the afternoon out of the office, chasing down prospective listings. James called to take her for lunch. She passed, not sure she wanted to face him, still confused about what had happened last night, but she promised to make it up.

When she returned to the office, just after 3:00, two policemen were waiting for her. They wore civilian clothes, the older one in jeans, a bomber jacket and a beard, the younger in a long dark coat with a sport coat and tie underneath. She led them back to her office as Tanya looked on with wide eyes.

When they were seated before her desk, she sat and waited.

The younger officer nodded slowly without smiling. "I'm Detective Harness, this is Detective Corisonni."

"Angello Corisonni," said the bearded officer with a very white smile.

"Can I help you?"

"We'd like to talk to you for a few minutes," Corisonni said.

"What about? Is it about Lydia?"

They both looked at each other and shook their heads.

"You had cosmetic surgery recently," Harness said.

He seemed to be studying her face for telltale signs or scars.

"Yes," Amanda said, frowning. "Why?"

"You saw Dr. Whitman?"

"Yes, at first."

"And then Dr. Lowell?"

"Yes. Why? What's this about?"

Corisonni looked at Harness, then back at Amanda. "Both Dr. Whitman and Dr. Lowell were murdered last night."

Amanda went rigid. Down the hall a phone rang, sounding distant and unreal. The room seemed to shrink, drawing in toward her.

"Are you all right?" Corisonni asked.

"I'm . . . I . . ."

"Dr. Whitman was killed while walking his dog, some time after 10:00 P.M., and Dr. Lowell was killed shortly after that. Within an hour, anyway. Both were shot twice.

"Oh, my God."

"We'd like to talk to you, because you're one of the few patients who saw both of them."

Amanda snapped her mouth closed and looked down at her desk. She took a deep breath to force her thoughts back in order.

"I moved from Dr. Whitman to Dr. Lowell."

"We know that. Would you mind answering a few questions?"

Amanda looked up at Harness. He looked grim. "Am I a suspect?"

"No," Angello Corisonni said.

"As yet we have no suspects," Harness said quietly.

"I mean, should I talk to a lawyer before I answer any questions?"

Harness said nothing for a moment. "If you feel that you should."

"Wait a second," Corisonni said. He looked at Amanda with his wide, brown eyes. "Mrs. Sanders, it's your right to have a lawyer if you want one. Personally, I don't think you need one. Not yet, anyway. We're talking to a number of different patients. You're not the only one who saw both Whitman and Lowell. Dr. Lowell was the kind of doctor who handled a lot of surgery that other doctors wouldn't touch. As such, he handled a lot of other doctors' patients. We're just trying to gather information. We're not trying to scare you, or trick you."

He smiled, and Amanda found herself relaxing, more at ease.

"Okay," she said.

Harness leaned toward her. "That said,

225

though, where were you last night at about ten?"

Amanda answered their questions as best she could, though for most of them she was no help. She had no idea if patients of either doctor had suffered severe complications, though she supposed it was a possibility. She had no idea if the doctors had enemies, or possibly even the same enemies. When Harness and Corisonni left, she was badly shaken. When she poured herself some coffee at the machine at the end of the hall, her hands shook and coffee spilled across the table.

Back in her office she drank the coffee quickly, scalding her mouth.

Her thoughts were forming patterns that she did not like.

With her tongue still stinging from the hot coffee, she picked up the phone and called the number she had scrawled on her jotter.

"Metro Police."

"I'd like to talk to Lieutenant Toni Kirk, please."

"I'll see if she's at her desk."

The phone clicked and buzzed for a few seconds. Amanda stared at the calendar above her desk. February showed a winter scene at some northeastern lake, ski tracks winding between trees and out onto the frozen water. It looked so peaceful, so serene, she wished she were there.

"Toni Kirk."

"It's Amanda. Amanda Burns-Sanders."

"Hello, Amanda."

Amanda took a deep breath. "You've heard about the two doctors who were murdered?"

A long pause. "Yes. Everybody has, I suppose."

"Two detectives were here, questioning me."

Another pause. "You were a patient?"

"Of both."

"It's probably just routine."

"That's what they said. But a thought occurred to me."

"Yes?"

"About motive, I mean."

"You have a motive?"

"No, not me. We talked before about Lydia trying to get back at me for becoming more like her. What if she blamed my surgeons as well?"

"Jesus Christ! Did you mention this to the detectives?"

"It just occurred to me."

"Who were they?"

"Harness and Corisonni."

"The Hardy Boys. Okay. Now, Amanda, I don't want you to worry yourself about this. I'm going to check into it. I'll talk to Harness and Corisonni. There's probably nothing to it."

"You still don't know who Lydia is, do you?"

"No. But I've got reason enough to get back on the case now. I'll keep in touch."

Amanda jabbed the last piece of sole with her fork and wiped it through the cheese sauce. She put it in her mouth and chewed methodically, slowly. James sipped from his glass of water.

"Why haven't you spoken to me since you got home?" James asked.

Amanda chewed. She swallowed.

"There's nothing to talk about."

"I think there is."

"I think there isn't."

"It's obvious that for some bizarre reason you blame me for what's happening."

Amanda sipped her water. She put her knife and fork together and pushed the plate away. On the other side of the table James was looking at her with an earnest, troubled expression.

"I don't blame you for anything, James."

"You're angry, then."

"Maybe I am."

"Why?"

She stared at him, astounded. "How can you ask why?"

"Because I don't know what's bothering you, that's why, and you're being childish by not talking."

"I'm not the one who had an affair with some tramp I didn't even know! I'm not the one who mistook his wife for that tramp right in his own home!"

"I knew you'd never forgive me. I don't know why I ever thought you would."

"Two people are dead, James."

"It wasn't Lydia."

"How do you know that?"

"How do you know otherwise?"

"I just know it."

"Well, excuse me for not having developed my own paranormal abilities!" He stood abruptly, tossing his napkin to the table. "I don't care what you think of Lydia, she'd never kill anybody."

"She tried to run me down, didn't she?"

"So you say!"

Amanda stiffened. "I didn't lie about any-thing," she said quietly.

James's expression changed to one of regret. "I didn't mean that you did. I just mean . . . we have to talk about things. We can't start blaming each other."

"I told the police I thought Lydia did it."

James turned pale. "You didn't."

"I did."

"Oh, Jesus, Amanda."

"What would you have had me do?"

He shook his head. Furious, Amanda stood and stalked past him. "You don't give a damn about me, or about those doctors. You're only concerned about yourself, and about Lydia!"

She went upstairs to the living room and

dropped heavily into the sofa. James followed her. He came up behind her and put a hand on her shoulder.

"Amanda, I'm . . ."

Amanda drew away. "Don't touch me!"

"Amanda, I . . ."

"Don't you see? If she killed those doctors, what's to stop her killing me?"

"Don't panic!"

"Why shouldn't I panic! You're closing your eyes to everything that's happening!"

He tried to reach for her again, and this time she backed away. He looked at her without saying anything, then left the room. Alone, Amanda put her head back and closed her eyes. Her heart was pounding and she felt nauseated. She knew that he was right. She was on the verge of panic. If she let herself slip even a little bit more, she would lose control.

She heard James go downstairs, and then heard him talking to someone. He did not return to the living room, but she wished that he would. She was frightened, and wanted him to reassure her. She wanted him to argue with her, to prove to her that she was wrong, that she was imagining things.

But he stayed away. She settled into the sofa, eyes closed. She turned on the television for awhile, but it was a docudrama about medical emergencies, and she had to turn it off. She tried reading, but the words turned to lines of ants marching across the page, without meaning.

When the doorbell rang she sat up straight, heart racing. She heard James's voice, then another voice, muffled by distance. Footsteps sounded on the stairs.

Shelly looked at her, then came to her with open arms.

Amanda fell into her friend's embrace, pressing her face into Shelly's shoulder.

"James called," Shelly said. "I'd heard about Dr. Whitman, but not about Dr. Lowell."

"It was Lydia," Amanda whispered.

Shelly pulled away and looked at her. "You can't know that."

"I feel it."

"You have to get a grip, Amanda."

"I could be next!"

Shelly pulled her close again. Amanda sensed the other presence, and pulled back. Patrick was standing at the end of the sofa, regarding her carefully.

"Patrick."

"How do you feel?"

"Awful."

"I heard what you said."

Amanda shook her head, not sure whether to feel terrified, or silly. She rubbed her eyes. "I don't know what to think. It's all so strange. What if it's true?"

"It doesn't sound likely," Patrick said.

"But two doctors. *Those* two doctors. It can't just be a coincidence."

"Of course it can," Patrick said. "And even if it isn't, that's a long way from pointing the finger at a perpetrator."

"Maybe Lydia had surgery, too." The thought had just occurred to her, but now she sat up straight as it gripped her imagination. "God, do you think that's possible?"

"I don't know," Patrick said, frowning.

Shelly looked from Patrick to Amanda, shaking her head.

"Will the two of you please stop it!"

Amanda sank back into the sofa.

"James doesn't believe me."

"James is worried about you, that's all," Shelly said. "He was frantic when he phoned. He thought you were on the verge of some sort of breakdown."

Amanda laughed quietly. "It was my fault. I blamed him."

"That wasn't nice," Shelly said.

"I know. Where is he?"

"He's downstairs. He didn't want to upset you."

"I should talk to him."

Patrick shook his head. "What you should do, is get some rest. You're distraught, that's all. It's understandable. You're mind is working too hard on this. It's creating theories out of the stew of troubles you've been through recently."

Amanda shuddered and took a deep breath. "You really think I'm being silly?"

"I really think," Patrick said, "that you've done all you can do about it. You told the police. Let them handle it."

She wrung her hands. "I can't sleep. I'm too worked up. Poor James."

"Don't worry about him. I brought something that will help you."

He lifted a small black case. Amanda looked at it, then up at his face. He was concerned, and nothing more. Her friends were worried about her. She felt ashamed and silly.

"My imagination ran away with me," she said.

"It could have happened to any of us. Come on," he said.

She let Shelly lift her to her feet. "I should talk to James."

"You can talk to him tomorrow. Sleep first. Doctor's orders."

Ten minutes later Amanda was in bed, sheets drawn up to her chin. Patrick had injected something into her arm. Already, her body felt tingly, her mind foggy.

"We'll come by, tomorrow evening," Shelly said from the door. "See how you're doing."

Amanda smiled, but said nothing. She heard the door close, and then the fog rolled in, and behind it a wall of darkness.

Something disturbed her, and she woke to the shadows of the bedroom. The fog had re-

233

ceded somewhat, though she sensed it at the edge of her vision, ready to flood back in. Her body still tingled.

Voices came from the lobby, or the living room. She heard James's, and Patrick's.

She swept away the sheets and blanket, and got up. On her feet she swayed, and held out her hands until she felt steady. Perhaps Patrick had not given her enough. She certainly felt calmer now.

At the door, dizzy again, she paused. The voices were clearer. She heard Patrick.

". . . talked to Lydia?"

"I can't." That was James.

Shelly said something that Amanda did not quite understand.

Then Patrick again, ". . . the damned police."

"Lydia would not do it," James said carefully. "I know it."

Amanda opened the door. She stepped into the landing.

The three of them were standing in the living room doorway, close together. Shelly's eyes widened when she saw Amanda, and a look of what might have been anger flashed across her face.

"I heard you talking," Amanda said, and heard the words come out as mumbles.

James turned to her, mouth open.

"Amanda!"

He moved toward her, but Patrick stopped

him. "It's okay. She's out of it. I'll put her back in bed."

He came to her, smiling, and held her arm. He took her back into the bedroom, and closed the door. He led her to the bed, pushed her down onto it.

"I heard you talking about Lydia."

"You were dreaming."

"No, I heard . . ."

"You're dreaming now."

He leaned over her, and she felt a prick on her arm.

"I'm not dreaming. I'm . . ."

"Yes, you are. Dreaming. Dreaming. Dream . . ."

His words brought the fog back. Dreaming. Dreaming. Yes, it had to have been a dream. It had to have been. Because if it wasn't a dream, then they knew something. Something awful. A terrible secret they were hiding from her.

The fog thickened, and the darkness swept in. Patrick's voice followed her down into it.

"Dreaming," he said.

Dreaming. Dreaming.

Yes.

Amanda woke suddenly. There was no easy transition through softening dream to the rudeness of reality, just an abrupt shift as if she had changed television channels inside her head.

235

She wondered how long she had been staring at the ceiling. A long arm of sunlight reaching across the room and down the wall behind her seemed awfully familiar. She must have been staring at it a long time.

She rolled over and looked at the clock radio. 10:47. My God, half the day was gone already! What, exactly, had Patrick given her?

Memories, vague, disturbing, unreal, flickered through her mind. There had been voices. She had heard the others talking. About Lydia.

But it had been a dream, hadn't it?

She pushed up and swung her legs out of bed. She sat on the edge of the bed and stared at her feet. No dizziness. No nausea. She felt good.

She moved to the end of the bed and looked into the mirror. As she saw her reflection, other memories came back. She remembered the police coming to visit, the deaths of Dr. Whitman and Dr. Lowell. Lydia.

Even in the bright light of midmorning, her suspicions seemed as strong as ever. Stronger.

She got off the bed and went to the door. No voices. She opened the door. The upper landing was bright with sunlight. A pillar of spiraling dust speared from the center skylight down into the lobby. From downstairs she could hear James, on the phone, his voice business-like, pleasant. The smell of coffee reached even up here. It felt like Sunday. A relaxed, lazy Sunday morning.

Hugging her nightgown around herself she closed the door and went back into the room. She ran the shower water as hot as she could stand it and stood under the scalding needle-spray until her skin was numb, then she turned the hot water off completely and stood in the icy stream until her skin had passed through a feeling stage and turned numb again. When she stepped out of the shower her skin glowed fiery red, but she felt more awake than she had in days, weeks.

She dried her hair in the bathroom and brushed her teeth. When she opened the door to the bedroom, Shelly was standing by the end of the bed.

"Good morning," Shelly said.

Amanda, towel draped around her breasts, stared at the other woman in surprise.

"What are you doing here?"

"No *good morning* for a concerned friend?"

"Did you stay here all night?"

Shelly sat on the edge of the bed. "No. I came by this morning to check on you."

"I'm fine."

"You were rather distraught last night."

"Distraught? You mean I was paranoid and terrified?"

"That, too."

"Well, I'm fine now."

Listening to herself, she realized she was sounding quite brusque, almost rude, and wondered why she did not care. Her dreams still tugged at her. Shelly had been in those dreams. But the dreams had not surprised her with something she had not already felt. From the beginning she'd suspected that Shelly and Patrick and James knew far more than they were telling her.

"What are you doing now?" Shelly asked, apparently undisturbed by Amanda's tone.

"I'm getting dressed. Actually, I wonder if you'd step out for a moment while I do it. I'll only be a few minutes."

Shelly tugged at her lower lip with her teeth. "I was going to suggest you get back into bed and sleep some more. Patrick thought it might be a good idea if you stayed in bed for a while."

"I'm fine, now. Let me get dressed and I'll be out soon."

"No, I was serious. Patrick thought if you slept a few hours more . . ."

"Shelly, I'm not going back to sleep. I feel fine. Please, just get out for a few minutes and let me get dressed."

Her tone left no room for argument. Shelly appeared to want to say something, but only nodded. She closed the door quietly behind her.

Amanda dressed quickly. She put on jeans and a woolen sweater her mother had made for her years ago. She applied her makeup with fingers that seemed to know exactly what to do without guidance. The casual clothes made the makeup look rather severe, and she stared at her reflection for a few seconds, shaking her head. The total look was rather startling.

"I don't know you," Amanda said to herself, voice quiet.

She sat again at the head of the bed and picked up the phone. She dialed the metro-police number from memory and asked for Toni Kirk. Toni answered sounding rather subdued.

"Toni, it's Amanda Burns-Sanders."

The pause was uncomfortably long, as if Toni did not recognize the name.

"Yes, Amanda. What can I do for you?"

"I was wondering if you'd talked to the other two detectives about Lydia, or if you'd found out anything."

Another pause. "Amanda, I'm not really at liberty to discuss an ongoing case."

Unnerved, Amanda said nothing.

As the pause lengthened, Toni spoke again, this time her voice hushed, urgent. "Amanda, listen to me carefully. We have no more information regarding Lydia. The opinion around here, nearly unanimous, is that she probably doesn't exist."

"But she . . ."

"Just listen. A couple of witnesses near Dr. Lowell's home stated they saw a woman in the vicinity around the time of the murder. Their descriptions match . . . both Lydia and yourself."

"Then she did it!"

"Amanda, don't say anything more to me.

239

Don't tell me anything else, not even in simple friendliness."

Amanda, uneasy now, said, "Toni, what's going on?"

"If you've got a lawyer, contact him or her now. If you don't have a lawyer, find one quickly."

"You don't think that I . . ."

"Corisonni and Harness will be talking with you again very soon. Be prepared. Get a lawyer."

"Toni . . ."

"Don't call me again. It would be improper."

The line went dead. Amanda slowly lowered the receiver. She felt dizzy, and realized she was breathing far too rapidly. She calmed herself, lowered her chin to her chest.

They suspected her. They thought that she, not Lydia, was responsible. What had Toni said? *Lydia probably doesn't exist.* What did that mean? That they thought Amanda had made the whole thing up?

Before she could panic, she stood and left the room. She found both James and Shelly downstairs in the kitchen with cups of coffee. James smiled anxiously when he saw her.

"Good morning!"

Amanda looked back and forth between them. "I have to go out for a while."

Now they looked at each other.

"I don't think that's a good idea," Shelly said. "You were very upset last night. Patrick thought . . . well, he left some pills for you to take, something to calm you down, and I think, Patrick thinks, you should take them."

"Patrick isn't my doctor. You're my friends, and I appreciate your concern, but it's not necessary. And I don't intend to take any more drugs that aren't prescribed for me."

"Really, Amanda," James said, "if Patrick thinks you should . . ."

"I'm going out."

"I'm calling Patrick," Shelly said.

Amanda stepped out of the way as Shelly moved to the phone. As Shelly dialed, Amanda moved closer to James.

"I'm sorry about last night. I didn't mean to accuse you, or blame you."

"You were upset."

"Yes, I was. I'm still upset, but I know that . . . what you did is done, it's gone. It can't be changed. Lydia is the problem."

"Amanda, I think you should wait here for Patrick."

"No."

Amanda left the kitchen and went to the vestibule. She put on her coat and boots. Shelly grabbed her arm as she was about to open the front door.

"Patrick is coming over. He wants you to wait here."

"Tell him thanks, but no thanks."

"I can't just let you go, Amanda," Shelly

said. "Patrick thinks you might be . . . he just wants you to wait, that's all."

"Shelly, let go of my arm."

Shelly's grip did not lessen. Amanda yanked free, and pushed the other woman away.

"Don't touch me like that, Shelly. I mean it."

Shelly stared at her, then at James. "James, you can't let her just go. She needs rest."

"I can't stop her," James said.

Amanda smiled sweetly at Shelly. "I'll be back later."

Eighteen

Amanda knocked once on the office door then opened it. Lincoln Fowler looked up from his desk as she entered. His face turned pale. He started to rise, then sat down again. His hand moved toward the top right drawer, then stopped. It took Amanda a few seconds to realize what his actions meant, and when she did she took a sharp breath.

"Oh, I'm sorry! This isn't what you think! I'm not *her.*"

He stared at her, not relaxing one bit.

"I don't know what you mean."

"It's me, Mr. Fowler. Amanda Burns-Sanders."

The suspicion on his face turned to one of outright shock. He continued to stare, and now he did rise slightly.

"Mrs. Sanders?"

"I'm sorry. I'd forgotten how I look now. I should have phoned to warn you."

"You just aged me ten years," he said. "This is a detective's worst nightmare. The surveil-

243

lance subject showing up and demanding an explanation."

Amanda went in and sat at the desk. Still shaking his head, still obviously disconcerted, Lincoln Fowler poured two cups of coffee. Amanda took the cup and sipped. The bitter brew made her grimace.

Lincoln Fowler sat behind his desk and stared at her unashamedly.

"You've changed."

"Cosmetic surgery, diet, makeup, clothes," Amanda said.

"Yes, but you've changed yourself into . . . I mean, you look almost exactly like . . ."

He opened his desk, riffled through some papers, and brought out a handful of photographs. He looked through them, shaking his head, and tossed one onto the desk. It was a photograph of Lydia. Amanda did not pick it up.

"Yes. I know. It wasn't entirely accidental, but it happened so gradually that I didn't realize until afterward."

"But why?"

Amanda sipped her coffee and looked away from him. "I wanted to keep my husband. I wanted to keep him happy."

"Jesus Christ."

She turned on him, angry now. "I didn't come here to be judged."

"I'm sorry. I'm just surprised, that's all. Why have you come?"

"I need to hire you again."

"Does it have something to do with her?" He indicated the photograph on the desk. "Is she still threatening you in some way?"

"Threatening is no longer an appropriate characterization of what she's doing."

"Okay. Tell me about it." He settled back into his chair, coffee cradled in both hands.

"It got worse after you gave me the photographs. That's when things really began to happen."

It took nearly half an hour to recount the past few months to Lincoln Fowler. He listened intently, eyes narrowed, mouth a thin line, interrupting only when he needed something clarified. He was a perfect listener, and Amanda found herself telling him things she had not told anybody else. The act of speaking, of organizing the incidents that had cast a pall over her life, brought things sharply to focus. By the time she had finished, all her doubts were gone.

"You think Lydia killed them," Fowler said. "Because she's angry that those doctors turned you into her? Made you look like her?"

"I know it. I can feel it. I think she was upset enough that I won James away from her, but that I did it by basically turning *into* her . . . she can't handle that."

"So she sets out to destroy everybody who helped in the process."

"I know it sounds crazy."

"I didn't say it sounded crazy. I'm just trying to get it straight." He sipped his coffee, grimaced at the coldness of it, and put the cup on the desk. "You're sure the police suspect you?"

"She told me to get a lawyer, not to talk to her again, and to prepare myself to be questioned."

"I should have done follow-up," Fowler said. "I should have done a complete ident package on her."

"That's what I want now. If I can find out who she is, then everything will be fine."

"You hope. Do you have a lawyer?"

"James's lawyer, I suppose. He handles a lot of things for James."

"I mean a criminal lawyer."

"No."

"I'm going to give you a name and a phone number. His name is Daniel Renton. He's very good, and he'll talk to you if you say I sent you."

"Should I call him now?"

"No. If you're too prepared, they'll suspect you that much more. Yes, it's your right, but don't do it. Wait until after they talk to you. They should suggest it. When they do, then call him. It will look better that way."

"What should I do in the meantime?"

"Go about your business. Be careful. I'll track down Lydia."

Amanda felt lightheaded with relief. "Thank you."

"And don't worry."

The smile stayed on her face as she left his building, but by the time she was sitting in her car it was gone, and the weight of worry had returned in full force.

James walked slowly through the skyway system, occasionally stopping to look out over streets glistening with melted snow. Over the past few days the temperature had risen dramatically. Despite blue skies, which normally indicated a high-pressure front and cooler temperatures, the days had been almost steamy. Cars below were black with dirt. Sellers of windshield-washer fluid had made a killing this week, he expected.

He felt anxious as he walked, and his hands sweated. His coat hung over his arm, and the weight of it made him weary. It was nearly 1:00 P.M., but he had been in the skyway system for more than an hour.

The few days since the murder of the doctors had been a great strain. Amanda had changed in a way that he could not quite put his finger on. She had withdrawn from him, it seemed. She seemed recalcitrant, almost. Stubborn, unwilling to listen.

The visits from the police had done nothing to improve matters. It almost seemed as if they suspected Amanda of something. They'd asked many questions about Lydia, but of course he had not been able to tell them anything. They had wanted to see his gun collection, and he had shown the two officers. Harness and Corleonne, or something like that. Corisonne, that was it.

They'd studied the rack of guns, taking up a full wall of the library, and Corisonne had whistled softly. James was always delighted when the collection impressed. It had taken him a lifetime to accumulate. They had touched the stocks and barrels of his rifles, had removed from its clip the special edition Colt .44 magnum and handed it back and forth. He had refused to allow them to handle the antique crossbow, or the Zulu assegai. Those were for show alone. But their questions had turned to other, more practical matters.

Did he own a .38 caliber handgun?

Of course.

Did Amanda own one?

No.

Did Amanda know how to handle a weapon?

Amanda, standing beside him, had nodded. She'd shot often in the country, as a girl. Rifles and handguns. She was quite proficient, actually.

But in the end they had left without giving any indication of why they had asked so many questions. Afterward, though James had wanted to, Amanda would not talk. He felt she was hiding something from him, but he could not blame her for that. He, after all, had hidden so much from her.

When the call had come from Lydia this morning he had been ecstatic. He needed desperately to see her, to talk, to question.

But now, walking through the skyway, he was nervous as a schoolboy. His heart fluttered, his forehead and hands sweated. He could hardly think.

At 1:30 he returned to the Radisson and booked a room.

He was lying on the bed, pondering the calamity of his life, when Lydia arrived.

"I knew you would come," she said.

"We have to talk."

"Yes, we do."

"You murdered those doctors, didn't you?"

"Everything I do, I do because I love you."

"Did you murder them?" Her perfume made him dizzy.

"Everything I do, I do because . . ."

"Don't touch me!"

"You want me to."

"I don't want you to. I want you to answer me."

"You love me, too. You always have."

"I love Amanda."

"I've loved you, and you've loved me, for a lot longer than you've known Amanda."

"That doesn't matter. Answer the question!"

"Everything I do, I do because I love you."

She touched him gently on the thigh. Her fingers moved up, slowly, stroking.

"Don't," he said hoarsely, but did not try to stop her.

"You love me."

He closed his eyes as her fingers encircled him. "Yes," he said.

"You must help me."

He tasted her lipstick, and her perfume surrounded him like a fog.

"I can't," he said.

"Yes, you can."

Late in the afternoon, her paperwork finished, Amanda relaxed in her office with some coffee. Fred Cooper stuck his head in the door and smiled at her.

"Howdy! Got more time now?"

"More time for what?"

"You rushed off so fast last night, I didn't even get a chance to say hi."

Amanda frowned up at him. "What are you talking about?"

He leaned on the door. "Last night. Around ten. You must have been showing a property or something over by my place. I saw you. You waved to me. I started to walk over, but you got in your car and drove away."

A prickly feeling spread across Amanda's back. "I was at home all night. Didn't step out at all."

"I'll be damned. I swear, it was you. It even sounded like you."

"What kind of car?"

"A red sports car. An Alfa Romeo, something like that. I thought it was new."

Amanda stared at him without speaking, the prickly sensation now rising up her neck, making her scalp tingle.

"It wasn't me, Fred."

He laughed now, shaking his head. "I wish you'd seen her, Amanda. She looked just like you. Spitting image."

Amanda tried not to let her shock show. She smiled nervously, but he seemed not to notice.

"They say everybody's got a doppelgänger somewhere," she said quietly.

"Well, if you see mine, tell him to give me a call. Maybe we can switch lives once in a while."

"I will," she said.

He left her office, closing the door behind him. Amanda turned back to the desk. Her hands were trembling.

Half an hour later, while Amanda was staring at the calendar above her desk, losing herself in the photograph of a snowbound cabin, Fowler called.

"Mr. Fowler?"

"Listen, I think . . ."

"She followed one of my friends! He thought

it was me, but it wasn't. She's going after my friends! She's trying to scare me, and it's working! She's . . ."

"Amanda, calm down."

"What is she trying to do?"

"I don't know. But I've found where she lives. Can you come and meet me?"

"What for?"

"I think we should have a close look."

"Shouldn't we just tell the police?"

"If they're going to charge you, we shouldn't offer them any information until we've talked to Daniel. Have you called him?"

"Not yet. The police didn't really accuse me, or suggest anything."

"We should probably call him anyway now. Especially with this new information. Let him decide what to do with it. Can you meet me?"

"Where?"

He gave her the address.

"That's downtown."

"That's right. About twelve blocks from your place."

"Oh, God."

"Don't think about it. Just meet me."

When she hung up, she felt nauseated, and her hands were still trembling. She took a number of deep breaths, closed her eyes, and calmed herself. She put on her coat and boots, took another deep breath, and left her office. At the reception desk she signed herself out on the board.

"I won't be back this afternoon," she told Tanya.

When she turned around, the office door opened. A gust of cool, moist air rushed in, followed by James. He stamped his feet on the doormat and grinned at her.

"I was hoping you'd still be here!"

Amanda clamped her teeth and tried to smile. "What are you doing here?"

"I thought I'd see if you wanted to go for a late, late lunch, or even just a drink."

His smile was so open, so hopeful, she felt terrible. "I can't, James. I'm on my way to a showing."

"Oh."

"If you'd called, maybe I could have . . ."

"That's okay. Don't worry about it. Maybe tomorrow."

"Sure. That would be nice."

He took a deep breath, shrugged, and smiled again. "Oh, well, a drink or two alone never hurt anybody, did it?"

"Not anybody I know," she said.

Outside, they kissed. A brief touching of lips. Almost reluctant.

"You won't be late home?"

"No. Probably not."

"See you later, then."

He waved to her as his car glided through the slush toward the entrance of the parking lot. She waved back with a tight smile. After he was gone, she walked resolutely to her car.

Nineteen

"We're not going to break in, are we?"

"We are."

From his pocket, Lincoln Fowler took a pair of clear plastic gloves and gave them to her. "Put these on. The last thing we want is your prints around here."

It took Fowler nearly five minutes to work the lock. When it finally turned, he grinned at her.

The inside of the apartment was nothing like what the decrepit state of the building had led Amanda to expect. Here she found furniture that could sit comfortably in her own home. A long, black leather sofa with two matching box chairs facing it, between them a steel-framed table topped by what looked like a slab of gray and black marble. On the walls hung Paul Klee prints. The color scheme was mostly dark. Purples, grays. The look was not austere, but the place felt empty—not lived in.

A jade ashtray on the coffee table was full

of cigarette butts, each smeared with dark red lipstick. The air smelled of tobacco smoke and Calantha.

A glass cabinet housed a respectable stereo system, but there was no television.

"Not bad," Fowler said, closing the door.

Amanda crossed the room to the window. On the sill sat a number of framed photographs. She looked at them and shook her head.

"Oh, God."

"What is it?"

Fowler came up behind her and held her arm.

One photograph was of James. It was a younger James, before Amanda had met him, but she recognized it from his mother's house. Another was of Shelly and Patrick being married. Another was of Petra. The final photograph, the one that took Amanda's breath away, was a duplicate of the one she had seen in the upstairs bedroom of Petra's house after New Year's. It was James's Aunt Paula.

Fowler leaned forward and stared at the photograph.

"Quite a resemblance."

"Is it Lydia?"

"Possibly. Similar features, but she didn't strike me as being that old." He looked at Amanda. "Maybe she's had surgery, too. That would explain why she looks younger than the photograph. If it's her, that is."

"If it's not Paula, then what are these pictures doing here? They imply she knows the family, don't they? It's just too horrible to think about!"

"This certainly bolsters that theory."

"It's awful."

Fowler began to look through the drawers of a roll-top desk against the wall adjacent to the window. His gloved fingers lifted papers, flipped through envelopes. Amanda turned away from the photographs and hugged her arms across her breasts. She felt cold, and unwelcome.

"Well, well, well," Fowler said.

"What is it?"

He motioned her over. He handed her a sheet of paper. Amanda stared at it, and after a few moments realized what she was looking at. It was a sales slip for a Mazda, dated less than a year ago. After she and James were married. It showed transfer of ownership for the amount of one dollar. It was signed by James. Lydia's name was not on the paper.

"Anybody could have this and say they owned that car," Fowler said. "He just signed it over."

"He bought it for her," Amanda said. She felt sick.

"Apparently so."

Fowler shoved the paper back into the desk, and continued to rake through the drawers.

"What are you looking for?"

"A gun. Anything interesting."

But a few minutes later he closed the desk and backed away from it. "Nothing."

They moved into the bedroom. Here they found clothes spread across the bed, and the floor, drawers hanging open, the closet open and disturbed.

"Somebody went through here in a hurry," Fowler said.

He looked at Amanda and frowned.

"Jesus," he said.

"What?"

"What if she's ditched?"

"Ditched?"

"Taken off. Flown the coop."

"Why would she do that?"

"Because the pressure's on. Because she knows we're getting close."

Amanda frowned at him. "That would be good, wouldn't it?"

"Not if the police need to talk to her. If she's gone, how do you prove she really exists?"

Amanda chewed her lip. She hadn't considered that.

Fowler proceeded to look through the dresser drawers. He pulled out panties, bras, stockings, and tossed them on the bed.

"How did you find this place?" Amanda asked.

"I followed her here."

"But how did you find *her?*"

He stopped what he was doing and turned to look at her. His expression was grim.

"The same way I found her last time."

Amanda stared at him, the meaning of his words finally coming clear.

"She was with James?"

"I watched him. It only took a few days."

"When was she with him?"

He turned away and started to look through the drawers again. "This afternoon. When she left him, I followed her. She came here. When she went out, I called you."

She thought of James showing up at the office, smiling, looking hurt when she had to refuse lunch and drinks. She gritted her teeth, biting back the fury that wanted to erupt.

"Where could she have gone?"

Fowler turned to her again. His expression was now mollifying. He smiled sheepishly.

"I don't know."

"Can you find her again?"

"Probably."

"How?"

He took a deep breath. "I'll follow your husband. He's bound to see her."

Amanda said nothing. Fowler came up behind her and touched her arm.

"Don't let this get to you."

"I'm not." Her voice was calmer than she had any right to expect.

"Let's get out of here."

She waited for him in the hall as he locked

the door. When he finished, he turned to her and pursed his lips.

"Where are you going now?"

"I don't know."

"You want to get a drink? I could use one."

She looked into his eyes, and though she recognized what she saw there, she smiled and nodded.

"I could use one, too."

Amanda stared at the ceiling. It was white, but she could see dark handprints on the paint. A child's handprints, where one had jumped on a bed. Thin cracks made a checkerboard pattern around the light fixture. She followed the cracks with her eyes as if they were roads on a map.

The room was dark, but light from the street leaked through glass covered only by a window shade. Yellow walls, cracked worse than the ceiling and peppered with nail holes, pressed close on all sides. The bed beneath her was soft, and the side on which she was lying seemed to have formed the shape of a body far different from her own. Fowler snored softly beside her, his pale, hairy back exposed.

Amanda breathed deeply, slowly, as she stared at the ceiling. She felt drained, in a bad sort of way, as if she had just come out of a fever, or had shaken the last of a cold.

When she closed her eyes she saw Fowler

bent over her, his face savage, shoulders tense, as he slammed her into the bed.

She had felt nothing. Nothing but pain, and had turned her face from him as he groaned and gasped in climax, his mouth and chin red from her lipstick.

His clock radio said it was nearly eight.

With a groan, and a great exertion of effort, she sat up and swung her legs out of bed. The floor beneath her feet was carpeted, but the carpet was thick with dust and tiny objects that poked into her skin. Somewhere in the house, it had not been an apartment as she had anticipated, a steam radiator started to hiss. Deep within the walls, pipes clanked and clicked. Behind her, Fowler snored softly.

Amanda put her elbows on her knees, then rested her face in her hands, covering her eyes. What had she done? She had just slept with a man she hardly knew, and she had not used protection. The stupidity! And for what? Because she was angry at James?

She shook her head. She sobbed without realizing it, and the noise startled her. She sat up straight.

Behind her, Fowler coughed and sat up. She could feel his eyes on her back.

"Listen, if you're worried about . . ."

"I'm not worried about anything."

"I haven't slept with anybody in nearly a year," he said with a dry voice, and I got tested six months ago. "I'm clean."

She let that sink in. It didn't make her feel any better.

"Thank you," she said anyway.

"I don't usually do this."

"Neither do I."

"Not with clients."

"Me either."

They sounded so stupid, she had to laugh. Her shoulders shook. The laughs nearly turned to tears, but she forced herself to rise. Without looking at Fowler, or at the spotted, streaked mirror above his dresser, she pulled on her clothes. He watched her silently. When she had her coat and boots on, she turned to him.

"I'll call you if I find anything," he said.

Amanda nodded, then turned and left the bedroom. She worked her way through the dark house, trying not to look at anything, trying not to see anything that might bring Lincoln Fowler's life into relief. She did not want to know him, or anything about him.

Outside, she stood on his front step and breathed deeply. The air smelled damp and dirty, and did not refresh her.

She walked to her car, but before she got there she stopped, bent over, and vomited. Still, there were no tears. Just a dry, painful anger. For herself. Disgust.

In the car, the engine running, she applied makeup while looking in the rearview mirror. When she had finished, she glanced toward the house. The bedroom light was on. The silhouette of a man filled the window. Amanda put the car in gear and drove away.

Amanda found James in the library, sitting in an easy chair, facing his gun collection. A half-empty glass of something amber hung from the tips of his fingers. He did not look at her as she came in, but his manner changed, his shoulders tensed.

"You know," he said, "I always thought this collection was my most prized collection. I've spent twenty years of my life acquiring it. Piece by piece. I know everything in here. I know the feel of it all, the weight of it. I can look at a piece and remember clearly what she feels like to fire. The whole thing is part of me. I used to think I'd die before giving it up. Can you believe that? *Die* rather than give up this collection of . . . inanimate junk."

Now he turned to her.

"But I know now I wouldn't die. I'd replace it all, piece by piece, if I had to. I could do it in far less than twenty years now."

Amanda was looking at the guns, and now she turned to James.

"James . . ."

He held a finger to his lips. "But one thing I couldn't replace, not in twenty years, not in a lifetime . . . is you. Is our marriage."

His eyes were wet and his voice choked.

"I don't want to lose you, Amanda."

Amanda felt the emotion in his words, and she had to force herself not to reflect it. Did he know where she had been? No, he couldn't. She had phoned him and told him she was going out for a drink, that was all.

"I know you saw Lydia today," she said, turning the tables of guilt.

He did not look surprised. "Yes."

"Why, James, why?"

"Because I was frightened. Because of the murders. I had to talk to her. To find out if it was true."

She stared at him, wanting desperately to believe what he was saying, but unwilling to let herself believe, unwilling to open herself.

"We found her apartment."

At that, his shoulders straightened. "You did?"

"Yes. With a private detective. He used you to locate her. But she's gone, now."

"Gone?"

"Where has she gone, James?"

He shook his head. "I don't know. You know more about her than I do, apparently. I don't know where she lives. I don't even know her full name."

There was no fraud in his tone. He seemed drained of the energy required for duplicity.

"I'm going to the police with what I know."

"Good," James said.

"You don't mind?"

263

"I want to be rid of her. I want it over with. I want us to get on with our lives."

She stared at him, still unwilling to commit herself to belief. She wanted to ask him questions about the photographs, about Lydia, but saw that he would have no answers. He was empty of answers. If they were going to get on with their lives, it would have to be tomorrow, or the next day. Tonight, she could do nothing.

"I'm going to bed," she said.

As she turned away he said, gently, in a voice that seemed thick with anguish, "Good night, Amanda."

Twenty

The following days were strained between Amanda and James. They hardly talked, and when they looked at each other they quickly looked away. It was horrible. Amanda began to wonder if they would ever return to normal. It seemed unlikely.

On Friday, Amanda woke to a bedroom swimming in sunlight. James snored on beside her. She did not wake him as she rose and showered. She did not even know what time he had come to bed.

Downstairs, she phoned her office, but got the answering service. She left a message for Fred Cooper to handle her calls. They had a standing agreement to cover for each other.

Amidst morning rush-hour traffic, she drove to Merit.

For nearly a full hour she subjected herself to a series of grueling exercises. Coming off the aerobic steps her legs and back burned, but she went immediately to the weights and began her curls. Finishing that, she advanced to the track and ran faster, and with more intensity than she had in her life. Images of Lincoln Fowler drove her on. She ached at the pain of the memory. How stupid, how ridiculous, how pathetic, to allow her emotions to manipulate her like that! Images of Lydia drove her even harder.

And so she tortured herself to the point of exhaustion, succumbing only when she could think no longer, when the physical signals from her body overwhelmed her mind. She stumbled into the shower and stood beneath a stream of scalding water. By the time she finished she felt almost feverish, and her skin was nearly raw.

Afterward, Chrissy stood her in a corner of her office and took a Polaroid photograph.

"I want to show you something," Chrissy said.

She held the Polaroid by her fingertips as it developed, then retrieved a file folder from her desk. With tape she stuck the photograph into the folder, then handed the entire package to Amanda.

Amanda looked down at the folder, and her hands shook.

There were two photographs taped to the inside cover. The one on the left had been taken her first day here. The one on the right was this morning's. The photographs were of different women. It was impossible to transform the first woman into this other woman. No diet could have achieved that. She looked at her old face and felt an ache of longing and despair so strong that her lips trembled. She remembered clearly the day she had come here, remembered the previous night of anguish as she had studied herself in the mirror, her self-image poisoned by her suspicions of James and by her talk with Shelly. And now, months later, she had become the very thing that had started it all. She was no longer the betrayed wife. She was the other woman.

She closed the folder and handed it back.

She had come to Merit to cleanse herself, but as she drove home Amanda felt as tainted as ever. This time, Lincoln Fowler had nothing to do with it. It was purely herself.

When she got home she found that James was not in his office. She could see the answering machine light glowing in the dim interior. She found him upstairs in their bedroom. A suitcase lay open on the bed, half full of clothes. He stopped packing when he saw her and they stood at either end of the room staring at each other.

"I thought you would be at work," he said.

"I thought you would, too. What are you doing?"

"I'm meeting a group of clients in L.A. tomorrow. I thought I told you. I'm sure I did."

"You didn't."

"It's been planned for a long time. I'm sure you've simply let it slip your mind."

"How long will you be gone?"

"Three days, four at most."

Amanda felt herself begin to lose control. She opened her mouth to say something, but could find no words. James turned away from her, obviously embarrassed by her discomfort. Finally, Amanda calmed herself, and found her voice.

"James, this is not a good time to go away."

"I talked to Shelly and Patrick. They'll keep in touch."

"There have been two murders, likely committed by a woman you were seeing. The police probably think I had something to do with it. You *can't* just go away now. Not now."

His face worked through a series of expressions as he folded a pair of pants and put them in the case.

"There's nothing to worry about, Amanda. I promise you."

"How can you know that?"

"I just know it."

The suspicion came on her like a chill and she took a sharp breath as it gripped her.

"You're going somewhere with her."

"Don't be ridiculous."

"You sent her somewhere, and now you're going after her. You're going to be with her."

"Amanda, that's not true. It's over between me and Lydia."

"You're lying, James. You've been lying from the start."

He shook his head and continued to pack his case. Furious, Amanda went to the bed and yanked out the packed clothes. She tossed pants, shirts, books to the bed. She held up a swimming suit, a bottle of suntan lotion.

"What's this for?"

"It's not going to be strictly work, of course. I always take these things with me. If you'll think about it, you'll see you know that."

"All that means is that you've taken trips with her before. It's true, isn't it?"

"No."

"James, you are a lying, snivelling, bastard."

He slowly repacked what she had unpacked, then closed the case. Unruffled, he looked at her with a sad sort of calm.

"I don't think we should talk about this now. I'll be back on Tuesday, Wednesday at the latest."

"Don't expect me to be here when you get back."

She stormed out of the bedroom and into the living room. It was nearly half an hour later that she heard him go downstairs. Heard the front door open and shut. Heard silence fill their home.

She picked up the phone and punched Lincoln Fowler's number from memory.

"Fowler investigations."

"It's Amanda. James is leaving the house. He's going to the airport."

"Now?"

"He just left."

"Did he say where he was going?"

"He said a business trip, but I think he's going with Lydia."

"Good. He'll have to come this way. I'll beat him there. I'll call you later."

"What if you see her? What then?"

"I'll call the police and see if they want to stop her. One way or another, I'll find out where your husband is going. If I were you, I'd take this opportunity to look through some of his things. See if you can find anything."

She stared at James's chest of drawers a long time before opening it. In the entire length of their marriage, she had never gone through his things. Not even to put his clothes away. She had never wanted to. Even now, at Fowler's urging, she could hardly bring herself to begin. A matter of trust hung in the balance.

Over the past months her life had been turned upside down, and her relationship with James had been dashed, but . . . they were still married. Marriage, whatever its problems, entailed trust. Perhaps James had betrayed that trust by seeing Lydia, but did that give her the right to do the same? What if she found something incriminating as she rummaged through his things? She would never be able to confront him with it. In a court of law any such evidence would be thrown out as illegally obtained, and in the court of her conscience the same ruling was being passed down.

Still, Fowler had asked her. More than simple trust was at stake here. Lydia was missing, the one person whose mere existence could extricate Amanda from a quagmire of suspicion and uncertainty.

She pondered the problem for nearly half an hour before deciding. The trust in their marriage had died long ago. She'd played her own part in that, hadn't she, when she had slept with Fowler? This was a matter of necessity.

She opened the top right drawer and looked down upon neatly folded underwear and socks. Even such simple items produced a strange feeling within her. It was like picking up a book you had thought to be thin and silly and finding it had far more depth than you had expected. Underwear and socks were so mundane, they immediately plucked James from the realm of the villainous and dropped him right back into real life. Villains didn't wear underwear and socks, did they?

Guilt renewed, she rummaged through the drawer and, finding nothing, closed it again quickly.

She looked at herself in the mirror, shook her head sadly, and proceeded to the next drawer. This one was full of old colognes, deodorants, an assortment of brushes, combs, and other grooming instruments. She found some folded papers at the back, but they turned out to be old electric and phone bills, along with a wallet-sized photograph of Amanda. The old Amanda. She shoved them back and closed the drawer.

This was silly.

What kind of evidence did she hope to find?

Still, as she went on it became easier, and exploring the subsurface of James's life became almost pleasurable. She knew the feeling well. Back in Joseph Walker Junior High somebody had gotten a copy of Xaviera Hollander's *The Happy Hooker*. Like a virulent tropical disease the book had raced through the class in a mere month. The feeling of discovering shining secrets you weren't supposed to find, not *yet,* had thrilled her. It was the same now. As James revealed himself to her through the recesses of his drawers and closet, she felt like a teenager on the verge of being caught.

The bedroom, however, for all its guilty pleasures, provided nothing of use. She came away from it simply with a stronger feeling for the reality of her husband.

She spent only a few minutes in the living room. One of the coffee tables had a drawer into which James often dropped spare change or loose papers. She sat on the ottoman and poked through the drawer. She found a number of old bills, pens, old photographs of her and

James, old airline tickets, loose keys that did not look familiar. Were they the keys for Lydia's apartment? More likely they were the unused keys for the front door.

Once, as a girl, she had raked through her father's desk, and this was the kind of thing she had found. She felt like that now—a child raking through her parents' things, enchanted by mysteries only half guessed at.

At the back of the drawer she found a sealed condom.

She pulled out the small package and stared at it, at once mortified and triumphant. They never used condoms. Did he use them with Lydia? She reached to the back of the drawer again, and found a blue handbill. It was from the Hennepin Area Aids Awareness Group. The photocopied sheet urged: "Use this rubber in good health!" Disappointed, she tossed both back into the drawer and closed it.

Nothing.

The library, though ostensibly belonging to both of them, was in reality James's private space, the lair to which he could retreat from the world. The books that lined three of the walls, like the weapons that hung on the fourth, had been acquired over a lifetime. After their marriage he had reorganized a few of the shelves to give her some space for her own books, but had not allowed her to simply mix hers in with the rest. Much of his collection was devoted to books about weapons, shooting, military history, and hunting, though he also boasted of having a number of classic first editions. Her own books were mostly book-club editions, and the two shelves he had put aside for her looked rather silly amidst the more serious surrounding tomes.

James insisted that the library remain generally free of loose papers and any accoutrements of work, and so she found little in here. Remembering the interest of the police, she stood before his gun collection and studied it. Nothing missing, as far as she could see. Most of the weapons were rather exotic, a variety of gunpowder weapons, some of them antiques. To the right were some more modern pneumatic guns James had become interested in over the past few years, and to the left a variety of bow weapons. To the extreme left and right he had examples of spear guns. The dart on the left-hand specimen was launched by a rubber loop, and the right hand one required a CO_2 cartridge. James often said he'd like to go spearfishing, but so far he hadn't gotten around to it.

By the time she reached his office, she had lost interest in the search. The rest of the house had yielded a dearth of incriminating material, but the office might prove a glut. She had neither the time nor the energy to search through all his drawers and files. Papers lay here and there on his desk, but a quick glance showed they were related to clients.

She had spent only minutes in this wing since she had moved into the building, and had seen it only briefly before the reconstruction, but now she was struck by something curious. Was the business wing *smaller* than the other three wings?

Why did James's office extend only to a line equal with the elevator, while their bedroom extended beyond it, and the library extended beyond it, and the kitchen extended beyond it?

She left his office and stood in the lobby, looking about herself, trying to regain her perspective on the building.

Only James's office, the lower wing on the north side, seemed truncated.

Why hadn't she noticed that before?

She pictured the outside rear of the building in her head. The old fire escape ran up the center of the building, and on either side of it windows ran from ground level to the second floor. There should be a window at the back of James's office, but there was not. What there was, was a closet in which he stored old files.

She returned to his office, curiosity piqued. During the reconstruction, had he simply walled over the window from the inside? Then why was the office truncated? Why didn't it extend the length of the wing. In her head she performed a quick calculation. There must be fifteen feet between the back of his office and the rear wall of the wing!

What was in that space?

With the pounding heart of somebody who believes she has uncovered a secret, Amanda opened the storage closet at the back of the office. To either side of the doorway, boxes were piled. But an open space showed the rear wall.

Amanda stepped into the closet.

She smelled Calantha.

"Oh, James," she said softly.

She pressed on the back wall. It creaked. She tapped on it. The sound was hollow.

In the darkness she felt along the wall, up and down, seeking any bump or recess out of the ordinary.

She was about to give up when the fingers of her left hand ran across a smooth shaft of cold steel. She fumbled for it again and found it. In the darkness it felt like a coat hook. She tugged at it, and it moved. She pulled down on it, hard.

A mechanism in the wall gave a click. Amanda pushed against the painted wood. The wall swung away from her.

The smell of Calantha became stronger, mingled with the odor of stale cigarette smoke.

Amanda groaned softly.

She stepped into the hidden room. An old sofa sat against one wall. Beside it an end table on which rested two glasses, one stained with lipstick. An ashtray sat in the center of a coffee table centered before the sofa. The ashtray was full. The ends of the cigarette butts were stained with lipstick. On the arm of the sofa sat a book. One of Amanda's books. She thought she had lost it.

The room, no bigger than a walk-in closet, had a comfortable, homey feel to it. The furniture was old, cheap, rickety, but it served its purpose.

Fowler had been right. Lydia *had* disappeared. But not into thin air.

She had been hidden.

In the last place Amanda would have ever thought to look.

With a choking sob she turned and ran from the room.

"Should we be in here?" Shelly asked. "Aren't there confidential files here, or something like that? James wouldn't like this."

"It's not in here. It's at the back. Please, come on."

Shelly entered reluctantly. Amanda opened the closet.

Patrick stuck his head in and looked around. "What? These boxes?"

"There's a hook on the back wall to your left. Pull it down."

Patrick looked at her steadily. "On the left?" he asked, at last.

"Yes."

He looked at Shelly, shrugged, and stepped into the closet. A few seconds later he grunted.

"Found it. Now . . . pull it down?"

"Yes."

The click was audible in the office.

"Jesus Christ," Patrick said softly.

The back wall of the closet pushed away and revealed the hidden room beyond. Shelly's mouth dropped open, and she stared at Amanda with an expression of shock that Amanda knew was real. There were some things, obviously, that even Shelly did not know.

"What is it?" she whispered.

"Go on in."

They filed into the room. Patrick was standing at the end table, looking down at the two glasses.

"I presume one of these isn't yours," he said.

"No."

"My God," Shelly said. "It's unbelievable."

"This is where he hid her," Amanda said.

"You don't know that, Amanda," Shelly said quickly. "This is nothing. This is just a room. It's . . ."

"Shelly, stop it."

Shelly's cheeks reddened, and she turned away from Amanda.

278

"I went back to that private detective."

Both Patrick and Shelly looked at her without saying anything.

"We found her apartment. James was still seeing her. But she had disappeared. This is where she went to. He hid her here, until he could make arrangements to get her away. She's a suspect in a murder investigation. So am I. And James is protecting her."

Neither of them said anything.

"You know what we found at her apartment?"

"No," Patrick said, averting his eyes.

"Photographs."

"Of what?"

"You and Shelly. Of James. Of Petra, and your Aunt Paula."

They stared at her. Shelly's lower lip trembled.

"Amanda," Patrick said softly, "this is as much a surprise to us as it is to you."

"Is it?"

"Patrick, I want to go," Shelly said. She turned and walked out of the small room.

Patrick pursed his lips, glanced once more around the room, then followed his wife. Amanda closed the secret door as she left the room.

In the lobby, Patrick and Shelly were talking in hushed voices. When Amanda approached they stopped and stepped apart.

"I know that you know something," Amanda said. "I know there's a secret you're hiding, to protect somebody."

Neither of them said anything. Shelly was obviously distraught. She would not look directly at Amanda.

"I don't know what it is, your secret, but if you were keeping it in the hope of saving our marriage, you can stop. We're finished."

"Amanda, you don't mean that," Shelly said.

"I do mean it. He saw Lydia only a few days ago. Fowler followed him."

Shelly lowered her eyes and shook her head.

"Sometimes, things aren't what they appear to be," she said in a hoarse voice.

"This seems pretty obvious."

"Does it?"

"Obvious enough. I don't know who Lydia is, but I do know that she's got a hold on James so firm that I can't seem to break it."

"What are you going to do?" Patrick asked.

"For my own protection, I have to prove that Lydia exists."

Shelly closed her eyes. "Can you honestly say that you no longer love my brother?" She opened her eyes again and looked directly at Amanda.

The question caught Amanda off guard. "I don't know. I know I can't go on like this."

"Do you still love him?"

"Even if I did, the situation is intolerable."

"Do you love him?"

"Yes, damn it!"

"Then don't take this any further. Call off your detective."

"Why should I? Who are you protecting? What are you hiding from me? Is it your aunt? Is it Paula?"

Shelly took a deep, trembling breath. Patrick put his arm around her. "If I've held something back from you, it's only because I love you, and because I love James, and because I want your marriage to work."

"Then tell me everything."

Exasperated, Shelly lifted her arms and looked to heaven. "Why, for God's sake? Can't you just let things settle? You've got so much, Amanda."

"I don't have James," Amanda said.

"You will, I promise."

"I don't think he'll be coming back," Amanda said. "I think he's gone to be with Lydia."

The look of shock on both their faces was almost comical, but Amanda did not laugh.

"You see, there are things I know, that you can't know. I think James put himself in a position where he had to choose between me and Lydia. I think he's made his choice now. The only thing left for me is . . . is to understand. To understand why my marriage has crumbled, why I look like the twin of the woman who caused it, why the police think I may have killed two human beings. And I'm going to understand. I don't care who it hurts. With or without your help, I'm going to know everything."

Shelly was pale now. Patrick helped her into her coat, and put on his own. They left without saying another word.

Twenty-one

James sat at a window table in the Sky-bound Lounge and watched the lineups at the ticket windows in the concourse below. He sipped his rusty nail and kept one hand on the two tickets on the table. This was his third drink, and he was feeling them all.

He needed the liquor, though. He needed to dampen the emotions swelling inside of him.

He could not get Amanda's face out of his mind. The look of hurt in her eyes kept popping up in front of him, accusing him, blaming him.

He glanced at his watch. Just after 3:00 P.M. The plane was scheduled to depart at 4:15. Lydia had better get here quickly or the passage through security was going to be a rushed nightmare.

He closed his eyes and took a deep breath. He was close to panicking. The decision he had made was, or would be in another hour or so, irrevocable.

He took another sip of the rusty nail and realized with a shock that he was down to flavored ice.

Lydia wouldn't have been stupid enough to go back to her apartment, would she? No. She knew how dangerous that could be.

He waved to the waitress and held up his glass. What the hell. A long flight stretched ahead. Two or three drinks too many wasn't going to mean much.

He looked around the lounge. Most of the tables were empty. A few lone businessmen sat in booths on the far side, one or two with papers open before them, one with a laptop computer beside his drink. At one table three flight attendants were laughing and drinking quietly. At the bar a lone man sat with his back to James, hunched over. All of them looked isolated, lost. Airports did that. He welcomed it.

When his drink arrived he took a deep swallow and closed his eyes again.

Damn it, Lydia. Come *on!*

At the sound of approaching footsteps on the carpet, James opened his eyes and sat to attention. A tall, fleshy man in a tan suit with a coat over his arm rounded the table, looking at him from the corner of his eye. He stopped and turned with a smile.

"James Sanders?"

James frowned and half stood, realizing the face was familiar from somewhere.

"Yes?"

"I thought it was you! How are you?"

"I'm fine. It's nice to see you . . ."

"Hank Wellen."

"Oh, Mr. Wellen, of course! Nice to see you!"

"Double nice to see you. I've been wandering around this place for over an hour without seeing a friendly face. I hate these damned places, don't you?"

James sipped his drink. "You get used to them."

Wellen was a client from Fargo whom he had met only once or twice over the past five years. Within a week from now Wellen and all his other clients would be informed of James's disappearance, and their portfolios would be transferred to a variety of institutions until matters could be settled. He liked to think the event would cause at least a mild ripple in the financial pond, but knew otherwise. He was a small fry in every sense of the word.

"Mind if I join you? My flight doesn't leave for two hours."

"Actually, I'm waiting for my wife."

"Amanda? Haven't seen her since that time two years ago, before you were married, you remember, the reception you threw at, where was it . . ."

"I remember, yes."

"How is she?"

"Fine, just fine."

"Lovely woman. In construction or something, isn't she?"

"Real estate."

"I'm amazed you let her work, with the amount you must make."

"I don't make her do anything. She wants to work."

"Liberated, huh?"

James sipped his drink and looked away with a grimace. There was no point getting defensive about Amanda. Not now.

"Suppose, if I had a wife who looked like that, I'd let her do what she wanted, too," Wellen said and chuckled.

James looked at him. A group of people pushed through the entrance of the lounge, laughing raucously for a moment, then quieting as heads turned. James scanned the group carefully. Amanda was not there.

As the thought registered he stiffened. *Lydia* was not there. Lydia.

"You okay?"

James nodded. "Yes, fine."

"You look almost sick."

"A touch of flu."

"You and Amanda off on a holiday?"

"Yes."

"Where to?"

"Cancún."

"Never been there."

James sipped his drink. The waitress brought

a beer for Wellen. He grinned up at her. "Thanks, honey."

When she left, he winked at James. "Now *that's* a woman."

James stood abruptly. "You'll have to excuse me. I have a number of things to do."

Before Wellen could respond he had picked up his carry-on case and had turned away. Wellen murmured something behind him, but James did not turn to find out what it was. Outside the Skybound he leaned against a pillar and forced himself to be calm.

My God, he was acting as if he'd robbed a bank.

Wellen's comments had turned his mind fully to Amanda, and he could not turn away.

He kept seeing Amanda on their wedding day, the white veil lifted from her face, the sparkling eyes, the loving smile. God, he had adored her. He had hoped she had saved him, and for a while it really seemed as if she had. But now . . .

He was giving her up. For her sake. For his own sake.

He was unsavable.

He pressed his back to the pillar and looked around. No sight of Amanda.

Lydia, damn it! Lydia!

With a groan he slammed his head back against the pillar. Stars danced behind his eyes and his teeth jarred.

I'm sorry, Amanda. You don't deserve this.

He brought to mind Amanda's face, the Amanda before the cosmetic and surgical changes. Inside himself he felt a warm glow, a welling of emotion that nearly made him sob.

He shook his head slowly. God, how he had loved her. How he *still* loved her. More than anything else in the world.

And then he knew. Knew without doubt, knew as surely as the sun rose and set, as surely as the stars burning in the sky.

He could not leave her.

He couldn't do it. Not now, not like this.

He clamped his teeth and closed his eyes.

His breath sighed out.

It was time to face the music. After all these years, it was time.

He felt amazing relief, as if his heart had been unshackled. His head blossomed with alcohol haze, and nausea swelled in his stomach.

Still, he felt better than he had all morning.

He would go to Amanda and tell her everything. Everything.

She would either understand, or she would . . . what? He did not know what.

His stomach roiled.

First things first. His stomach was lurching from the excitement, from trepidation. He needed to vomit. He spotted the washroom sign past the duty-free gift shop and headed straight for it.

* * *

Lincoln Fowler waited a full minute after James Sanders left the Skybound Lounge before following him. He felt no special hurry. He knew the flight Sanders intended to take, and felt confident that Lydia would be meeting him. He could afford to be slightly lax in his surveillance.

He finished off his beer, left a five-dollar bill on the counter for the tab, and walked nonchalantly to the exit.

It was now 3:35.

He looked both ways along the shopping mezzanine, past duty-free shops, magazine counters, coffee shops. No sign of Sanders.

He walked to the railing and looked down to the concourse below. It was a quiet afternoon at Wold Chamberlain Field. Only a few of the agents had lines. A woman with six small children in tow tried to corral them around a flight-insurance island, but the screaming little monsters seemed reluctant to be controlled.

Could Sanders have met Lydia during the few seconds he had alone up here? He doubted it, but the possibility made him nervous. He needed to ID Lydia before the pair of them went through security for boarding. After that, they were on their own, unless he called in some help.

He walked the length of the mezzanine, looking inside every shop, but saw no sign of Sanders. He walked back, more slowly this time, scanning from left to right. A security guard patrolling alone eyed him suspiciously. Fowler averted his eyes, realizing he was looking peculiar.

Sanders had disappeared.

"Christ."

He had muttered to himself, but a young girl walking along with her father heard him and looked up. He turned away.

He leaned on the railing and looked down to the concourse below, trying to gather his thoughts. Okay, so assume that Sanders had met Lydia the moment he stepped out of the Skybound. Where would they go?

He walked quickly toward the boarding gates. The corridor leading to the departure lounge was divided into narrow security lanes. Lineups extended from each one, as security personnel passed carry-on luggage through x-ray scanners, and passed each passenger through metal detectors. No sign of Sanders or Lydia.

He stood on tiptoe and craned his neck to see beyond the security line to the lounge beyond, and though he got a decent view he saw no sign of Sanders. His agitated state finally attracted a security guard, who came up beside him with a pleasant smile.

"Can I help you with anything?"

Fowler smiled back. "I was supposed to meet somebody. In the Skybound. She hasn't shown up."

He blushed on cue, and the guard nodded knowingly.

"Try the lounge again. Maybe she's waiting for you now."

"Good idea."

He walked back toward the Skybound, feeling the guard's eyes on his back the whole way. At the lounge he poked his head in the door, simply to appease the guard's curiosity. Sitting at a table with a view of the concourse, sipping some sort of red mixed drink, was Lydia.

After taking a couple of deep breaths, amazed at this fortunate turn, Fowler moved back to the bar, sat up on a stool, and ordered a beer. He watched Lydia in the mirror behind the bar, reflected between bottles and glasses.

A long black coat hung over the arm of the chair. She wore a beige skirt and a dark brown blazer. As he watched, she checked her watch, looked toward the entrance, and sipped her drink. She drew on a cigarette and exhaled a cloud of smoke.

Where the hell was Sanders?

Somewhere along the line they had missed one another. Fowler checked his watch. It was 3:50. If she wanted to make the flight, she would have to hit the security check very soon.

She slowly looked around the restaurant, and Fowler averted his eyes toward his beer and hunched his shoulders. When he checked again she was emptying her drink. She stood and picked up her coat.

Fowler watched her, entranced. It was hard to believe how closely Amanda Burns-Sanders had come to resemble this woman. He sipped his beer. She left her table and walked toward the door. For a moment, as she crossed the lounge, her eyes seemed to glance toward him.

My God, was it Amanda?

He swiveled in his chair and watched her walk out. Could it be? Had she come down here to find Lydia and her husband?

He left another five on the counter and followed immediately. She was walking toward the security check, coat hanging across her arm. He watched her behind swing beneath the smooth fabric of the skirt, and remembered Amanda's face and body from earlier in the week.

No. Lydia was slightly taller. Wasn't she? It was no wonder the police suspected Amanda. If Lydia had been at the scene, any witness would pick Amanda from a lineup without hesitation.

Disconcerted, he followed. Even fifteen yards behind her he could smell her perfume. The same as Amanda's. As he approached the security check he saw that she had not entered a line, but was standing back and watching. Waiting. For James.

Fowler moved aside and stood by a banking machine.

Lydia checked her watch. It was 4:00.

A voice came over the public address system and announced the final boarding call for the flight to Cancún.

A now obviously distressed Lydia began to pace back and forth.

Where was Sanders? Had the bastard backed out at the last minute? He wouldn't doubt it. He'd seen it happen many times. He could imagine Sanders sitting in that lounge, sipping his drink, contemplating all he was leaving behind. It might not seem worth it after some levelheaded thought, and probably it wasn't. But in a way, he wished Sanders would show up, wished he would meet Lydia, kiss her, calm her, and lead her through security. He did not like to see a woman distressed like this.

But Sanders did not show up.

At 4:15 the flight to Cancún was removed from the departure screen. Three of the security desks closed down.

Lydia looked shocked, disbelieving. Fowler was tempted to walk up to her, to introduce himself, to see what would develop. He wanted to console her. Sanders was a bastard, that was all.

She waited until 4:20, then, head high, stiffly erect, she walked back toward the Skybound Lounge. Fowler turned away as she passed him and pretended to withdraw cash from the banking machine. He followed her at a safe distance, still smelling her perfume.

She entered the lounge. This time, Fowler did not follow. He walked to the edge of the mezzanine, leaned on the railing, and waited. There was only one exit from the lounge.

She was still waiting, waiting for Sanders, not daring to believe he had deserted her. It was pathetic and sad.

What the hell was Sanders playing at?

The security guard who had questioned him earlier approached again, this time in the company of a younger, female guard.

Fowler smiled and tried to look relaxed.

"Did you find your friend?"

"No, not yet."

"Check the lounge?"

"Yes. No sign. She'll show up, I'm sure of it."

"Are you waiting for a flight?"

"Uh, no."

"What does your friend look like. Maybe we've seen her."

"Short, petite, blonde, around twenty-five."

They both shook their heads. They were blocking his view of the lounge, and he leaned sideways to see around them. Both of them turned to follow his view, then stepped in to block it again.

"I wonder if you'd care to come to the security office? Perhaps we could locate your friend for you."

They thought he was trouble and they wanted him out of the way. He'd seen this operation enacted too many times to mistake it for anything else.

"I'm not waiting for anybody," he said. "I'm a private detective. I'm watching a woman right now who's in the lounge, waiting for somebody else."

He dug out his license and handed it to them. The young female guard checked the picture and looked at his face. After her partner had checked the ID he handed it back and leaned forward.

"Anything we can help you with?"

Fowler shook his head. "No, but I'll call if I think of anything."

"We'll just be down there a little ways."

They walked away, looking back at him over their shoulders.

He had attracted attention now. Others were looking at him, wondering who he was, wondering why security was interested.

Swearing softly, he moved to the entrance to the lounge and poked his head in. It took only a few seconds to ascertain that Lydia was not there.

He stepped into the narrow alcove leading to the washrooms and opened the women's. It was empty.

He leaned his head against the wall and breathed deeply. This was getting ridiculous. Two subjects lost while under surveillance. In the same fucking day.

He left the lounge and found a row of pay phones by a magazine stand down the mezzanine. He dialed Amanda Burns-Sanders's home number. It rang fifteen times without answering. He hung up and tried again with the same result. Then he checked the phone book for her work number. He dialed and waited. The receptionist said that Amanda had not been in all day.

Once again, he wondered if the woman he had seen had been Amanda. Could it have been?

"Does she have a pager?"

"Yes, she does."

"Could you send her a message for me?"

"Certainly."

"It's important this goes to her word for word. Please, it's very urgent."

"I understand. What's the message?"

He told her, and after he hung up he shook his head, angry at James Sanders, angry at Lydia, angry at the security guards who had distracted him, and angrier still at himself.

Son of a bitch.

He would give the area one more sweep. One more careful, thorough sweep. Hell, maybe he'd find the two of them holed up in the concourse watching pay television, nuzzling each other's necks. That would be real nice.

Otherwise, it would be time for plan B. Whatever the hell that was.

Twenty-two

Fred Cooper was standing outside his car in the driveway of the house on Sheridan when Amanda arrived. He opened her car door for her and helped her out.

"I'm sorry I had to call you for this," he said.

"Don't be sorry, I don't mind."

"They said the only time they could see the house was at five, and I've got another showing at five. I've worked six months to arrange this, and I can't miss it."

"Don't worry, Fred, I don't mind. It's good to be out of the house."

"You're sure?"

"Positive."

"I've got to run. Good luck."

"You, too."

She waved to him as he drove away, then opened up the house. Like many properties in these days of flat sales, it was empty, the vendors having moved on, or having been relocated by their companies. Empty houses, though easier to arrange to show, were much harder to sell. Buyers liked to see what a home looked like when it was lived in.

She turned on all the lights, both upstairs and downstairs, and in the basement, and turned up the heat a little. She found a dirty ashtray in the kitchen and emptied it. The tap in the downstairs bathroom was dripping slightly, and she twisted it as hard as she could to get it to stop.

At 5:00 on the nose a car pulled up outside. She opened the front door to greet the buyers.

"Mr. and Mrs. Ferguson?"

The couple were in their late forties, Amanda guessed, well dressed, but casual. The car was a new Buick Park Avenue. Good signs, all.

"You're Amanda Burns?"

"That's right. Would you like to look around outside first, or come in and have a look?"

"Inside first," said Mr. Ferguson.

Mrs. Ferguson said nothing, but followed her husband into the vestibule.

Amanda led them slowly through the house, pointing out what she considered the pluses (marvelous spacious living room, open fireplace, huge eating area in kitchen, great bathroom both upstairs and down), and the drawbacks (older cupboards in the kitchen, some flooring ready for replacing in the upstairs bedrooms, some windows in need of upgrading). It paid to be scrupulously honest with buyers.

"You think we could get it for eighty?" Mr. Ferguson asked as they returned to the main floor.

"It's possible. If you wanted to offer, we could lowball at seventy and let them counter."

"Where are the vendors?"

"They were relocated to Detroit. The company now owns the house. They might be willing to let it go low."

The Fergusons nodded thoughtfully. Amanda's pager beeped. She tapped it with her finger to save the message and cut off the noise.

"Well, we'll think about it. You think it's likely to sell in the next few days?"

"I don't know."

"How long has it been on the market?"

"Only two months."

Mr. Ferguson nodded. "Well, thank you for your time."

He accepted one of her cards, and took his wife outside. From inside the house, as she turned off lights, Amanda watched them enter the back yard and look around. They were talking animatedly. Another good sign.

When she returned to front door, their car was gone.

Before leaving, she checked her pager. The message marched across the LCD line by line.

LYDIA MAY STILL BE HERE.
GO HOME.
STAY HOME.

BE CAREFUL.
FOWLER.

Amanda stared at the pager, mouth dry. She ran the message again.

"Oh, Jesus," she said softly.

She dropped the pager into her purse, left a light burning in the vestibule, and went outside. She locked the door, then stood on the front step, unmoving. It was getting dark now, and streetlights were flickering. The air was chill.

The memory of the night when the car had nearly run her down came upon her, and she found herself frozen, heart hammering.

She forced herself to be calm.

What had Fowler meant? Had he seen Lydia? Where?

She finally forced herself to leave the steps, and walked toward her car. At the street she stopped and looked both ways. No cars in sight. Still, she hurried across the street and into her own car.

There she turned on the engine, sat a moment, and pulled away from the curb. She wanted brighter lights, other cars.

When she hit I-94 she breathed a sigh of relief. It was near the end of rush hour, and traffic was thinning. The drive downtown was not nearly as bad as the drive out here. The city glowed in the dusk, looking vibrant, alive, and safe.

By the time she reached home it was fully

dark, and the clouds seemed to be coming lower. The tops of many of the downtown buildings were cut off, as if they'd been sheared, by the unblemished ceiling of gray.

Until she was inside the house her skin crawled, and she felt that at any moment someone might jump out at her. If anybody had said "hello" to her, she would have screamed. Inside, with the lobby light turned on, she leaned against the door. She locked it, then bolted it, and clamped the chain to its clip.

Only then did she allow herself to relax.

She wondered for a moment if she should call the police. What would she say? She was frightened, that was all. There was no evidence, really, that she was in danger. She went upstairs and into the bedroom. She had told James she would not be here when she got back, but now, looking at her things, she did not know what to do. Should she pack something? Should she prepare to leave?

She needed to talk to Fowler. Needed his advice badly. The phone rang and she jumped. She let it ring three more times, heart pounding, before sitting down on the bed and picking it up.

"Hello?"

"Amanda?"

It was Fowler. She nearly sobbed with relief.

"Thank God you called. I was . . ."

The line went dead.

"Hello? Lincoln?"

301

No answer. Then, ever so softly, another click.

One of the extensions.

Amanda slowly hung up with her finger, then lifted it again. No dial tone.

Somewhere downstairs, something thumped.

Amanda stared at the bedroom door, unable to breathe.

Somebody was in the house.

All she could hear was the hum of the furnace far below, the clicking of warming metal ducts, and the rush of warm air from vents.

Could she have imagined the soft click on the line? *Something* had cut Fowler off. If it had been at his end, wouldn't he have called back by now?

She had not moved from the bed, and realized with a start that she was wringing her hands so tightly her fingers were numb.

Calm down, she told herself. It was nothing. You're safe here. This is your home.

She took a deep breath, released it, took another.

She picked up the receiver again and raised it slowly to her ear. Silence. But not the silence of a dead line. This was the echoing silence of another room. An extension was off the hook. She kept the receiver to her ear, focusing on the emptiness at the other end. There were phones in the library, the living room, and the kitchen, all the same line. It could be any of them. Dead or off the hook, it didn't matter. Either way, nobody would be getting through.

Still listening, she closed her eyes.

A small sound came from the receiver.

Amanda started. Had the sound been a breath?

Her reflection in the mirror stared back at her with wide, glassy eyes.

The sound came again. Longer, softer. It *was* a breath.

Somebody was on the other end of the line.

But what room?

"Hello, Amanda."

The voice reached from the receiver like a hand to grip the back of Amanda's neck. She stiffened so tightly it was almost painful. She recognized the voice. It had been the voice that had called for James that day, so long ago. Lydia's voice. Soft, sensual, mysterious.

Amanda forced herself to speak. "Get out of my house."

"I thought it was time we should meet."

As Lydia's voice trailed off, she heard something else. A metallic rattle that sharpened into a buzz.

The refrigerator!

The kitchen!

Amanda hung up the phone and ran to the door. She opened it and stepped onto the landing. Downstairs, the lobby was mostly dark, illuminated only by a swath of pale yellow light from the second floor.

Hadn't she turned on the downstairs light?

The kitchen door opened. Another slab of light reached across the hall. A shadow grew.

Amanda bolted for the library. She fumbled for the light switch then slammed the door behind her. Beyond the door, only silence. She leaned against it, eyes closed, ears filled only with the beating of her own heart, the rush of her own blood.

Be calm, she commanded herself.

You're safe for now.

Lydia was here! Here!

Why? How?

What had Fowler's message on the pager said?

Lydia may still be here.

Had he seen her at the airport? Had he seen James? Had Lydia met James?

She wanted desperately to talk to Fowler now, to understand what was happening.

Two people were already dead, and she knew in her bones that Lydia was responsible. Lydia had killed them. And now Lydia was here in the house.

I thought it was time we should meet.

This is what I wanted, Amanda thought. The face to face.

From downstairs came a sound of furniture being moved. Metal clanking. Or a glass.

What was she doing?

Amanda's mind was blank. She couldn't think. Lydia's presence had frozen her like a rabbit in a car's headlights. She was easy prey.

Think! Think!

She had to call for help. Call the police. She had to let somebody know that she was in danger.

She needed a phone.

The library phone sat upon a bronze stand to her left. Only a few steps away.

Another clanking sound came from downstairs. Somebody stumbling about.

Amanda left her leaning post at the door and went to the phone, but when she picked it up there was no dial tone. Over the phone she heard movement, soft and stealthy.

Fascinated, almost hypnotized, she kept the receiver to her ear, even when the sounds stopped.

"Amanda."

Amanda gasped. She slammed the receiver into its cradle and backed away from it as if it were a giant spider.

Back at the door, she leaned again into the wood, as if her weight could keep it closed forever.

With the kitchen phone off the hook, every extension would be dead. None of the upstairs phones would work.

"God damn it," she whispered to herself.

Alone in the house with a murderess, with no way to call for help!

She felt pathetic, and helpless, and silly, and useless. She wanted to be a little girl and sit down and cry, but knew that she could not succumb to the desire. She needed to stay alert now—needed to think her way out of this.

She had to get out of the house. Simple as that. Get out, and think about getting help after that. But that meant she had to go downstairs, which meant getting past Lydia.

She realized with a start that she was staring at James's gun collection. Exhilaration surged through her.

"Oh, thank you, God," she muttered.

She left the doorway with a shudder and turned to look at it. What if Lydia should burst in? If only the door had a lock!

From the table in the middle of the room she took one of the high-backed chairs and pushed it against the door. She wedged the back under the handle. That should do. For a while, anyway. How much force would it take to dislodge the chair? Probably far less than she thought. This always seemed to work in the movies, but then, a lot of things worked in the movies.

She went to the gun rack and for the first time in her life studied it with more than casual interest. She needed a gun.

She chose a U.S. Armed Forces .45 caliber automatic, a relic of the Korean War. With trembling hands she lifted it from the rack, surprised at its heaviness.

She held the gun in both hands and studied it. James often took this gun with him to the shooting range. It was one of his favorites. There was a story behind it, about a POW he had known. This gun had killed people, had taken the lives away from walking, talking, thinking, breathing humans.

What else?

Ammunition.

Where did he keep it?

Beneath the display were a number of oak panels that opened up on drawers. She kneeled and fumbled at one of them, but realized that it was locked. She tried the others. All locked.

"Shit!"

Why did James have to be so damned careful with this stuff!

She kicked at the panel and succeeded only in scuffing it. It would not budge. The oak was heavy and solid. It had been designed to keep out burglars who might decide to use the weapons against the owners of the house. The keys were on James's key ring.

She hefted the gun, reassured by its weight, but knew that it was useless without ammunition. A toy.

But Lydia wouldn't know it was not loaded, would she?

She tried to imagine her own reaction if somebody waved this thing at her. Loaded or not, the sight of a gun staring her in the face would likely reduce her to a quivering wreck. Guns were meant to kill.

Okay. Okay. So Lydia wouldn't know.

Lydia would think it was loaded. Who would be so silly as to carry an unloaded gun?

She took a deep breath, trying to calm herself. Her chest felt tight. Her arms tingled.

At the door, she paused and listened.

Silence.

The noises from downstairs had ended.

She closed her eyes and forced herself to count slowly to ten. Do this properly. Don't panic.

She unwedged the chair and pushed it aside. She rested her hand on the knob a full thirty seconds before turning it.

Teeth gritted, she peeked around the edge of the door. The landing was empty.

With the gun held out before her, she stepped out of the room. She looked toward the elevator, but decided against it. Only a smaller space in which to be trapped. She moved toward the top of the stairs.

Downstairs, light leaked from the closed kitchen door. Her own shadow reached down the stairs ahead of her, adding to the general darkness of the lobby.

Her heart pounded, and it took every ounce of will to force her legs to carry her downward.

She was halfway down the stairs when all the lights went out.

Twenty-three

Lincoln Fowler cursed himself for a fool as he drove north on Hiawatha toward downtown. He had lost both James Sanders and Lydia at the airport, had seen not a sign of them during his final sweep. Where they hell had they gone? Could Sanders have boarded the plane for Cancún? If so, he had done it without Lydia.

He wondered how he was going to explain this to Amanda.

He debated for a few moments not charging her for the time spent, but rejected the idea quickly. It wasn't his fault that Sanders and Lydia had done their best to lose him. Christ, he should charge her double for the effort!

These thoughts, he knew, were simply camouflage for the deep unease he felt. He had phoned Amanda to warn her that Lydia might still be around, but the phone had died in his hand.

Thank God you called!

She had sounded frightened. Panicked.

And something had cut her off.

Damn it. He should have called the police, sent them over to her place. Deal with the consequences later if it turned out to be nothing. He just hadn't been thinking clearly.

He was feeling things toward Amanda Burns-Sanders that he should not be feeling. He should never have slept with her. That had been a big mistake. The detective-client relationship altered horribly under those circumstances. He became, instead of her employee, her protector—felt toward her . . . well, far more than he should be feeling, that was for sure.

Likely the dead phone was nothing important. Lines went down all the time at this time of year. Sudden icing, or the collapse of a gutter under the weight of melting snow, often tore phone lines out of walls. Anything like that might have happened.

So why did he keep seeing Lydia with a pair of scissors cutting the phone line?

"Jesus, you idiot," he said to himself.

The night was misty, the air full of dirt. The windshield wipers on his car left great muddy swaths on the glass. He hated the end of winter, that dirty, wet, miserable period before spring arrived. Forty below would be better than this.

He heaved a sigh of relief as he approached the exit for East Franklin. Only ten or eleven blocks now until the Sanderses' place on Park

Avenue. The mist thickened as he drove, and sleet spattered against the windshield. He activated the wiper and washer, but the washer pump groaned dryly. The wipers turned the glass into a sea of mud through which he could see nothing.

"Damn!"

He slammed on the brakes. A horn blared to his left, and a car roared by. He pulled over to the side of the road. He got out of the car and with his sleeve tried to clear the window. That only made it worse. His coat turned black.

He was only three blocks from Park Avenue now, and he could cut through Peavy Park to save some time. He turned on the car's blinkers, locked it up, and started to run.

This is crazy, he thought.

Everything is fine. I'm panicking for nothing.

But he ran harder, sucking harsh breaths, arms and legs churning.

He crossed Hiawatha amidst a hail of honking horns, and entered the park. He hadn't counted on the melting snow. Slogging through the park was a nasty, difficult business. He fell twice, once tripping headlong into a vast, icy pool.

When he hit Park Avenue he was soaked, filthy, disheveled.

Amanda was going to think he was nuts.

He could see as he left the cover of some

trees that the Sanderses' building was dark. Pitch black. Not a light on in the place.

Amanda had gone out.

He crossed the street and stood at the front door, shrouded in shadow. Though soaked to the skin, he was hot. Steam rose from his collar.

He stared up at the dark building.

Who the hell could live in a building like this? He had never been inside, but imagined it was one of those renovated jobs. A rich guy like Sanders would do something like that. Take a slum and turn it into his palace.

He walked along the front of the building and looked into the alley. A car was parked in one of the stalls. A Buick. Amanda's car.

Was she inside? Had she hit the sack?

No, impossible. It wasn't even eight yet.

He went back to the front door and rang the bell. He waited a few seconds, then rang it again.

He heard nothing through the door.

He lifted his fist and knocked hard.

This time, he heard something from inside the house. A muffled noise. He tried the door. Locked.

He knocked harder.

"Jesus Christ."

He stepped back to look up at the building. Solid black. No sign of life.

Had he imagined the noise?

He was not sure what prompted him to look

down at the pavement, but the cigarette butt caught his eye like a silver dollar. He reached down and picked it up. The white end was stained crimson. He rubbed the lipstick smear. Still moist. He smelled the cigarette. Fresh.

The lipstick was the same shade as Amanda's. But Amanda Burns-Sanders did not smoke.

"Oh, shit," he said with a sigh.

He hammered on the door, waited, hammered again.

"Amanda!"

No answer. Then the doorknob turned. Latches clicked. But the door did not open. From beyond the wood and steel came a muffled cry. He tried the door. Still locked.

Fowler swore softly. He ran along the front of the building to the alley. A few steps into the alley he found the low, basement window. Barred, but only with flimsy, self-installed things.

He swore softly.

He kicked in the glass, and cleared the edge of the frame with his boot. Then he kneeled down and started working on the bars.

Darkness swirled around her, liquid, alive.

Amanda bit hard on her lower lip, tasted blood. She was hanging in space, no frame of reference by which to anchor herself. She crashed against the wall and fell to the hardwood stairs, but even the pain could not stop the swirling sensation.

She pressed herself against the wall and half rolled so that her face was touching the edge of a step. She squeezed her eyes shut. The gun had slithered away from her, but now she grasped tightly to the edge of the step, breathing deeply. It felt like hours later, but she knew it was only seconds, since the falling sensation had passed. She rolled again, still gripping the step, and sought any sign of light. Some indeterminate distance in front of her she saw a blue glow. The glow suddenly brightened, and she recognized the frame of the window above the front door. With that one reference point she anchored herself. She craned her neck. Another patch of haze, octagonal. The skylight. The stairs became solid beneath her again. She let out a trembling breath.

She reached out and patted the step, searching for the pistol. It had moved, somehow, to the side of the bannister. She picked it up and wondered, again, how useful it was going to be. No ammunition, and now, in the dark, invisible, too. Still, the solid feel of it gave her some comfort, and she did not let it go.

Gripping the bannister, she moved slowly down, feeling with each foot before planting it. Her eyes were growing accustomed to the dark now, and the liquid around her was filling with familiar shapes and outlines. She could see

James's office door below and to her right, the kitchen door a few yards to the right of that.

Where was Lydia?

To have turned off the lights, she must have entered the basement. The fuse box was there, at the bottom of the stairs. How much time did that give her?

Still tasting blood from her bitten lip, Amanda moved more quickly. Dark or not, the steps were there. They were solid. They would not disappear. Trust reality.

Gripping the bannister, she hurried down. As she touched bottom, something made a soft noise to her right. She froze, breath caught, and listened.

She listened so hard that her own rushing blood became a roar through which nothing could penetrate.

She released her breath in a sigh and took another.

Nerves. That was all. Just nerves.

She calmed her breathing, nodding once to reassure herself, and moved toward the front door. The blue square of the window seemed to rise, as if by magic, into the darkness above her. Her mind provided the perspective, and when she reached out her hand the wood of the door was right there. She almost cried out with relief.

She fumbled for the knob, found it, twisted. The door would not open.

And then, as if she were dreaming, a voice from beyond the door.

"Amanda!"

Fowler! He was here!

She scrabbled at the two dead bolts, twisted them open, tried the knob again. Still, the door would not budge. A small whimper came from her mouth, and she bit it back angrily. From the other side, Fowler tried the doorknob.

She closed her eyes and breathed deeply. Silence. If Fowler had been outside the door, he was quiet now. Had he heard her fumbling with the locks? What would he do if he had?

Perhaps he had only seen the darkness and thought the house empty. In that case, he would simply have left.

She fought of the black wave of panic that threatened to dash her senseless.

Think.

The dead bolts were released. The chain . . . a quick check revealed it was not latched. Then the door should open . . . but it didn't. Which meant . . .

A sudden chill gripped her neck and she groaned quietly.

The front door was also equipped with a dead bolt operated by a key from both sides. She and James never used it. In the case of a fire, or any emergency, it made escape too difficult. She was not even sure where the keys were kept. Could Lydia have one of the keys? She remembered the keys she had found in the living room. She stared at the darkness where the stairs should be and knew that she could not climb them.

Once again, she tried the dead-bolt latches, then the chain. The door would not open.

"Damn!"

She turned and pressed her back to the door.

Her mind had gone suddenly blank, and she stood, thoughtless, fearless, for nearly ten seconds, aware of the darkness around her, the shapes growing clearer and clearer.

What now?

Try the phone in James's office. It was not part of the house line. Call for help.

She fortified herself with another breath and edged away from the door, back pressed to the wall. A sudden sharp noise, as of something heavy dropping, came from somewhere beyond the kitchen. Amanda froze, listening.

She had to hurry. Had to use what time she had. She had no wish to confront Lydia in this darkness. Had no wish, in fact, to confront her at all. Not any more. Nothing was worth this. Not James, not her own self-esteem, certainly not her marriage.

Her hand knocked against the edge of the office door and she grabbed the knob and twisted. Locked.

"Oh, damn it!"

In the darkness, her voice sounded very loud. She pressed her back to the wall again.

Footsteps padded across the lobby, directly in front of her, then to her right.

She did not move, did not breathe.

"Amanda."

The voice had come from toward the stairs. She stared hard into the darkness until she made things move, but saw nothing.

"I've got a gun! I'll use it!"

More footsteps. To her right, then her left.

"I mean it! I'll shoot!"

A solid footfall came from the direction of the stairs. Then another. A step creaked. The step fourth from the bottom. Lydia was on the stairs!

Amanda moved quickly toward the kitchen, hands held out in front of her. If she could make it through the pantry, then into the rear storage area, she could try the back door, the old emergency exit. Once, before James had owned the place, a hallway ran directly from the front door to the back, a straight line of sight. She wished it were so simple now.

As she reached the kitchen doorway, scuffling sounds came from behind her. Lydia had left the stairs.

Panic gave her a sudden surge of adrenalin, and she rushed forward, careless of any obstacles. Her knee cracked into one of the kitchen chairs, sending it clattering to the floor. Her left arm knocked a glass from the table and it smashed on the linoleum.

The panicked sounds that filled the darkness

were from her own mouth, but she could not stop them.

She maneuvered past the table, past the work island. Behind her, pieces of broken glass crackled. Amanda spun. The darkness was impenetrable.

"Stay away from me! I'll shoot. Damn it, you bitch, I will!"

In the sudden silence, she used her fingers to move the pistol's slide. The click of metal sounded terrible and loud, an exclamation to her threat.

"Stay away from me!"

She backed away. One step. Two. Footsteps padded across the kitchen.

Had Lydia gone? Had the threat of the gun frightened her away?

Amanda did not move, but kept the unloaded pistol held out in front of her. She was trembling now. Her breath came in harsh little mouthfuls that shook her shoulders.

After a time, she lowered the weapon. Silence. Deathly silence. No electric hum, no hiss of furnace air.

Amanda stepped backward.

"Amanda."

Warm breath touched her ear. She spun, but a rough hand covered her mouth. She tried to swing the pistol, but another hand grasped her elbow and held it fast.

"Damn it, stop moving! It's me! Fowler!"

Amanda slumped into him, into his arms, breathless, shaking, hardly able to stand.

Fowler slowly removed his hand from her mouth. Amanda whimpered softly, but made no other sound. Her knees were weak. All her strength seemed to have dissipated. In the darkness she could hardly see him, but she could smell him, and she could feel him.

But Fowler pushed her away and forced her to stand. A flash of light came from her right, and she saw that he had a penlight. In the quick burst of light she saw that he was standing very close to her, face intense, eyes narrow.

"Don't fold now," he said urgently.

Amanda reacted to his words by taking a deep breath. She nodded sharply.

"Are you okay?"

"Yes. I think so."

"Are you *hurt?"*

Amanda shook her head. "No."

"Good. Then let's get out of here."

He reached to take the pistol from her hand. The light flashed. His hands took the gun.

"Is this thing loaded?"

"I couldn't find any ammunition. I thought, if she saw it, it might scare her."

"It probably did. But I've got the real thing. Now we can more than scare her, if we have to. How's the front door?"

"Locked by key. It won't open."

320

"Same with the back. Feel like climbing out a basement window? On second thought, forget it. We'd be sitting ducks. Is there a key for the front door?"

"Upstairs, in the living room. But I'm not sure."

"Then let's go get it."

"But . . . Lydia."

"We're all in the dark. She's probably as frightened of us as we are of her. Come on."

"She's not. She's not frightened at all. She *made* it dark."

Suddenly he was holding her shoulders, twisting her to face him, and again she felt his breath on her face.

"Amanda, we've got to get out of here. We don't have many choices here. The longer we stay, the more danger we're in. This woman has killed two men already. I want to face her about as much as you do, but we've got to do something. At least we're armed."

Amanda nodded slowly, then realized the motion was invisible in the dark. "Okay. Okay."

"Keep a hold of my arm. I'll lead."

He edged away from her, waited until she had grasped his arm, then started moving again. Broken glass crunched under their feet, but Fowler did not slow down. When they reached the kitchen doorway, he stopped and turned to her.

"Shhh."

"Can you see?"

"No, but I will in a second."

"But if you shine that flashlight, she'll . . ."

"Don't worry."

He pulled her through the doorway, then stopped again. For a few seconds they were absolutely silent, and still. Amanda's heart began to beat faster.

The flash came from her left. Fowler had held the penlight at arm's length and flicked it on. In that moment, the entire downstairs seemed to be illuminated by some powerful searchlight, though in reality the penlight sent out only a meager few candles. Shadows leaped and jumped, stretched, bent and curled.

"Okay," Fowler said. "I got a bearing on the stairs."

The flash came from their right, slightly elevated, somewhere on the stairs. The crack of sound that followed it hurt Amanda's ears. She leaped backward, pulling Fowler with her. He pushed her behind him, and they both fell to the floor.

"She has a gun, too!" Amanda cried. "Jesus, Fowler!"

He was struggling to get up. His fingers touched her arm, and he handed her the penlight. Amanda took it up and fumbled with it. Should she use it? They weren't in the open any longer, but . . .

She twisted the top, flicking the light on for a moment. In her lap, Fowler glared up at her. His look was much angrier than it should have been. His right eye gleamed, locked onto her. His left eye was an empty hole from which dark blood leaked down his cheek. The left side of his head was a bloody pulp.

His neck convulsed as she looked upon him, mouth opening and shutting but saying nothing.

Amanda screamed and kicked him off. She scrambled away from him, her hand pressing down on the broken glass on the floor. She ignored the pain, pushing herself away, pushing, pushing.

Although she knew the danger, she could not help herself. She aimed the penlight and turned it on. Fowler, curled up by the doorway, had stopped moving now. His tongue lolled from his mouth.

Amanda clamped a hand over her own mouth to hold back another cry.

From the lobby came the sound of footsteps. Amanda crawled toward Fowler. She found his revolver at his side, hanging from his hand. With trembling fingers she took it from him.

She stood, gun held out in front of her, light spearing into the lobby. The feeble cone of light crushed shadows into the corners, making them darker. As she stepped forward the shadows flowed, moving and elongating. She stepped into the doorway, light swinging.

A shape scuttled toward the stairs.

Amanda pointed the revolver and fired. The sudden flash made the lobby brilliant. She fired again, and again. The smell of gunpowder surrounded her.

From the stair came a cry and an answering flash. Amanda fell to the floor as the wall behind her exploded plaster shards. The penlight rolled away from her, its beam pointing directly into her face. She held up her hand, blinded.

Footsteps pounded across the floor.

She was a perfect target, pinned by the light.

Blind, terrified, furious, she raised the gun and fired at random. Once, twice, three times. Then a click on an empty chamber. There were no answering shots.

Amazed she had not been fired upon, she fell back through the kitchen doorway, into darkness, realizing as she did so that it was all over. She had lost the light, and she had used all the bullets in the gun.

Still, she cried out in triumph. "Come closer! I'll kill you! I'll kill you!"

More footsteps. And then a sound she hardly dared believe. The sound of a key turning in a lock, and the front door opening.

The voice that cried out from the darkness almost made her weep. It was James.

"Lydia! What . . . Lydia!"

His voice receded. The sound of traffic reached her. Then more footsteps.

"Amanda!"

James again.

"Amanda! For God's sake, Amanda!"

She stood by pulling herself up the back of

one of the chairs. Then, on wobbly feet, she stumbled out into the lobby, nearly tripping over Lincoln Fowler's body.

Light streamed through the open front door. A car rushed past on the street, its headlights momentarily illuminating the shape standing there. She recognized James's posture immediately, and moved toward him. He ran to her, arms held out, and she fell sobbing into his embrace.

"Oh, God, darling, you're all right! I couldn't go. I just couldn't leave you."

But Amanda was beyond hearing him. Holding tightly to his arm, she let him lead her to the stairs. He sat her down and kissed her face.

"Sit. She's gone. Don't move. I'll turn the power on."

Amanda only nodded. Silent.

Twenty-four

Amanda could not stop her hands from shaking. She sat on the bed, back pressed to the headboard, and willed herself to be calm. It did not work. The shaking progressed to her shoulders, as if she had an abominable disease, and finally she could only hug herself and press her chin to her breasts, waiting for the spell to pass.

James seemed to be in as great a state of shock as herself. After leading her upstairs he had sat down at her dresser and covered his eyes with his hands. He had tripped over Lincoln Fowler's body in the kitchen, and now his knees were dark with the detective's blood.

Where was Lydia? Amanda wondered. Were they really safe now?

"Where are the police?" she wondered aloud.

"It won't be long," James said.

"I *hate* this. There's a body downstairs. I just *hate* this. Oh, God."

The sound of her own voice was like a

wave beneath her, carrying her, lifting her to new heights of panic. She was a train derailing, totally out of control.

"Who was he?" James asked, looking at her in the mirror. "What was he doing here?"

His voice was almost petulant, and a sudden stirring of anger pulled Amanda back from her own edge.

"He was helping me," she said. "He was a private detective."

"Did you call him here?"

"He followed you to the airport. He was trying to locate Lydia, so we could call the police."

"My God," James said softly, shaking his head.

He lowered his gaze again, staring at his hands in his lap. He looked disheveled, lost, confused. He hadn't even taken off his coat yet.

She wondered why she felt so little anger at him. Tonight's horror was a direct result of his continuing infidelity. If he'd ended it with Lydia when he had said he'd ended it, none of this would have happened. Or would it? Was Lydia simply a woman scorned?

God, what wrath!

But James now seemed so pathetic. He looked lost, defeated, guilty. He knew what had happened, and he knew who was responsible. In a way she felt sorry for him.

"You know more about Lydia than you told the police, don't you?"

He looked at her again. He looked about ready to cry. He nodded and looked down again.

"You'll have to tell them everything now."

"Yes."

She thought of the body in the kitchen, poor Lincoln Fowler, shattered and destroyed in one bright instant. What portion of blame should she shoulder for that?

"If only . . ." she began, and faltered when he looked up at her. "If only you hadn't tried to protect her."

"I can't tell you how sorry I am for what has happened."

She shook her head. "Not sorry enough. You've ruined our marriage. A man is dead. *Three* men are dead! God, and look at me."

"I'm sorry."

"God damn it, where are the police?"

She stood up and paced back and forth by the bed. James watched her warily, as if she were a tiger.

"Are we going to try to . . . fix things?" he asked quietly.

She stopped her pacing to stare at him, taken aback by the question. This morning she had planned on leaving, had intended him to come back, if he ever came back, to find the place empty. This morning, she had given up on her marriage. She had wanted only to hand

Lydia, a living, breathing, *real* Lydia, to the police, to clear herself.

"I don't know," she said.

The question seemed so silly, so unimportant. A man was dead downstairs. Killed in their home.

"I want to," he said without looking at her.

"Do you?"

"Yes."

"I just don't know."

He squeezed his hands and looked down at them. "I really did try to end it with her, you know."

Amanda sat down on the bed again and stared at him. Despite the obvious emotion in his voice, she could not make herself believe him. She made a noncommittal sound.

"It's just, I've known her for so long, I couldn't. It just wasn't as easy as I thought."

Amanda leaned back against the headboard again and closed her eyes. She was exhausted, and her head seemed foggy.

"Didn't you know what she was like? She's crazy."

With her eyes closed, the feeling of fatigue reaching all her extremities, she could almost believe that nothing had happened tonight, that she was simply waking up from a dream, talking to James, ready to face a new day.

"I know now."

"James, when did you first meet her?"

"When I was younger."

"How young?"

"Sixteen, I suppose. Around there."

"Sixteen?" She opened her eyes now, shocked, and stared at him. "But you told me . . ." She shook her head, disgusted and confused. "You've known her a long time."

"Yes."

"I need a drink."

"I'll get it."

"I'll get it myself."

She wanted to be away from him, out of his sight. She felt as if she hardly knew him, and did not know that she wanted to at all. She got off the bed, left the bedroom, and went into the living room. At the liquor table she poured herself a stiff brandy and sipped it. The liquid burned her mouth and made her eyes water, but she swallowed and made herself have some more. She shuddered as the liquor slid into her stomach.

She looked at the living room doorway and thought of Fowler downstairs.

Where *were* the police!

Angry she stalked to the phone and picked it up. She dialled 911 and waited. Nothing happened. She hung up with her finger and listened. No dial tone. She slammed the phone down and stalked from the room.

As she burst into the bedroom, she said, "James, the phone's not working. When you called the police did . . ."

He stared at her in the mirror. For a moment she was not quite sure what she was looking at. He was holding one of her lipstick tubes to his mouth. His lips were angry red.

"What are you doing?"

He put down the lipstick and lifted her eyeliner pencil to his face and deftly marked his eyelids. His cheeks were already rouged. He put down the eyeliner, placed his hands flat on the dresser, and stared at her.

"He's known me longer than he's known you. Longer than he's known any woman," he said.

The voice, so soft, so smooth, so rich and feminine, was the voice that had called to her in the darkness, the voice that had spoken to her over the phone.

The muscles in Amanda's shoulders and neck suddenly crawled.

"James, don't."

"Don't what?" That same voice, full, now, of contempt.

"James . . ."

He stiffened and his eyelids trembled. In his own voice he said, "Amanda?"

Then he started, and stared at the phone by the bed as if it were ringing. It was silent. He continued to stare. He stood and went to it, picked it up gingerly. He held it to his ear.

"No," he said, in his own voice. "No, Lydia. I won't do it. No!"

He hung up, looked at Amanda, then returned to the chair by the dresser.

"That was Lydia," he said. "She wanted me to . . ." His voice had changed again.

Amanda was frozen, chilled to the bone by that voice. James swiveled in the chair to face her. He was beautiful. Beautiful in the way he liked, in the way she herself had become. His thin, boyish face was transformed by the makeup, transformed into something utterly feminine. He reached into his coat pocket and pulled out something black and glistening. He put the wig on his head and straightened it expertly. This was the Lydia from the photographs Fowler had brought her, this was the face that stared back from her own mirror when she stared into it. This is what she had become.

She felt a terrible dissonance, as if the world had suddenly shifted on its axis, as if she had stepped out of her own body and were watching *herself* and not James.

"He bought this house for you," James said. "He rebuilt it . . . for you. He never did that for me. You saw where he made me stay."

"Oh, God, James."

"My name is Lydia."

"Oh, please . . ."

She backed away and found herself against the wall. She could not move. She could only stare, as James stood.

Her mind was turmoil—was storm—was a thousand brilliant fragments suddenly swirling and coming together—was the room downstairs full of Lydia's smell—was Fowler's photographs—was a Lydia that did not exist.

Lydia was here. Lydia had always been here.

The other woman was standing in front of her, standing with her husband, one with her husband.

The woman who had invaded her life, who had broken her marriage.

The woman of James's dreams. Of Amanda's nightmares.

Here. Now.

"Do you know what they tried to do?" James asked, stepping smoothly toward Amanda. "They tried to make you into me. And he let them. He accepted you. Do you know how that made me feel?"

"Don't do this, James. Please, stop it."

Jame smiled. In that painted face Amanda saw his mother, his sister, his aunt. The family resemblance. The women who had raised him. The women he had wanted her to become. The woman she *had* become.

She felt suddenly sick, nauseated to the core.

James's long fingers, the fingers Amanda had so often thought were feminine and gentle, now slowly unbuttoned his coat and untied its belt. As it opened she saw he was wearing a camisole, stockings, black panties. Not sexy underclothes, but utilitarian, like the things he had bought for her, like the things she was now wearing.

He was erect, and now one of his hands gently cupped his crotch and squeezed.

"At first I thought he would get over you. He's had other women, but they've all fallen short of his expectations. But you . . . he tried harder with you. He wanted you to save him. From me."

James eyes filled with tears. Black mascara rolled down his cheeks. Amanda could smell the perfume he had put on. Calantha.

"I know you can hear me, James. I know you can stop this."

"He tried to make me leave. He thought he could abandon me."

"Stop it!"

"But I wouldn't. I couldn't."

He moved toward her again, and she saw that he was carrying a revolver, held loosely at his side. He raised it and pointed it at her.

"Get away from me!"

"He's mine. You can't have him. He can't have you."

Flame leaped from the barrel, and an explosion rocked the room. The bullet sizzled through Amanda's hair and smacked into the wall behind her. She screamed.

Instinct, anger, horror, pure blind luck, and a night of terror, all rolled into a billion-megavolt jolt of adrenalin, drove her forward. With a cry she smashed her knee into James's groin and

334

he buckled to the floor with a gasp. The revolver discharged again. This time the bullet slammed into the floor only inches from Amanda's foot. She fell away from him, onto the bed.

He tried to follow her and she kicked savagely at his face, crushing his nose, smearing his lipstick.

"Get away from me! Get away from me!"

She pulled back her foot for one final blow to his face, but suddenly found herself staring into the black hole of the revolver's barrel. She froze, mouth open to cry.

"He's mine," James said.

Amanda saw his finger begin to squeeze the trigger. She closed her eyes. He was out of reach. She was dead.

When the shot did not come she opened her eyes. He was staring at her, tears flowing down his cheeks. He seemed to be struggling with the gun. It wavered in the air, one moment pointing at her, the next sliding away. As she watched, the gun slowly, inexorably, moved away from her until it was pointing at the wall.

James's face was contorted now, a face caught in a moment of supreme exertion, the face of a weight lifter jerking five hundred pounds. His lips quivered, his eyes bulged, and veins throbbed in his corded neck.

"Amanda," he said through gritted teeth. "I . . . love . . . you . . ."

The voice, changed by exertion, was his own. Feeble, hoarse, hardly audible, but definitely his own.

"James . . ." she reached for him.

"Don't!" Lydia's voice again.

The revolver swung and discharged. Amanda fell to the bed as the headboard splintered behind her.

"Amanda! Run! Before she . . ."

Amanda jumped from the bed as James swung at her, transformed again. As she lunged through the door the gun exploded behind her and a piece of the doorframe splintered in her face. With a cry she dodged to her right, away from the stairs, toward the library. She realized too late that she was trapping herself. Behind her, James rushed after her. As Amanda slammed into the library door a piece of wood next to her hand exploded outward. The bullet smacked into the books on the opposite wall.

Amanda ran to the gun display. She needed a weapon with ammunition. Something that would work.

She lifted one of the spear guns from its rack. The one with the rubber loop. She grabbed the long spear beside it, and fell behind the easy chair.

The library door opened.

"It's over, Amanda," Lydia said.

Behind the chair, where she could not see James, she could believe that he was not present at all. The voice was all Lydia.

"If you come closer, I'll kill you," Amanda grunted.

She used her foot to cock the firing mechanism, straining to stretch the thick, pale rubber. It locked with a satisfying click. She sat the gun upright between her thighs and slid the dart down its tube, so that the base rested against the catapult cup.

"He's mine, now. He'll always be mine."

A cloud of feathers and splinters erupted around Amanda's head. The roar of the shot filled the library. She rolled away as the back of the chair exploded again. She landed on her knees, and jumped to her feet.

She lifted the spear gun as James turned toward her.

"Stop!"

Her husband's painted mouth quivered. He stared at her, and slowly raised the revolver. Again, the transformation came over him. His face strained.

Through gritted teeth, he said, "Amanda . . . shoot . . ."

He stumbled toward her and came up against the chair. Leaning against the shattered back, he fought for the revolver with both hands. It shook in the air.

"I'm . . . sorry . . . Amanda . . ." he said.

The struggle being enacted within his body was titanic. It shook him. Spittle flew from his mouth. His eyes bulged as if they were going to pop out.

"James, stop her! Stop her!"

And for a moment, he seemed to win the battle. He stared at her and slowly raised the revolver. Amanda cringed as the barrel swung past her face, and uttered a cry of horror as it lodged itself beneath James's chin.

"Amanda . . ."

He squeezed the trigger. The hammer clicked on a spent round. His face twisted into an expression of fury and terror.

"No!"

Lydia was back.

If James had been present moments ago, he was gone again, relegated to some deep, powerless corner of his mind. It was Lydia who now advanced on Amanda, pushed past the ruined chair, reached for her with hands turned to claws.

It was Lydia who grinned as she swung the revolver at Amanda's face.

Amanda twisted the spear gun. As Lydia's hand touched her breast she squeezed the trigger. The rubber sling whipped forward with a whine and a sudden slapping sound. The dart launched up past Amanda's chin, brushing her with cold air.

Lydia released a high whistling sound, half scream, half sigh. The dart punched through her throat and out the back of her neck, coming to a sudden jarring halt.

The claws slid down Amanda's breasts. Lydia stumbled away, hands reaching for her throat.

She tugged at the dart, twisted it, pulled it, until her fingers slid from it on a gushing torrent of blood.

Then Lydia stiffened. Stood straight. Trembled.

And for a moment, Amanda was staring into James's eyes.

James's face.

And it was James's arms that opened to her. James's fingers that curled in agony, beckoning her.

"James . . ."

He collapsed to his knees. Blood pumped from his throat and down the camisole within his coat.

His eyes gleamed.

Lydia was gone.

As he fell to the floor the final expression that crossed his face, his painted, ruined face, was one of triumph.

He trembled and was still.

Amanda dropped the spear gun.

She turned and left the room, making sure the phone was hung up. Moving like a robot, she entered every upstairs room and hung up the phones. Finally, in the kitchen, she lifted the receiver and got a dial tone.

She dialled 911 with a steady hand, and explained to the emergency operator that there were two bodies in the house with her and to please send somebody out. The operator asked her to leave the phone off the hook, but she told him she could not. She hung up and dialed Shelly and Patrick's number.

"Lydia is dead," she said. "You had better come over."

She refused to answer questions, and hung up the phone.

Then she sat at the kitchen table, hands clasped in front of her, to wait.

Twenty-five

Amanda was too drained, too exhausted, too shocked and emptied to cry. The choking sobs of Shelly meant nothing to her, nor the words and entreaties that Patrick offered. She listened, and heard, but could not respond. She felt neither anger, nor sympathy. She felt nothing.

The words that came from her own mouth seemed to be spoken by somebody else, somebody detached from the circumstances, somebody impartial.

"You knew all along," her voice said.

"I'm so sorry, Amanda. We never meant it to come to this. Please, believe me."

"You protected Lydia."

"I protected James."

"It's true, Amanda," Patrick said, holding Shelly tightly.

The living room was crowded with people that Amanda did not know. Men in suits, men and women in uniform. They asked questions, they poked and prodded her, they tramped here and there.

Petra made a brief appearance. She studied James's body, then left the house without a word to either Shelly or Amanda. Shelly had watched her mother with hard eyes, tears rolling down her face.

Shelly blurted the story amidst violent sobs, as Amanda and Toni Kirk and two or three other police officers listened in amazement.

It had started after James's father had died. Petra had changed. Had gone into a state of shock. Soon after, she had turned to young James, poor, fourteen-year-old James, for consolation. For more than consolation.

The boy, already under his mother's thumb, had succumbed, had given what she asked. It had gone on for less than a year, until Paula, Petra's younger sister, had threatened to expose the perversion. A year and a half later, Lydia had made her first appearance. James was quickly diagnosed as schizophrenic, manifesting a multipersonality syndrome. Despite years of treatment, even occasional remissions, the personality of Lydia persisted.

"Dr. Jensen told me it was James's way of dealing with mother. In his mind, she wasn't Petra any more. She was Lydia. She was another woman. Someone from outside the family. A stranger. It was his way of cleansing the perversion. It had never been Petra, it had always been Lydia. Lydia was real for him, Amanda, and like mother, she controlled him."

Through his entire adult life, James's relationships with women had failed. None of them could live up to his adolescent memories of Petra/Lydia. For him, Lydia still existed. Someone real. The perfect woman. The woman of his dreams. When things went wrong with his real relationships, or got difficult, he turned to Lydia.

"But you were different, Amanda," Shelly said. "We thought you had cured him. He honestly loved you. I'd never seen him so happy as when he first met you, and then when you got married it was the real James back again. Lydia was gone."

"But she came back."

"Last year. James phoned me, terrified. I tried to get him to see Dr. Jensen, but it was too late. Lydia had him. He fought her, Amanda, really he did. With everything he had. But he kept losing. And I kept remembering something that Dr. Jensen had said. Something about James only being truly cured when he could possess the *real* Lydia."

"So you tried to change me into her. You wanted me to become his real Lydia."

"No, no, that's not true. I wanted you to become *like* her. There's a difference."

"Not much."

"Amanda . . . I did it for James, and for you. I thought that . . . I wanted you to be

343

happy. I never dreamed that Lydia, James's Lydia, would react so violently."

"You used me," Amanda heard her voice say, surprised even to hear a twinge of anger.

Shelly nodded. "Yes."

"I thought you were my friend."

"I was your friend. I am your friend."

"You turned me into Lydia. You turned me into something unreal."

Shelly burst into tears. Patrick, holding her tightly, also cried.

"I did it for my brother. My brother, Amanda. Do you understand? He was only fourteen! She destroyed him! He deserved better!"

Amanda looked on, cold, empty.

It was well past midnight when the house finally became quiet. Shelly and Patrick were two of the last to leave. Amanda stood at the door as they stepped out into the cold night.

Shelly turned to Amanda, face swollen from crying, ugly in her despair.

"Can you ever forgive us? Can you forgive me?"

"I don't know," Amanda said.

Shelly turned away, tears flowing.

Toni Kirk came up behind Amanda, and stepped out.

"Some night," she said.

"Some night," Amanda agreed.

"What are you going to do?"

"Go away. Back home."

"Judging from what I heard in there, you've got grounds for one hell of a lawsuit."

"I don't want to sue. They're family."

"Some family."

"Yeah, some family."

After Toni Kirk was gone, the house was silent. It closed in on Amanda, oppressive, alive, waiting.

She tried to sleep, but imagined she could smell blood. Imagined she could hear footsteps.

At three in the morning she packed a single bag and left the house. She drove to the Holiday Inn in Roseville and booked a room.

She slept a dreamless sleep. Dead to the world.

February turned into March, and March to April. Spring brought colors to St. Cloud that Amanda had not seen in a long, long time. From her old room in her parents' house she watched the trees and flowers bloom in the yard and street, watched children shed clothes and slowly slip into summer mode.

For a while, there were reporters to deal with, and even attention from national television media. The story appeared, sans any input from Amanda, three times on "Hard Copy," and once on "A Current Affair." Both shows used the photograph that hung on the wall of the MRS office, and both compared it to photographs of Lydia taken by Fowler.

"From this all-American girl next door, to heart-crushing vamp?"

Amanda watched the stories with wry amusement. She imagined what strangers must make of it all.

"A legacy of incest and insanity led this girl-next-door to become . . ."

It was almost funny. It didn't seem real at all.

Her father took it all very hard. He talked little, went out less. He did not know what to say to people when he met them, and when he returned home after going out, he was always surly.

Her mother, as usual, accepted it all with stoic good humor.

"Well, at least you know he wasn't *really* cheating on you."

"Thank God for small mercies," Amanda had said.

But the withdrawal of her father hurt. Hurt her far more deeply than she could reveal.

She had very few visitors, and those who did drive up to see her, she screened thoroughly.

Shelly drove up in mid-April, alone. Amanda sat on the front porch with her sister-in-law. They watched children bike past, watched pedestrians stroll along, watched clouds drift by overhead. They said nothing. After an hour, Shelly stood, gave Amanda a long, hard hug, and left. Amanda went back inside, went up to her room, and wept.

Her only regular visitor was Fred Cooper.

He drove up twice a week and told her hilarious stories about real-estate goings-on that must, she knew, border on the slanderous. They walked together, talked together, got to know each another.

Once, in late March, they went for a drive and booked a room at a motel on the edge of town. They tried to make love, but it didn't work very well. Afterward they both laughed.

"Friends we'll stay, I guess," Fred had said.

But Amanda wasn't so sure. She thought she'd like to try it again sometime.

She slowly put on weight. Her angular appearance softened somewhat, and without makeup she soon began to look more and more like her old self. There was nothing she could do about her nose, however, or the high, permanently perky breasts. A cosmetic surgeon she visited in Minneapolis assured her that over time the effects of the surgery would disappear as her skin naturally sagged.

Amanda couldn't wait.

James's estate was settled quickly, contested by neither Petra nor Shelly. By late summer, Amanda was going to be very wealthy. She did not know what she was going to do. Something.

On the last Sunday of April, a beautiful sunny evening, Amanda sat alone on the front porch, a paperback open in her lap. She breathed deeply of the cool, northern air, and watched the sky turn bloody in the west.

Her father came out to the porch with two beers. He looked at her a moment, then sat down beside her on the old sofa. He handed her one of the beers.

She took it, not daring to look at him, and stared across the lawn.

"Your mother and I are thinking of driving out to the Rockies next month, get a good look before the tourist season kicks in."

"That sounds really nice."

She looked at him and smiled. He frowned and sipped his beer. Amanda sipped her beer.

"Your mother was thinking, maybe, since you're not really doing anything, that you'd like to come along."

She looked at him, then away.

"I don't know . . ."

They both sipped their beer.

"Amy . . ."

She turned to him, startled.

"What are you looking so shocked for?"

"You haven't called my Amy since I was thirteen."

"I'm your dad. I can call you what I want, can't I?"

She nodded, looked away, unsure of what to say.

"Amy. I'd like you to come, too. Do us all